The Innocence of Power

by N. K. Hart

Tangible *press*

THE INNOCENCE OF POWER

Copyright © 2013 N. K. Hart
Published by Tangible Press
www.tangiblepress.net

ISBN: 0985814012
ISBN-13: 978-0985814014
Library of Congress Control Number: 2013948692

Cover design by L. R. Pollock

Printed in the United States of America

Dedicated to my one true love…
JMH

And to SP-P, who always knew
there was a book in me

THE INNOCENCE OF POWER

ACKNOWLEDGMENTS

There have been many people who have helped and encouraged me throughout the writing of this book. I only hope that, in time, I'll be able to properly thank each and every one of them. For now, I would like to especially thank John Howells who has been a steady supporter right from the beginning and has allowed me the freedom to create this work. Thank you to Sus Pollock for her steadfast friendship and sincere encouragement of my endeavor and guidance in my transformation. Thank you to my beautiful niece, Teal Conroy, who has offered valuable advice and has helped me beyond measure. Thank you to my sweet niece, Amanda Hart, who provided a proof edit beyond amazing. Thank you to Lindsey Pollock for her kindness and friendship and beautiful sense of art, without which this book would not look so damn appealing.

Thank you, thank you, thank you.

THE INNOCENCE OF POWER

The
Innocence
of
Power

THE INNOCENCE OF POWER

1
Smoke And Mirrors

It was a few minutes before dawn and the view from the large picture window in the overly large, well appointed office, outlined a dark cityscape against the hazy gray-violet of the new day.

For Mark Sturgess, Executive VP in charge of Operations and Client Interests for The Hartfield Connection, LLC, a sort of personal brokerage company, his day would start the minute he stepped out of his office, but for right now...his thoughts were his own. He was standing quite still, looking out without much interest on the beginnings of the day starting to move about far below. There was a haze that hung over the city starting at the easternmost rivers edge that crept inward several blocks. It resembled a cloak that was hiding the filth of the streets and the stench of desperation. Or so went the thoughts running through his mind.

As he gazed down toward the streets, Mark thought of all the people down there living their little lives, running in their little circles. He was so glad to be on top of his world, above all of that. He felt that he deserved his place in The Hartfield, and more. He knew that he had the talent and the brains for the work. If only he had a free hand.

Mark thought of the steady progress that he had made since coming to work at The Hartfield. Or more correctly, since he chose The Hartfield as the business he would bestow his talents upon, on his way up to greater heights. Mark took pride in the fact that he had expanded the legal department by giving senior executives the power to negotiate directly with clients. He organized a crack research team whose only function was to develop background information on all potential clients. He virtually eliminated Azekiel Hartfield's "gentlemen's agreement" whereby nebulous commitments were promised before all was known or contracts drawn up. Oh, everyone still shakes hands, and for almost any reason. It's just that handshakes don't mean much until the ink is dry on the signature line.

Yes, a lot had changed. Mark Sturgess could see where the business had benefited by his presence. And he saw where he might make further improvements...if only he had a free hand.

◆　◆　◆

The Hartfield Connection was more than the man who owned it. It was the building, the furnishings, the well-appointed interiors. It was the clients and it was everything that Azekiel Hartfield, the absolute ruler of his empire, thought it should be.

The building itself was a combination of early English Gothic Spanish Baroque and Modernism. A sort of neo-early European architecture with a North American modern twist. It rose out of the city center to loom over most of the neighboring buildings within the twelve-block radius it dominated. While the muscle and bones of the building were of the strongest steel and cables, with the stability of the structure well beyond current building codes, it was the architecture that communicated to the world that this building was special, this building was to be reckoned with and that this building was here to stay.

The building occupied an entire city block, in fact, taking up two original blocks worth of space in its entirety. Rising up ninety stories, the floors of offices were graced with banks of windows that were tucked into alcoves and, alternating with those jutting out, that maximized on views of the cityscape. The top-most building suite was stepped back from the outer walls allowing a generous amount of space that had been designed as a private patio and gardens including a pathway that meandered around the perimeter.

The gardens would rival any of those well talked about gardens belonging to country estates...closer to terra firma. Flowers were planted to provide seasonal blooms and shrubs and trees that could be viewed from every suite window, provided windbreaks for the outdoor seating areas. Mood lighting and path lighting added spectacular illumination to the gardens at night. The care of these spaces was entrusted to a master gardener who excelled at coaxing second and third blooms from her charges. On occasion, cut flowers in crystal bowls were added to Azekiel Hartfield's desktop. He was a man who appreciated the finer things that life could provide.

On the north side of the rooftop was a private helicopter pad and a small but adequate workspace for the two chopper pilots and a mechanic.

From the rooftop suite, the building continued upward another one hundred feet, boasting the most amazing English Gothic architecture reminiscent of churches built during the medieval times of the Normans. It simply took ones breath away to look at, and to see it up close revealed details not evident from the street. This beautiful tower and spire were bathed in art lighting from dusk until dawn. It so impressed city officials that they used its silhouette as part of a skyline decoupage on city letterheads and logos.

Surrounding the Hartfield building, at street level, were manicured gardens and swept walkways with benches for the enjoyment of the employees working there. Its beauty was for the appreciation of the general city population, but the spaces were private property and non-Hartfield persons were not made welcome.

The overall architecture of the building, with its lighted tower and spire, was further complimented by the elaborate baroque façade. The craftsmanship was exquisite. Two pink marble columns, sitting atop black marble plinths, flanked both sides of the huge double, etched glass entry doors. Next to the set of columns was an area of relief that not only framed the façade but tied it into the rest of the building's face.

There is a winged dragon, coiled as if to strike, spewing flames and smoke from its throat. Plumes and leaves and shells and vines rose to join with banners that entwined a huge ornate sword that pointed to the heavens and supported a capital made to resemble laurel leaves on their branches. The columns supported a unifying extension of travertine and South American granite. Above all this beauty and stone and skill was mounted a relief depicting a leaping stag on a field of moss green across a battle shield with the words "Au Vainqueur va le Gâte" written in black onyx. "Hartfield, to the victor go the spoils."

All the spaces within The Hartfield were designed according to their needs with one sense ruling the others: the use of contemporary furnishings within traditional walls. The one exception to this rule was the Hartfield penthouse office suite. There, traditional and masculine styled furnishings took precedence over good design, although design and style were running a close third and forth and nothing had been left to chance. After all, this was Azekiel Hartfield's place of power.

◆   ◆   ◆

The Hartfield Connection, referred to by company contemporaries as The Hartfield, was a company concerned with advancing its wealthiest clients interests, whatever they be. The business was image consulting and tailoring, and the clients were all rich and extremely powerful people who were usually looking for the next logical step: control. There was a slogan used by The Hartfield that was found quite widely throughout the business: Strategic Communications With Insight and Intelligence - Building a Better "You" Through Technology Tailoring. In fact, this slogan was written in very large golden letters on the expansive Italian marble façade in the building's entryway. Yes. Technology Tailoring. It would be a very funny slogan if not so ironic.

The company's public face was a shining example of personal marketing. The client list was impressive, long, and included such dignitaries as past Presidents and foreign Prime Ministers, corporate Ps and VPs and Hollywood royalty, all of whom needed a periodic boost to gain or to keep favor with the public and keep the media satiated with their goodness and charm. In this fast-paced world with its ever-changing fads and fashions, it wasn't uncommon for public persons to be interested in keeping themselves well known and likable and to seek The Hartfield's services. For the most part, they all needed guidance in the arts of persuasion and personal and professional strategies. There were varied levels of involvement that The Hartfield would gladly provide.

Hartfield's basic service was an individual and very personalized coaching session, where the client was trained in speechmaking and appearance. Several levels of service above this were concerned with the absolute handling of every aspect of a client's life and business. The Hartfield provided each of their clients with a team of professionals focused on image makeovers and media control and proper deportment for each and every public situation that would occur in the clients' life. This included future plans that affected the client, their lifestyles and public perceptions. This level of service was what The Hartfield had maintained for several years and was constantly working to advance. It was the main focus right from the start. Visionary, Azekiel Hartfield was the man who brainstormed the beginning of The Hartfield Connection. He was the one who saw a real need for personal coaching among the top-level managers and executives after many of the greatest institutions in the United States and abroad fell into one of the worst economic downturns of the new millennium. Many corporations took a public beating and were brought to public shame over controversial and financial issues that The Hartfield was, frankly, not interested in. This same visionary also saw how he could manufacture a need for his new Public Relations firm's services. He foresaw how business and political leaders would come to depend upon his help and subtle guidance to create better business relations in every aspect of their lives. The current client base represented the wealthiest of the world's population and if there was one thing that The Hartfield Connection had learned from its inception to this very moment, it was that the wealthy were not content to be merely wealthy. They also wanted power and control over everything and everyone around them and were willing to spend a great deal of their wealth to get it.

◆　　◆　　◆

Mark Sturgess thought he was just the man to guide the helm of such a corporation. At 37 years old, he was still a good looking, 6'1" tall man, with well-toned muscles and ice-cold blue eyes.

Mark was polite but had a savvy intelligence about him. To meet him casually, you would never suspect that he could be ruthless in his business dealings. One had to be if one was to rise to the level that Mark enjoyed all so well. The power that he wielded and the vast influence and persuasion he had with many high-level clients and governments seemed to suit him. There was a worldly air about him and an undeniable penchant for rich tastes and fast but calculated living.

It was just after dawn and Mark, as he was known only to Mr. Hartfield, and Mr. Sturgess as he's known everywhere else, began the daily rounds of his business world. Stepping outside his office he was greeted with "Good morning" and "How was your evening" from his personal staff that were already busy at work. Mark nodded his acknowledgement of these greetings and smiled slightly as he made his way out of his department and into the wide, plush hallway that connected all other offices and departments on this floor to large, well stocked, conference rooms and well appointed anterooms adjoining the major vertical transports. Today he would visit several of the lower departments on his way to the highly secured floors located below ground level.

Mark's rise to VP of Operations and Client Interests didn't happen overnight, but it did happen as a natural step in his carefully planned career path. He was first in his class at Yale and graduated Magna Cum Laude. He immediately put his life-plan into action: he would work one year for a management team in a large international company, meet those persons he knew to be part of something bigger and take his pick of which corporation he would work for. The idea of an eventual corporate takeover was never far out of his thoughts, and indeed, it had been the basis of Mark's senior graduate level thesis.

He didn't have to dream of a corporate takeover, as he had

already worked out many of the details. It was just a matter of putting it into action. The easiest part was to identify the weakest area of a corporate structure – this included everyone at the top, too. The fewer people at the top who were making decisions, the better. Basic finance 101 would tell him how much cash and assets were available and, of course, one good read through their business model would show the level of risk the corporation could withstand...with Mark at its head. It was just a matter of studying his opposition, biding his time, then exploiting all identified weaknesses while maneuvering himself into the owner's big office on the top floor. Mark considered this strategy to be "business as usual" and had not wavered from it at all.

It was about four years ago that The Hartfield Connection came into Mark's view. At that time, Mark was employed by an up and coming Personal Relations firm, Burgit & Maine, that might have been considered a competitor to The Hartfield had they not, at that time, taken a loss on the acquisition of a smaller firm that was so heavily in debt that it cost them their AAA rating. Burgit & Maine was looking to partner with Hartfield but on Mark's advice, Hartfield bought the company outright, rewarded Mark with a management position and promptly dismantled what was left of Burgit & Maine, consigning it to the history books.

Once inside The Hartfield, it didn't take long for Mark to work his way to an executive VP position, and by his reckoning, wouldn't be much longer before he was in position to squeeze Hartfield out and assume leadership entirely.

With a smile across his face and a knowing nod to himself, Mark thought of his first act of business when The Hartfield Connection was finally his...rebranding the company.

2
Business As Usual

It was just another day in the world of fast business transactions coupled with fast gains and high expectations for The Hartfield Connection. When Hartfield is well, everyone is well.

At precisely nine fifty three that morning, Travis Stratton stepped through the outer doors of The Hartford Connection and gazed around in wonder. His one step through the overly large, very heavy etched glass doors had revealed further proof of Hartfield's success: the brand...the words, "The Hartfield Connection ~ Strategic Communications With Insight and Intelligence". This logo had been written in a beautiful script font, two and one half feet high, covered in 18-karat gold leaf and had been backlit mounted on a sea of travertine tiles. Here and there, the lettering had been inset with carved moonstones that resembled twinkling stars. Underfoot there were hand-made field tiles imported from Milan with a black granite and iridescent glass tile border around the entire vestibule.

Smiling to himself, Travis introduced himself to the pretty young woman sitting at the desk. The receptionist busied her fingers on a small keyboard and within a few seconds had looked up Mr. Stratton's impressive biography, had paged Mark Sturgess to come to the lobby at his convenience and had sent the mini-bio to Mark's phone. With a broad smile, the receptionist escorted Travis Stratton to a private waiting room near the lobby, where she motioned him to an overstuffed leather chair and poured him a glass of Louis Roederer's Cristal.

Travis was impressed that the company so quickly recognized

that he was special. Indeed, he flattered himself that the treatment he received and the friendly smile of the receptionist was because he was young, good looking, energetic and brilliant. And he was all of these things and more.

His school years were fast-paced and filled with wild social situations. Travis found his classes almost too easy and volunteered as a student teacher for most of his junior and senior years. He found he was a skilled organizer and put together handpicked teams of science students to build the most remarkable series of robots M.I.T. had experienced in the last twelve years. With Travis as team captain, he and his various minions won first place in every competition they entered. M.I.T. couldn't do enough for him. He brought fame and fortune in the form of large donations to the school, and in return, the school gave Travis the run of their labs and resources.

When he wasn't designing robotics or teaching classes, Travis immersed himself in the wild nights of student living. The rowdy all-night parties served as a stage for the development of Travis' appetite for beautiful women and a pedestal on which he placed himself – above everyone else.

Graduating with honors at the absolute top of his class, Travis was asked to give the valediction at his graduation ceremonies. It took all of thirty minutes to write and less than twelve minutes to deliver, but what a twelve minutes they were! Because of his small but growing fame, the auditorium was filled to capacity with the influential parents of other students and alumni and powerful representatives from the electronics industries here and abroad. From the podium, to a hushed and expectant crowd, Travis launched into what could be called a Twelve Minute Résumé, citing his perfect grades, all the glory he had won for the school and actually giving the dollar amount ($18.5 million, to be exact) of the donations that wouldn't have been possible without him and his work. He felt that the school should be deeply grateful to him and he was sure his name would ring throughout M.I.T.'s hallways for the next five or six generations. In summing up his speech, he spread his arms, in a gesture suggesting a possessed holy-roller, and in a loud voice, called out, "Thank you!" He waved to the stunned audience, and walked off the stage. This was the last day that Travis was part of the private educational system.

The number of days Travis spent looking for gainful employment was one. There were fifteen messages on his e-device by the time he drove off campus and twenty more before he reached home. One week later, he had a short but lucrative contract with one of the largest technology conglomerates, his own lab, no budget ceiling, and was about to move into a penthouse on the Upper West Side.

Now, as a young man of twenty-six with dark Italian features whose gold-flecked brown eyes danced in the light, Travis was used to turning the heads of young women and being the center of attention when he entered rooms. After graduating, he dominated the fast changing field of technology with a rapid succession of engineering marvels in the field of robotics. He developed advanced mathematical matrices software for two theoretical models of robot: ornithology and bipartite.

Travis' first self-powered mechanical design was ornithological in nature. He named it Strato-Soar-One to accurately reflect its lofty capabilities. The assembly of parts and materials into a smooth and beautiful machine was enough to get the type of attention Travis sought. With a small amount of thrust, his ornithological device spread its wings and, beating them in a rhythmic pattern, lifted up off the ground and into the sky. The small fuel converter was a top secret that no one but Travis understood. The on-board circuitry controlled flight through a myriad of sensors and command signals that safely guided the hybrid machine through changing air patterns and past looming obstacles. Travis closely guarded his algorithmic equations. They were the foundation for all that had come before and were certain to support all that would came after.

Along the way, Travis managed to step on a few toes, but none of that seemed to bother him. He burned through people without recognizing their potential value, using them to his own advantage at the time. He threw lavish parties but when he grew bored or distracted, he would order everyone out except the few who still managed to entertain him. He would carouse with those few until most were in a stupor and regale the remaining ones with stories about how he "did this" and "managed that" and was always the boy wonder whose talents were highly sought after.

For the past two years he had enjoyed a level of entrepreneurial ownership of several businesses and had built a bastion of wealth beyond his wildest boyhood dreams. Now he had his sights set on a ten year, one hundred fifty seven billion dollar government contract to provide multi-point processors with on-going maintenance. There was a lucrative yearly sub-contract worth additional hundreds of millions of dollars, to create control-ware for a bullet-proof worldwide security system that would be negotiated separately. All this led him to The Hartfield Connection. With their reputation and resources they should be able to make the name Travis Stratton respectable and dependable in spite of his reckless walks on the wild side, his big ego and sometimes big mouth.

In spite of everything, Travis Stratton's star was still rising.

♦   ♦   ♦

Mark Sturgess' leisure tour of the Internal Affairs and the Acquisitions Departments had been interrupted by a call from reception about a potential new client that he should meet and interview and who was now ensconced in the Continental Room and working on a second glass of champagne.

Stepping off of the vertical into the lobby, Mark strode past the receptionist, giving her a slight nod with a wide smile thanking her for the timely notification and data on Mr. Stratton. Upon opening the conference room door, Mark had adjusted his smile and held out his hand for a greeting and, as the catch phrase goes, said, "Now what can we do for you, Mr. Stratton?"

Travis launched into a brief, but rehearsed, speech on his graduating top of his class, the awards for his inventions, his short but prosperous backing of several entrepreneurial ventures and his desires to increase his wealth as well as his visibility on the world stage.

"I'm here today, Mr. Sturgess, to see if The Hartfield Connection can provide the kind of resources I will need to complete the next phase of my career. I'm also looking for guarantees of your success because a partial success, or worse, a failure, is not an option for either of us."

Sturgess took this in stride. He had heard this kind of bluster from potential clients before. The over-confidence displayed in these early meetings was always due to a kind of inept social grace resulting from an egocentric lifestyle. There was always a fearful child at the root of all the bragging. Mark could feel the meaning behind his own smile. He was turning into the confident cat ready to pounce on the hapless mouse.

"Mr. Stratton, The Hartfield Connection is fully capable of managing your success far beyond your expectations. I'll be able to provide you with further information after we come to

21

agreement of the terms and conditions of our business partnership."

Mark's e-device chimed, and after a quick glance at the face, turned to Travis and said, "You will be escorted up to the 52ⁿᵈ floor for a short meeting with the corporate lawyers and then, if everything is to our mutual satisfaction, you will be introduced to your personal team of handlers for preliminary discussions. If all goes well, it will culminate in an agreement to a working relationship. As for your financial security, I assure you, Mr. Stratton, Hartfield understands that a successful client is the basis for a successful company. We wouldn't guide you to do anything that would jeopardize your current profile, and I can say with all honesty, that your wellbeing is our wellbeing. Now, if you will excuse me, Mr. Stratton, I have an urgent meeting I must attend. I'll have someone from our legal staff escort you up to a wonderful meeting room where you can discuss your concerns and develop the legal foundations of our future relationship."

Travis set down his third glass of champagne and rose from his chair. After a broad smile and a hardy handshake, Mark nodded in happy agreement and stepped out through the conference room door, closing it gently behind him.

As Mark crossed through the lobby, he nodded to the receptionist, and lifting his e-device up to reading level said, "Thank you for the heads-up."

As the mini-bio and financial data of Elizabeth "Liz" Preston streamed across the screen of his e-device, Mark made his way to the verticals. Miss Preston had been shown to one of the larger conference rooms on the second floor and, upon her request, had been served high pulp orange juice over crushed ice. According to the mini-bio, Elizabeth Preston was an aspiring political figure. She was 38-years old, 5'7" tall with auburn hair, fair skin and green eyes. Her pictures did little justice to her strikingly handsome figure and composed demeanor. However charming she appeared in public, her public persona did not give away how cold, unfeeling and calculating she could be.

◆　　◆　　◆

As a child, Elizabeth would set herself in competition with her neighborhood friends to be first in everything. And if one of the other girls were to trip on the jump rope, well, so what...she was clumsy. If another girl got a new doll for her birthday, well...Elizabeth had a better one.

In high school, Elizabeth excelled in political science and was head of the debate team for all four years. She learned, all too well, the art of twisting a person's words to the point of harming them. This gave her a feeling of accomplishment that encouraged her to hone her craft further.

In college, she took to Poly Sci and the study of corporate law like a fish to water. She found her element and excelled with alarming speed. She had few friends, more like close associations, but Elizabeth was unconcerned with that. Her eye was on a prize further out, just a few years of premeditated work and it would be hers.

Elizabeth Preston's desire for power barely outweighed her desire for fame and money. Shortly after starting her graduate studies in law, Elizabeth realized she had a talent for arguing whichever side of a dispute she took part in. This side or the other side, high or low, right or wrong – it didn't matter. She was good and she usually won.

In her third year, Elizabeth took part in a mock trial staged as a theatrical drama by one of her law professors. The professor thought it would be entertaining for the first- and second-years to witness what it would be like for them after they had acquired a bit of legal acumen.

Elizabeth had been chosen to act as the prosecuting attorney in a case involving a corporate CEO accused of systematically embezzling funds and defrauding company clients to the tune of $6.5 million. She took her part seriously, studying law and researching precedence. In her desire to win, she unwittingly made assistants out of several classmates and routinely burned the midnight oil preparing her case and writing her opening statement.

The campus theatre was booked and the stage dressed to look like the interior of a state supreme court. And as the house lights dimmed and the curtain started to go up, Elizabeth was hardly surprised to find that her excitement levels had also started to rise. She became cool and relaxed as the trial progressed and more focused than she remembered being in a long while. And as the trial neared its conclusion, Elizabeth's expectation that she would win became even more clear to her. It spoke to her of the future.

Mock trial or not, Elizabeth Preston knew she had found a clear direction and it went straight through the legal system and out into the world.

Elizabeth Preston's rise through the political ranks started with her recruitment into one of the largest law firms in the country. She became a full partner within eighteen months, but within the following year found that she was restless and bored. Nothing new and exciting presented itself. It was the same dry court system with its quasi-formality and stuffed shirts. Elizabeth used her restive moments to look about for another opportunity and within weeks, she had started working for a local politician. Elizabeth was quickly and thoroughly seduced into the world of media fame and government expenditures. It didn't take long for her to notice that cameras loved her and she played to it with relish. She enjoyed the public attention and soon realized that she made a better opponent to the local politician who had hired her into his campaign and quickly changed sides, winning debates and making over her public image. From there it seemed that she was riding on a jet train straight into a state level Representative's seat and was now looking to gain the next important step: the United States Senate.

She had spent the past eight years on a fast track through the political scene in her efforts to maneuver a Senatorial position within the Federal Government. Her intentions were clear. She was aiming high and it seemed that there wasn't too much of anything that would stop her. The list of her defeated opponents, as well as her discarded playthings, read like a Who's Who of wannabes from some of the wealthiest corporate and political families.

◆　　◆　　◆

As Sturgess walked past the glass enclosed meeting room to the door, he noticed Miss Preston standing at the windows looking out, not down at the street activities, but out over the treetops and at nothing in particular. He wondered what must be going on in her mind at that precise moment, but those thoughts quickly vanished as he turned the handle and entered the room with a smile and his hand extended in greeting.

Taking Elizabeth's hand in his and holding it for a moment before letting it go, Mark said, "Miss Preston, I'm Mark Sturgess. Welcome to The Hartfield Connection. I trust you've been made comfortable?"

"Yes, I'm fine, thank you for asking. You have a beautiful

building and helpful staff at reception. I must tell you that I'm fully aware of Hartfield's reputation and am looking forward to an association that would benefit both myself and your company."

Mark heard the distinct sound of cash being deposited into his hands and it made him hungry. "I'm sure we can come to an agreement on that point. But, tell me what brought you here today, Miss Preston."

"It's all rather simple, Mr. Sturgess, I plan to include a senatorial position to my professional résumé, and would like to know how your company will assist me in accomplishing that endeavor. Hartfield's reputation is well known among my circle of colleagues and has come up more than once in conversations with my overseas contacts. One gentleman, in particular, The Honorable Montigue Amaya, told me I should not hesitate any longer – that I was to contact Hartfield immediately. He seems to hold your company in high regard, Mr. Sturgess. I'm hoping that in time I will too."

Noting the authority in Elizabeth's voice and the way she held herself when addressing him, Mark sized her up as controlling and manipulative and a bit of an ice queen. Using his warm corporate smile, Mark stepped to the door, held it open and indicated with a gentle sweep of his arm that they were ready to leave. Turning to Elizabeth, Mark said, "Miss Preston, I have no doubt our business arrangement will make us both very happy."

At the mention of Montigue Amaya's name, Mark decided to personally take Miss Preston in hand. Amaya's name was well known in the highest circles of influence throughout the United States and, internationally, throughout Europe. Mr. Amaya was from old money, very old money and was a very important person. Too important to let the mention of his name slip past with little or no notice. As Mark escorted Miss Preston into one of the verticals and up to the 52nd floor to meet with legal representatives, he tapped out a brief message to legal, requesting a team be assembled and waiting for them in the Skyline conference room. Mark also wanted them to be prepared to negotiate and finalize all contract content and, when that was completed, arrange for Miss Preston to meet with her new team of handlers four floors above.

On the way from the vertical to a more private meeting room, they happened to walk past another well appointed meeting room where Mark noticed a small team of lawyers and two supervisors were listening intently to whatever Travis Stratton was saying. The sound proofing of the meeting room ensured that no voices were heard from the hallway but Travis' mouth was working steadily, so whatever story he was telling must have been an earful and Sturgess smiled to himself with mild amusement at what the meeting recordings would ultimately reveal.

THE INNOCENCE OF POWER

3
Concerns Are For Those Who Worry

After Mark Sturgess introduced Elizabeth Preston to her new family of handlers, he had advised them to construct Phase 1 of their strategy, outlining the initial three-month course of action with a one-month follow-on suggestion and to deliver this to his desk before three that afternoon. He then turned to Miss Preston, took her hand in both of his and held it firmly while he assured her that her destiny would be well guided and if she had any questions or concerns she was to bring them to his personal attention. He smiled one of his disarming smiles and stepped out of the meeting room into the relative quiet of the hallway. Immediately his e-device signaled an incoming message. It was from the VP of Security Operations who was requesting a moment of Mark's time. Mark was not particularly fond of the Security VP. He found Jack Abourn mealy-mouthed and weak, unable to form an original thought and constantly looking for reassurance whenever he made a decision. The only thing Mark did like about him was that he offered little resistance to Mark's strongly worded suggestions about how to run the Security Department, thereby making it an auxiliary department to his own.

Several key clicks later, his affirmation sent, Mark went through Legal to the verticals and descended to the floor just below street level where the company's Security Department was located. After traversing the various levels of eye scans and other recognition protocols, Sturgess was finally in the outer offices of Security Operations and was directly ushered into the plush but overly electronisized VP's office. As he entered the office, he recognized that, in addition to himself, there were four other Department Chairmen in attendance: Personnel, Marketing, Accounting and Internal Affairs. He knew immediately that this wouldn't be good but he took a seat and was handed a sheaf of papers by the VP's executive assistant.

Jack Abourn, began the briefing with a quick background about a young woman who was recently hired into the Financial Department as the Private Executive Secretary to Tom Ashton. As Abourn droned on, Mark built a mental picture of Anne Whitman. She was 22 years old, 5'2" tall, with blond hair and gray eyes. She had graduated at the top of her class late last year from Stanford with a degree in business engineering. She possessed several very impressive references and was hired into the Financial Department less than a month ago. Mark's thoughts started to drift back to his daily routines but brought his attention back to the meeting when Abourn cleared his throat with a loud rasping noise. Abourn was trying much too hard to sound authoritative, although to Mark, it was all affected and fake.

"It is believed that this Anne Whitman stumbled upon sensitive computer files that could implicate The Hartfield in several legal gray areas as well as link several top names in U.S. politics and worldwide businesses to those gray areas. We think that she downloaded these files to a sidecar drive in order to remove them from the department. Two days ago she failed to come in to the office at her regular start time and upon inquiry, we found that she has not been seen since leaving the office the evening before."

Mr. Miller, the Personnel Department Chairman, spoke up, "Is Mr. Ashton aware of this situation?"

"Yes. Following the initial briefing given to Mr. Hartfield, Mr. Ashton was summoned to his office where, I believe, a thorough debriefing as well as a question and answer period was conducted. Mr. Ashton has been transferred to an undisclosed company location until further notice."

Mrs. Lang, head of the Marketing Division, asked, "How bad is the situation – has it spread beyond the company?"

"The situation has been classified as Code Yellow and is being contained within corporate. At this time I would like to introduce Frank Joiner from our Internal Affairs Division." Gesturing with a nod of his head, Abourn brought everyone's attention to Frank Joiner, IA Specialist, who was seated off to the side and watching the meeting with fixed attention. Frank nodded to the small group to communicate a curt hello but also to clearly tell the group that he was aware of them and was watching.

Frank Joiner was a bit of a perfectionist. He looked for that quality in everyone he met. He would eye them suspiciously and judge whether they met with his approval or not. He would look straight into the eyes of whomever he was talking with to see if they would squirm with guilt or return his gaze steadily and with reassurance. He rarely met his match and liked to brag that he could always spot a liar.

Abourn cleared his throat and continued, "Internal Affairs has taken a focused interest in this matter and Mr. Joiner will be leading an investigation that will no doubt include all departments represented here, as well as any others deemed necessary. Mr. Hartfield expects that you will lend your full cooperation, and upon Mr. Joiner's request, instruct your staff to do the same. Frank, do you have anything to add at this time?"

Mark watched passively as Frank Joiner stood up and stepped toward the group.

"Yes, I do and thank you, Jack."

Frank looked from one face to another as he intoned a short

introduction, "Most of you know me from flow charts and hearsay and for the most part I like it that way. When our department becomes involved with a situation, our job is to sort it out by locating all the facts, putting them together to bring focus and to make recommendations to Mr. Hartfield about how best to ensure it doesn't happen again."

Although Mark would rather focus on the integration of Travis Stratton and Elizabeth Preston onto Hartfield's client list, his attention was now on Frank Joiner. Mark wondered how many cases Joiner had actually solved or if he was just a blowhard. He looked around the room and noticed that Mr. Miller seemed a bit agitated as he was fidgeting uncomfortably in his chair.

"I would like to start in the Personnel Department." Shifting his stance, Frank squared himself to directly face Miller. "I'll need full access to all information your department has on Anne Whitman. This means all records, background checks, investigations, interview records, voiceprints and anything else I've not already mentioned. There's no need to alert your entire department, just those directly involved with Ms. Whitman's employment with The Hartfield. I'd like to start low key. Would it be convenient, Mr. Miller, to begin in one hour?"

"Ahem. Yes, yes. That would be fine."

"Thank you. One hour, then. Your office." Joiner turned to face the other managers, "I'll notify you and other Department VPs as needed. Thank you for your attention. I'm confident we will get to the end of this investigation with as little disruption to your departments and their daily operations as necessary."

Turning to Abourn, Joiner nodded and moved back to his place at the edge of the assembly. Abourn pursed his lips and released an audible exhale slowly through his nose, all the while looking at his hands as he flexed his fingers. After a moment, he stood up and stepped around to the opposite side of the seating area and, trying to look authorative, squared his shoulders and said, "All departments are hereby notified that Lock Down Level Three has been implemented and that no one will be granted permission to exchange information with any outside source. This includes disclosure of anything that may raise questions, or worse, bring any media attention to us at this time."

Looking around at the faces of the department heads, Abourn added, "Are there any questions for me?"

Mrs. Lang, from Accounting, asked, "What exactly has been done so far and what will be done by your department to resolve this problem?"

"Well, as you can see, we're aware of Ms. Whitman and are in the process of accumulating as much information as we can on her and her activities to fully understand the level of sabotage she may be involved in. We're working with Internal Affairs, assisting their investigations and my department has formed two teams of security specialists who have my fullest confidence in their ability to locate the girl and the missing information. Be assured, everyone, that we're looking into it and plan to have this all wrapped up within the week."

With a clear note of irritation in his voice, Mark added the last word, "Yes. By all means, look into it."

◆　　◆　　◆

Mark Sturgess was born Marek Stern in Reedsville Pennsylvania, the only son of poor working-class parents. His father worked as a clerk for the town, issuing building permits and filing papers. His mother was an English teacher at the local high school where she taught her students to speak with style and elocution. She constantly maintained that they could rise to something greater than their small community. It was a big world and had many opportunities.

The lesson was not lost on Marek. He watched his father work diligently, year after year, with little praise and no real reward. He watched his mother spend her days in the classroom and her evenings looking after the family and grading papers and preparing for the next day's lessons. Neither parent complained about their lives, both were relatively happy people, but they were helpless to change their situation without throwing it all to the wind.

Marek loved his parents, but as he grew older and wanted more than what they could provide, he gradually lost respect for them. At times, in the privacy of his room, he would silently rage against them for not advancing their work. Why wasn't his father the mayor? Why wasn't his mother the school's Principal? These thoughts were a driving force in Marek. He vowed to himself that he would get away from Reedsville. He would not be content until he had it all: fast cars, fancy clothes, and a supermodel girlfriend.

4
Gaining Momentum

The phone at the Malloy Agency rang again. That was the fifth ring so whoever was on the other end was either serious or had fallen asleep. Either way, it was going to be interesting.

Pete Malloy was tall with light brown hair that had a hint of gray at the temples. He was a tailored, nicely buffed, 52-year old father of two grown boys, who adored him. His first son was a topnotch attorney specializing in federal regulations and prosecuting corporations for thwarting the law. He was very happy putting the bad guys in jail, or at the least, taking away their expensive toys as a way of making them pay for their wrongdoing. Pete's other son was a writer who happened to love fiction. He also wrote poetry and had written many very good poems over the years. Two of his books of fiction had been published and his first book of poetry had just gone into its third printing. Between the two boys, Pete was able to provide a balance between the logical and the artistic sides of life. The advice he had been known to give to them at one time or another included being serious and having fun but to always know which to apply at what time.

Pete had been widowed for several years and while it had been difficult for the three of them to get back on their feet, they had all managed to become at ease with their personal loss and more comfortable with their lives now.

The experience that Pete brought to his job was varied and his personal résumé highlighted a brilliant career in military strategy and law enforcement. He was self-possessed, not prone to emotional outbursts, and very calm and controlled under fire. His many years in the field made him well connected among police agencies and local private investigators. When he opened his office ten years ago, his experience made him the perfect go-to guy when things got too tangled for the regular police to get involved with.

On the seventh ring, Pete picked up the receiver and after introducing himself, listened intently to the polite introduction from the potential client on the line. Malloy's interest sharpened when he heard the words, "Hartfield Connection" quickly followed by "Our daughter is missing, will you help us?"

"Yes, can you come to my office at one this afternoon to discuss the matter in detail? Fine, I'll see you then."

♦　　♦　　♦

After earning a college degree in Criminal Justice with a minor in Law, Pete Malloy entered military service. His interest in investigative work began in his early twenties when he was training for a position with the Marine Corps Special Forces Black Ops unit Omega Eight. Part of the training required that the team ready themselves for a four-day deployment to a foreign city where they would receive further instructions. The intel received would outline a situation they were to clear within forty-eight hours and return to base with zero losses. The project was to be accomplished as stealthily as possible, virtually unnoticed and leaving no trace. Pete was chosen to lead the four-man team, which he gladly did, bringing the project to a more than satisfactory conclusion. Out of the entire project, it was the detective work in the foreign city that piqued Pete's interest and set him on a life-long career track.

◆　　◆　　◆

At approximately the same time Pete Malloy was talking with his soon-to-be clients, another meeting was taking place among a very elite and highly secretive group of three U.S. Senators. The Senators were joined by Martha Gainsbrook, a top ranking and highly decorated CIA agent. Ms. Gainsbrook was their choice to lead an investigation into several questionable practices by one of the nation's largest corporations: The Hartfield Connection. Since hiding in plain view always seemed to work best, the meeting took on the appearance of a casual golf game at a local private club.

◆　　◆　　◆

Now in her mid-forties, Martha Gainsbrook was 5'5" tall with dark blue-gray eyes and she was a very good-looking woman. She wore her hair short but styled and appeared fit and trim due to her regular workouts. She had a reputation for being smart, cunning and tenacious.

During her pursuit of a bachelor's degree, Martha elected to take several classes in information technology, analytical skills and European languages. She became fascinated with the world of information technology and became enthralled with anything that had to do with technology, what it could do and how it was changing.

In the course of her studies, Martha had learned that many aspects of technology could be modified to solve virtually any problem. During her second year, she wrote a moderately complex set of software instructions that impressed her instructor and had set her up for her Master of Science in Information Technology degree studies. Her elaborate set of software code, when uploaded to three separate computer platforms, retrieved the contents of all three hard drives and organized the information into a relational database on the originating computer system. For this, Martha won a coveted undergraduate award for her outstanding contribution to the overall excellence of the Computer Science Division.

After graduating at the top of her class Martha delayed her entry into the work world. She decided that after four tough years of classes, study and tests that she would take some time for herself, to reward herself with a bit of travelling. Within two weeks of graduation, Martha had packed a small bag and flew to Europe, where she found herself touring a string of small, newly independent countries with unstable governments. She surprised herself by finding it all so intriguing. After five months of observing the fringes of small governments grapple with the balance of criminality, freedom and military power struggles, Martha was sure of her career path and took the next flight home.

Martha applied to and was accepted into the CIA as a trainee in their introductory level agent classes. Martha not only completed her training within the prescribed amount of time, several of her completed class assignments had been adapted by the instructor into class curriculum. It was no surprise that Martha earned top honors for the courses and the attention of the Director of the National Clandestine Services Office.

Following her tour of duty as a CIA covert agent in several of the world's hot spots, which earned her the respect and trust of many top-ranking FBI and CIA officials, as well as one or two international law enforcement agencies, she applied for and was granted a top secret clearance with special considerations. It was those special considerations that kept her interested in her work.

♦　　♦　　♦

As the Senators slowly made their way through the first three holes of the course, they welcomed Martha Gainsbrook, assuring her that they were aware of her stellar reputation. They reminded her that she was participating in an extremely sensitive and somewhat oblique operation wherein secrecy and expediency were of the utmost importance.

After unloading their golf bags at the tee box for the fourth hole, the group of Senators took turns in the explanation of the problem they wished to be solved.

After squaring his golf tee and balancing his Titleist, the first Senator took a moment to face Martha and said, "Hartfield has ties to many top officials in government and private industry. They're worth billions. In the past ten years, they've gone from a standard business to a multi-national presence with 'alumni' in the highest places."

Returning to his ball, the Senator took a powerful tee shot, sending it straight down the course to the fourth hole.

The next Senator added, "Recently one newly appointed junior senator has come to our attention. Shortly after confirmation, he began exhibiting the type of behaviors that we strive to guard against: greed, sedition and the complications that surface when one is working toward a private agenda instead of the common good. Secret meetings, 'midnight oil' sort of stuff."

The Senator set up his tee shot, took a moment to steady his form and brought his number 3-wood down with a swooshing sound. The audible pop the wood made as it smacked the ball sounded like a tree branch cracking under its own weight. The Senator made a small sound of disappointment in the back of his throat as he watched his ball as it flew straight into the rough about three quarters of the way down the course.

The third Senator stepped to the tee and spoke up.

"Hartfield's rapid expansion from a PR firm in a nice neighborhood to having a presence on the world business scene sent a red flag to our core group of members. We set in place a few monitoring schemes and spent six months watching the newest Hartfield building being constructed. Several levels were excavated from the site for what we thought would be underground parking but that never materialized. Instead, we've estimated that there are at least four, maybe five, underground floors to the building."

Taking his number 1-wood from his bag, he stepped to the tee box and readied his Callaway atop a new Flytee and with near-perfect form, sent it flying high above the fairway to land just outside of the putting green.

Smiling to himself, he turned to the small group and continued, "We've never been able to determine what those underground floors are being used for, but for weeks following their construction, we observed many truck-loads of equipment being delivered under cover of darkness, as if to hide what they were taking inside."

Martha set up her tee shot and chose her number 3-wood calculating that she would need the lift it would provide to her ball if she was to make this shot to the green. She calmed her mind and clearly visualized the fairway and where she intended the ball to land…on the green. Slowly letting the air from her lungs, Martha swung her club down and connected with the ball, sending it high. She held her breath as she watched the ball shoot toward the right then angle back to land about ten yards from the right-hand side of the green.

As the group gathered their bags and started the walk back to the carts, the first Senator said, "It's well understood that the government has a strict policy of intolerance toward any of its elected members indulging in any activity that may be construed as an unfair practice. It's spent a great deal of time and even more money…taxpayer dollars…correcting any situation it encountered – even if it was only a perception – and assuring the American public that their elected officials have only public interests as their focus."

The two golf carts made their way along the winding asphalt path. Martha, sitting quietly beside one of the Senators, was listening to him talk about the par needed to win the hole and watching the backs to the other two Senators as their cart bounced along the path.

When they reached the location of the ball in the rough, the little carts pulled up to a stop along the fairway. The second Senator got out, chose his club and chipped the ball out of the rough to place it fifteen feet into the green.

Turning back to his companions he said, "There's still hope! I can sink that putt with ease." After returning his 9-iron to his golf bag, the group moved on to the number four green.

After a smooth ride, the small golf carts pulled up and parked slightly off the path. With the group now loosely assembled along the outside of the putting green, the second Senator turned to the group and said, "There's a strong indication that The Hartfield Connection may have found a way to circumvent government safeguards, but we need irrefutable proof. We would also like the opportunity to prepare a formal proposition that would guarantee additional safeguards that, if put into motion, would prevent future ingress."

Two of the Senators were testing the turf by poking at it with their putting irons, while Martha stood aside with the third Senator who was warily eyeing his ball's alignment to the cup.

Since Martha's shot was furthest from the hole, it was understood that she would make her putt last. As she waited to the side of the green, she addressed the group, "I'll call my right-hand man as soon as we finish this hole and have him gather my top five agents and set up a briefing for six tonight. This project will need surveillance, equipment, a cover story, support, personnel, logistics and all the intel and background that you can provide."

The Senator standing off to her left turned to face her and said, "We have continued to monitor the situation but have been unable to make any in-depth moves for fear of exposure. If any of our actions were to become public knowledge, it would set us back years and could mean the forfeiture of our careers. An operation such as ours, as good as our intentions may be, would not be viewed favorably by the American public."

Two putts sunk and two left to go. Martha felt a twinge of excitement start to build as the Senator's story started to wind down and her strategy formed. Aligning her shot and tapping her putter into place behind her ball, she said, "Gentlemen, let me say first, that I'm very much interested in participating in this project, and second, that I have the finest team ready to begin work. I would like to offer you this...in addition to your surveillance, I will establish another level that will bring the visuals and taps to a more detailed point". Keeping her focus on her ball Martha slowly swung her putter and with a firm tap, sent it rolling into the cup.

The Senator holding the flagstick smiled and said, "Nice shot, well played. I believe that puts you in the lead with one under par."

One of the Senators ventured a question, "Martha, would you be able to accomplish a more detailed surveillance without the need for judicial intervention?"

"I believe so." Martha replied, "But Senator, if I were to ask that a court intervene on our behalf, would you be able to make that happen?"

"Yes, within moments of your asking."

Martha continued, "We'll tailor a cover that will allow me access to The Hartfield Connection by way of the front door. All necessary support will be identified and put into place. I'll keep you posted by way of a secure web address where you can access our intel when it's convenient for yourselves."

Quietly watching a Senator take his turn at his shot and sinking a long putt, Martha turned to the group and said, "I would like your assurance that I and my team have your full authority and will be granted anonymity during and after the operation." Each Senator, in turn, nodded their consent to her request.

She smiled and looked from one Senator to the next and studied their faces as they took a moment to ponder her words and their putting distance to the cup.

By the end of the ninth hole, all four players were satisfied that results would be quickly forthcoming.

The senior Senator spoke, "Ms. Gainsbrook, we love what we're hearing and support your ideas fully. From this point forward, consider us to be your patrons. We don't anticipate that there will be any difficulties along the way, unless, of course, the player with the highest par doesn't agree to pick up today's lunch tab."

◆　◆　◆

Pete Malloy's meeting with the parents of the missing girl, Anne Whitman, was strained to say the least. Her mother frequently broke into uncontrolled fits of sobbing and her father was beside himself in a strange mixture of anger and bravery. He vacillated between blaming Azekiel Hartfield for his daughter's disappearance and showing real concern for his wife, who continually wiped tears from her eyes.

Anne's father spoke in an even tone, "Anne was so excited about her new job. She just bubbled when she spoke to us about her position as an Executive Assistant; she even bought new clothes, wanting to look dignified and mature. Anne wanted everything to go well. She was hopeful about submitting her résumé and was thrilled when she was contacted about interviewing. After all the paperwork and face-to-face sessions were completed, she was so confident that she had gotten the job that by the time the offer letter arrived at her flat, she had already planned her work attire and readied her valise."

Pete watched Mr. Whitman as he sat on the edge of the couch fidgeting with his wedding band, twisting it around and around his finger as he spoke.

Mrs. Whitman made a tiny mewing sound and dabbed at her eyes on the last dry corner of her tear-soaked hankie. Both men looked at her for a moment before Pete broke the awkward silence with a question, directing it to Mr. Whitman.

"What can you tell me about the days leading up to Anne's last phone call to you?"

Mr. Whitman pulled in a long breath, filling his lungs. Slowly letting it out in a controlled manner seemed to calm his body and organize his thoughts. Then he began.

"The first week of her new job went as well as any, I suppose. Anne talked about establishing new habits and adjusting her commute timing. Overall she was happy with how things were going. About the second week, Anne mentioned that she had received access to the secure corporate site that included a wide range of privileges, something that surprised her a bit."

"What made that a surprise for her?"

"She had made friends with another woman in her department who mentioned in passing that full system access was never granted to anyone who hadn't already been working there for several months. Apparently, The Hartfield Connection wanted to test their new employees before letting them in."

Mrs. Whitman managed to calm herself once again and started to speak but her voice broke so she coughed a bit to bring it back. Pete got up from his chair and strode to a large armoire that stood along the wall adjacent to his desk. When opened it revealed a small cooler and clean stemware. He produced a bottle of sparkling water and filled a glass. Glancing at Mr. Whitman, Pete held up the glass as if to ask if he would like one too. Mr. Whitman gave a small shake of his head to decline the offer. Returning to Mrs. Whitman, he placed the glass in front of her and said, "Please, take your time."

Mrs. Whitman sipped the water and after another small sip, spoke.

"It was into that third week when Anne's bearing started to change. She has always been such an upbeat girl. Always cheerful, always mindful of how others may perceive her. But during that third week, her outlook had started to change a bit, started to become more serious. She mentioned that something felt odd to her, that something was not right but that maybe it was her imagination, maybe things were fine. Two days later she was very upset and left a message on our home line saying that things were not fine and that she needed to think seriously about quitting her job."

Taking another sip from her glass and trying to calm her

shaking hands by fidgeting with her hankie, Mrs. Whitman looked up at her husband and said, "That troubled me because it meant she was unhappy."

Mr. Whitman added, "That was on a Friday and after a late night phone call to her, we suggested that she take the weekend to consider her options, not to make any rash decisions. When we spoke again on Monday evening, Anne had calmed down considerably, almost as if a wave had enveloped her. Her voice took on a level of seriousness not typical for her. Anne had always been eager and positive about her life but the serious tone of her voice just raised red flags for us. And it was what she said next that gave us real concern. She said, 'I'm okay now. I know what I need to do.' Then she begged off and hung up."

"But not before we made her promise to call us the next day," said Mrs. Whitman.

"Yes, but," said Mr. Whitman, putting his arm around his wife's shoulders as she had started to sob again, "she didn't call us and we've been unable to contact her since. This brings us to the phone call to you, Mr. Malloy. Mr. Ed Burnett, a P.D. acquaintance of mine, gave me your number. You are highly recommended. Is there anything you can do to help us find Anne?"

"Yes, there are several things that I can do," said Pete. "I'll call my friends on the police force to see what they have, inquire into Anne's hiring through Hartfield's personnel department and things of that nature. I'll need a few days to gather some baseline facts but I'll keep in touch with you along the way."

Pete handed Mr. Whitman a pad of paper and a pen.

"Write down all your contact information for me. Also, I'll need a current photo of Anne and a list of her friends and their contact information. Now, please, go home and try to relax, there's nothing more you can do right now. If you think of anything else, call this number."

Pete handed his business card to Mr. Whitman who looked at it, nodded, then put it into the inside breast pocket of his jacket. Mrs. Whitman had again composed herself and allowed her husband to help her up from the couch. As they made their way to the outer office door and out into the hallway, Mr. Whitman thanked Pete for his time and managed a sad smile and held out his hand. Pete grasped the offered hand and said, "I'll look into this and keep you updated as I find information to share with you. Don't worry, and hope for the best."

♦   ♦   ♦

Anne Whitman was a pretty, young wisp of a woman, and at 22 years old, she considered herself fortunate to be newly employed at The Hartfield Connection. She had taken her university courses in business engineering very seriously and in the weeks following her graduation, researched several top businesses. She sent off polished and well thought out résumés to the four companies that interested her most. The responses she received were varied but Hartfield's letter was the most positive. The letter was printed on embossed stationary with the company logo in the letterhead appearing in raised golden ink. The letter complimented her on her university accomplishments and requested that she schedule for an interview at her earliest convenience.

The interviewing process went quicker than she had anticipated, culminating with an employment offer after only two meetings: one with Personnel and one with the department leads from Finance and Accounting.

Anne was thrilled when the employment proposal came in the

mail. She had been offered a job with the Finance department, starting as a junior level analyst and working under the direct supervision of the department's Chief Financial Officer, Mr. Tom Ashton.

The first weeks of her new job flew past. Anne felt like a kid in a candy shop. She was excited about going to work every morning. Excited about setting up her area. Excited about meeting new people. Excited about being asked to look at an accounting spreadsheet and to give her opinion about it. Excited about working directly with Hartfield's CFO. Anne was just plain excited.

She had been given a modest desk and workspace inside Tom Ashton's large office on the 21ˢᵗ floor. Ashton thought that he would undertake her training, himself. He felt that they should work closely for a time and when Anne was ready to assume full responsibility for the design of a new business model for Hartfield's financial department, he would see that she was moved into a nice office of her own.

Things moved along at a rapid pace as Anne became more familiar with how the department operated and her responsibilities. Ashton encouraged her to expand her role as analyst by developing opinions on various reports and accounting practices and discussing those opinions with him at their weekly progress meetings.

On one particular morning, Ashton had been watching Anne as she worked diligently over several reports. He leaned back in his overstuffed leather desk chair, propped his foot up on a lower desk drawer handle and said, "Anne, I think it's about time we put that fancy college degree of yours to work."

Anne looked up from her work, her concentration broken, and said, "Yes, Mr. Ashton, how's that again?"

With a wry smile on his face, Ashton continued, "I'd like you to review the financial records for this quarter and make at least three recommendations about how we can economize company expenditures. Do you think you can do that?"

Anne's mind raced. "Of course! When would you like me to start?"

Ashton thought for a second and said, "We'll have to get you cleared for access, but otherwise, right away."

Anne was very happy when her clearance was granted, so happy that she mentioned it to a coworker the next day during a coffee break in the department's kitchenette. The response from the coworker was that of mild astonishment, mentioning that clearances usually took months to go through. Anne let the comment pass, assuming that what Mr. Ashton asked for, he got.

It wasn't until a week later that she started to notice several line items on the accounting sheets that looked a bit out of place. Worried that her questions would make her look unprofessional, Anne kept them to herself, hoping that an obvious explanation could be derived further into the quarter's accounting. As Anne continued to work, the questionable line items continued to appear with alarming frequency and her belief that something suspicious was going on, continued to grow.

It didn't take long before Anne knew, almost beyond a doubt, that The Hartfield was financing some uncertain ventures. As her suspicions turned to certainty, fear started to manifest itself in the pit of Anne's stomach. Her conversations with coworkers became infrequent and her interaction with Tom Ashton was strained. Anne tried to cover her sudden stress with explanations that she was serious about doing a good job and wanted to complete the analysis of all quarterly data before giving her considered opinion about efficiency improvements and updating processes.

One evening, in the dusky quiet of her flat, Anne thought about all she had discovered and considered her options. Should she continue forward and build a big future for herself as a senior analyst and business designer? After all, The Hartfield Connection was a huge and powerful company. Surely they knew what they were doing. Or, should she set her fears aside and risk her future by becoming a whistle blower?

The longer Anne thought about it, the calmer she became. She managed to replace some of her fear with a steady resolve that only grew as the hour became late and a strategy started to form. The hours ticked by until a decision had been made:

Anne Whitman would do the right thing.

5
It's All About The Details

After the Whitman's left Pete Malloy's office, he sat in silence for several long minutes thinking about all he had just heard and guessing at the parts he hadn't heard. In his mind, he could see the facts all floating about in space in an irregular line and he was trying to fit them together like a jigsaw puzzle. As the facts slowly moved about, making their way onto a time line, gray areas and questions emerged to fill in the blank spaces. Pete made his own narrative out of the jumble of information and updated his notes to record the additional details he had gathered from the meeting.

What Pete didn't know would fill a book, but what he could intuit from the facts was this: Anne found something at The Hartfield Connection that frightened her enough to make her disappear – either on her own, with help or by force. Which way was of little importance at this time. The fact that Anne Whitman was missing clearly indicated that she was in possession of information that could be damaging to Hartfield or to any of his clients.

Pete picked up his phone and touched a series of lighted buttons that connected him with a good friend at his old precinct.

"Hello, Ed. It's Pete. How are you?"

Ed Burnett was one of Pete's better friends and a good poker buddy and greeted Pete in return.

"I'm doing as good as I can. What's up with you?"

"Thanks for the Whitman referral. I've just had a meeting with them and it seems that it isn't just a missing persons case." Pete shifted the handset to his other ear and reached for his notepad and a pen and continued, "Their daughter, Anne, took a job with The Hartfield Connection last month. She was offered a fairly lucrative position in the finance department and jumped at it. After a couple of weeks on the job, she made a phone call to her parents and dropped a hint that she was starting to have second thoughts about the job."

Ed asked, "Did her parents ask her anything specific about her feelings? Did they get a sense for what it was about?"

"Not really," Pete said. "At first, they let it go, thinking that maybe Anne's trepidation was nothing more than new job nerves and wanting to look good."

As he continued, Pete referred to his notes. "One week after that, she called again when her parents weren't home and left a garbled message...something about her being right about The Hartfield and suggesting that very soon she may have to quit her job."

"How long ago was that?" asked Ed.

"That was three days ago."

"Hang on Pete, I'll get my notes." Pete heard muffled sounds coming from the phone's earpiece and after fifteen seconds, Ed returned.

Pete took the opportunity to write a few sentences on his pad and refocused his attention when Ed continued

"Her parents became alarmed when they couldn't reach Anne and tried to reach her e-device, calling every few hours after she disappeared. They had been to her flat and noted to me that there was evidence that Anne had hurriedly packed a few clothes and left, taking her passport with her."

"Something is definitely wrong here." After a second of thought, Pete said, "I'm betting that The Hartfield is involved more than we know. Anne Whitman is running scared."

"Well," Ed said. "After speaking with Mr. Whitman, I transferred his call to our Missing Persons Department. Give me an hour and I'll talk with them to see if they can add anything to our little mystery."

Pete signed off with, "I'll wait for your call here at my office, and thank you, Ed, and I owe you one."

Thirty minutes later, the phone atop the big wooden desk in the third story office space of the Malloy Agency rang once before Pete snapped up the handset.

"Yo, it's Pete" and concentrated as Ed filled him in on what had transpired during his conversations with others in the P.D. Pete listened with intent to the voice on the wire and as his pen flew across his page of notes, more pieces were being added to the puzzle.

The phone wire sang. "A call to Hartfield's personnel department and a shunt to the department manager, resulted in a denial that Anne Whitman was hired into the company at all, in fact, they said they've never even heard the name before and have checked their unsolicited communication files for a résumé or some other communiqué but found nothing. They were so sorry that they couldn't help."

"This doesn't make any sense at all. Why would The Hartfield deny Anne Whitman's employment? The act itself is suspicious. They're trying to hide something. Anne worked in the finance department. It's my guess that she saw or heard something that she wasn't supposed to see or hear. It's the only thing that makes sense right now."

Ed continued, "A search of police files yielded three other complaints of recent hires gone missing from The Hartfield with the one previous to Ms. Whitman occurring late last year. The company has denied all three. All three had been worked on by my department but with no results and are now classified as cold files."

That last bit of intel raised the biggest question for Pete and as he pondered the implications of what he had just heard, Ed continued.

"And hey, two CIA big shots were here this morning in a meeting with brass. I don't know if it means anything or not but something's up. It's all hush-hush and we've been told that we're to stay out of the way of their investigations. A couple of us have tried to find out what that means but brass isn't talking."

"The connection isn't that clear," Pete said, "The CIA could be there for any number of reasons. Just for arguments sake, let's say that there is a connection and that the CIA is there because of The Hartfield. Their finance department may be under scrutiny due to, I don't know, financing something that the government doesn't like. Maybe funneling money into the corporate takeover of another firm, much like their handling and dismantling of that Personal Relations firm, Burgit & Maine, several years ago."

Ed continued, "I do have good news for you though. We spotted a job posting on Hartfield's personnel page. They're looking for a Security Auditor to run leak checks on their entire system. We've managed to block the post from being viewed by other outside queries – don't ask how we do these things – and have submitted your name as the qualifying candidate. If you hurry, you can make your 4:30PM briefing with the VP of Security. Ask for contact 437 at reception, and good luck!"

Pete set his pen down next to the notepad and shifted his weight in the chair to straighten his back. "Ed, thanks for that very interesting information. I especially like the part about the other missing new-hires. This case is already getting larger than I first thought and probably much larger than Anne Whitman's parents think. I'll keep you in the loop."

After disconnecting from the phone line, Pete grabbed his coat, his Private Investigator badge and his wallet full of credentials. He unlocked the top middle drawer of his desk, removed his PA-48 from its charger and flipped open the chambers to make sure that all rounds were present. Before he took another step, Pete set the safety and ensured that the slider on the left side of the weapons barrel was set to single shot. Checking the laser tracker and satisfied that the weapon was in top condition, he holstered it and left the office, careful to secure the door behind him.

THE INNOCENCE OF POWER

6
Leave Nothing To Chance

In a fashionable, well appointed loft office on 38th Street North, Martha Gainsbrook prepared to brief her team on why they had set up such an appealing ruse in one of the nicer buildings in the downtown.   Martha felt that in order to play a convincing undercover role to the fullest extent, she would need an organization surrounding her. A faux company was needed to set the stage for the subterfuge.

The six-story building architecture was a pleasing mixture of mid-last century gothic and modern contemporary. The top four floors were loft spaces with Martha's team occupying the top most floor. At 16,250 square feet, there was more than enough space for a faux entry and a behind-the-scenes area where all the work would be done. The building was the tallest in this small industrial complex so prying eyes were not really a problem. The top loft also had exclusive rights to roof access, which Martha had thought might come in handy at a later time. Plenty of natural light flooded in from tall windows that surrounded the space on all four sides.

Seemingly overnight, Martha's command center had sprung into being and it was a thing of beauty. Lucite tables, oak desks and ergo-chairs had been arranged to best suit the tasks to be performed: surveillance, analysis, and communication. Each area had been equipped with its relevant electronic needs and atop each station sat a state-of-the-art laptop with all required supplies neatly stored along side. There was no clutter. All the cables had been tied back and stowed and the artificial lighting fully integrated. Around the entire loft, and situated about the computer networks and the soft constant hum of electricity, stood large and small potted live plants. This uncommon addition to the work place, beautiful lush green plants, was the result of an empirical study done by Martha herself, on the development of the human psyche when required to live in a total electronic environment. She found that the calming, steadying effect of nature facilitated better judgment and decision making actions and promoted overall better mental health among her teams. A side benefit turned out to be the pleasing visual impact perceived when entering the workspace – it set the pace for the work ahead. And as such, became a standard setup for Martha's teams.

Gathered in the main meeting area, Martha's team listened as she began her overview of their new mission.

"You have been assigned to this team on my request. I've worked with many of you in the past and it's nice to see familiar faces." Martha stood in front of the group, leaning back against the front of her desk with her feet lightly crossed at her ankles. "The project we'll be working on has been presented as a substantiated suspicion that The Hartfield Connection is involved in several highly lucrative, but very questionable, activities. Details about The Hartfield are in your briefing papers. We are to penetrate their well-established wall of secrecy and extract enough information to do the largest amount of damage possible."

"As much damage as Stone did on the last mission?", poked Mitchal.

"All that smoke and no mirrors!", added Rosen.

"Yes," Martha smiled, "Stone was very enthused about his task."

Laughter rippled around the group but they quickly settled down and Martha continued.

"We are interested in obtaining as much evidence as possible that will implicate The Hartfield in any and all illegal stratagems they are involved in. Our approach will be that of a potential client." Martha continued.

"My cover name will be Mrs. Jennifer Harstaad. The widow Harstaad. My poor deceased husband was one of Norway's largest manufacturers of titanium, which you may know, is a necessary component used in the steel industry. Harstaad owned a great deal of that industry, too, hence the great wealth I am now at liberty to enjoy." As Martha spoke, she shifted her weight as she continued to lean against the edge of her desk and un-crossed her ankles.

"Several partially vague stories of my globetrotting life-style as well as hinting about my late husband's other holdings – such as precious gems, possible weapons sales and other such shady practices – have been placed in some of the more prominent e-papers. Some of these clips date back three years, others are more recent."

Flipping a page in her folder, Martha continued, "Apparently, I'm tired of my liberated, if somewhat boring, life-style – after all, one can only traverse the globe so many times before the romance and excitement are gone." She looked up with a smile and was greeted back with smiles and knowing nods from the team.

"Therefore, I've decided to enter U.S. politics. But my recent past, and maybe one or two questionable walks on the wild side during my twenties and thirties might be showstoppers." Martha straightened up and took a couple idle paces across the front of her desk. She turned to face her team before continuing.

"This is where The Hartfield comes in. I'm going to need their help and all my money practically guarantees that they will give it. I want to see how far they can reach, how deep their influence is with foreign governments and international organizations, and, above all, how far they will go to ensure success."

As she reached for her cup of water, Martha continued her briefing, "One hour from now, I'll enter The Hartfield and request a meeting with a company rep. My cover is that of a very wealthy lady of questionable character wishing to enter U.S. politics and it's up to The Hartfield Connection, with the generous support of my deep pocket, to see that that happens. I have a back-story in mind that will give them something to think about and will give me a measure of their power."

"From there, my Gazelle encoder will transmit my conversations and movements. You are to track and map my every move. My Trapping encoder will tag every e-device within a one hundred foot radius and you are to track and map those persons too. I expect highlights to be sent to me by way of the encrypted contact number without delay. I'll decide what to use and what to toss, you just send the data."

Martha looked over the faces about her and spotted one of her technical people. She smiled and asked, "David, do you need anything or are you ready to go?"

David, a tall slender man of about twenty-eight, looked up from his papers and returned her smile. "Don't need a thing. Thanks. Your Gazelle and your Trapper are ready when you are."

After checking her notes, Martha continued, "We have surveillance on the streets and have been given online access to all private security systems within a ten-block grid surrounding The Hartfield building. I've assembled four tactical Ready Teams that will mobilize within one minute of our signal, or more specifically, within one minute of my signal to you. I believe we're more than ready to go and if you would, please take a moment to read the project details in your briefing doc. Any questions or comments?"

The rustling of paper was the only sound heard for a number of seconds and the excitement of expectation hung over the group. A few glances passed between the team members, but there were no pressing questions.

"Okay. That's it for the moment, except, thank you for your time and for all the hard work you are about to do for me." Smiling, Martha watched as everyone filtered back to his or her workstations then turned her attention to the continuous stream of intel appearing on her laptop screen.

◆ ◆ ◆

Stepping over to the Communication area, Martha addressed the lead tech, "Sam, after powering up my bugs and devices run them through a quick diagnostics to make sure they're working and test the network transmission rates. You might verify that the pass codes have been activated. And thank you."

Excusing herself, Martha made her way through the work area to the ladies lounge where she changed into a tight fitting and slightly revealing dark blue business dress, clasped a string of fresh-water pearls around her neck, placed a gold Movado watch on her wrist and slipped on a pair of dark brown Manolos...the ones with the three inch heels. After adjusting her makeup and hair, Martha put on a light but stylish overcoat, picked up her handbag and prepared to leave.

She retrieved her e-devices and spoke again with Sam, "I'll tap out a message to you when I reach the Hartfield building. The rest of my visit should follow our strategy planning. I'll be in touch along the way."

Sam nodded as he handed Martha her laptop and two sidecars and said, "Don't worry, boss, we'll be here ready to go. Take care."

Martha stepped off the vertical into the newly renovated office-building foyer and nodded to the doorman. He rang the car service station and within a minute, Martha's chauffeured vintage Rolls Royce pulled up to the curb just outside the wide expanse of lobby windows. Settling into the soft leather seats, she centered herself by watching the streetscape roll by her door window. Sitting quietly in the comfort of the rear seat of the Rolls always calmed her mind. It created a managed buffer between her mission and her cover. When these times were available, Martha used them to envelop herself deeper into character, to bring substance to the fabrications, to bring believability to her stories.

She sat passively, feeling the car rock back and forth as it glid forward and noted the tall trees in planting areas at each corner, surrounded by flowering shrubs, and illuminated by the late afternoon sun. *Jennifer Harstaad. U.S. citizen and recently married to one of the world's biggest magnates.* Several cars were lined up on a side street waiting for the light to change. *I've had a wild life but am now bored and looking for a change, something more challenging than a social dinner party.* The afternoon sun was reflecting off the windows of an older downtown high-rise building. It made it look like it had been constructed of gold. *Be on guard. They'll be scrutinizing everything.*

The Rolls Royce rocked gently to the right as it pulled into a lane of traffic and rolled forward.

7
The Gathering Storm

At exactly 4:29PM Pete Malloy stepped into the spacious lobby of The Hartfield Connection and presented himself to the receptionist. With an air of authority, Pete asked to be announced to Contact 437. With a neat smile and a slight tilt of her head, the receptionist replied, "Yes, of course, Mr. Malloy, Security Operations is expecting you. You are to take the left-hand vertical to their floor. Just press S1, where you will be met and escorted to the Vice President's office."

Pete nodded his acknowledgement and as he turned toward the verticals, he heard the rapid fire clicking of keyboard keys behind him and knew that he has just been announced.

The ride down was quick but before the doors slid open, Pete took note that there were three additional floors below Security: L1, L2 and L3. All were accessible by a key slot on a separate panel. When the doors opened, two people met Pete. The first was a hard-edged and rather big man in a guard's uniform whose steady stare put Pete on alert. The second was a much more pleasant looking woman wearing the clean lines of business fashion, who greeted him with a soft smile and a light handshake.

"I'm Miss Ebbert and I'll be your escort until your access coded badge is delivered." She glanced at her watch and continued, "Which will be in approximately one hour. We're running reference checks, you understand."

Smiling another soft smile, she said, "Let's get started, shall we?"

Miss Ebbert extended her arm to point the way down the

narrow hallway, took a furtive step and waited for Pete to fall into step beside her. As they walked in silence to the door marked "Office of the Vice President of Security Operations", Pete noticed the camera surveillance along the corridor and the extensive security verification stations at every door. A pesky little thought occurred to him...*Why would a public relations firm need such a high level of security?*

◆　　◆　　◆

When the Rolls was within three blocks of The Hartfield Connection, Martha instructed her driver to call ahead to announce that she was arriving on time. By the time the chauffeur had eased the car up to the curb, Mark Sturgess was standing on the sidewalk, waiting.

With the gear in park and the key turned off, Mark watched as the driver got out and made his way to the curbside rear door. He tipped his cap to Mark and then stepped up to the door, placing his hand upon the door latch. He hesitated for a second or two before Mark, with a shadow of a question forming across his face, took a step forward. Just then, an audible clicking sound emitted from the door, the chauffeur pulled the latch and the door swung open. The chauffeur extended his gloved hand and helped Martha out of the car. Mark smiled and was about to extend his greeting when he realized she was talking on her e-device. He pulled himself up short and took a half step backward, almost tripping as he did so.

"Yes. Yes. Yes. Please have that ready for me by 7PM. I'll have someone pick it up. Yes. Thank you." Martha pressed a button, looked up at Mark, and with a teasing smile said, "Forgive me, a small piece of business that needed to be taken care of."

Extending her hand to Mark, she allowed herself to be guided in the front doors directly to the verticals and straight into business.

◆　　◆　　◆

Mark led Martha to a beautiful conference room on the twelfth floor. The room was arranged into two separate spaces tied together by a huge bank of windows that were covered in a haze of sheer material. One side of the room was arranged with a beautiful maple table and enough comfortable chairs to seat at least twenty persons. The wall at the head of the table was faced with stone except for a wide area in the center that showcased a piece of artwork depicting tall snow-capped mountains surrounded by trees and blue skies. The entire wall was awash with soft lighting that naturally guided the eye to the art centerpiece.

The other side of the room had been set up as a more intimate seating area with large upholstered chairs, a leather love seat and mahogany tables. Martha noticed a beautiful hand-cut crystal flower bowl with one almost perfect yellow bloom in it had been placed in the center of the low coffee table.

Martha took a chair facing the large expanse of windows that framed a view of the city skyline. Mark seated himself on the end of the small sofa closest to her.

Martha adjusted herself in the chair, being careful to place her e-device in her lap, and after she had settled in, addressed Mark.

"Mr. Sturgess…"

"Please call me Mark."

"Okay, Mark. I'd like The Hartfield Connection to assist me in my efforts to gain a position in public office. This would be a career change for me and I'm afraid I lack the basic knowledge of how exactly to start." Martha watched Mark closely and saw his mouth turn upward into a slight smile before he spoke.

"Mrs. Harstaad, you've chosen the right company for the job. Hartfield has a solid reputation for successfully launching its clients into their chosen careers." Mark reached into his pocket and brought out his e-device and said, "Mind if I take a few notes as we talk?"

Smiling politely, Martha said, "Not at all. As long as they're accurate." She watched Mark's reaction and noted that while he appeared to take her statement in stride, a small twitch of his jaw gave away his true feelings: he didn't like it.

Martha spoke, "Let me begin by giving you a brief overview of my life so far." Adjusting herself deeper into the chair, and smiling to herself, she asked, "May I have something to drink? A sparkling water perhaps?"

Mark immediately rose from his seat saying, "Certainly. With or without ice?"

As he strode to the sideboard, Martha called out, "With ice. Shaved if you have it."

With his back to Martha, Mark felt his eyebrows knit together in an expression of derision as he thought *I don't doubt you would like shaved ice*, but he quickly adjusted himself before turning back to her and smiled pleasantly.

"You were saying?"

Martha continued her story, "As I was saying, I graduated middle of my class from the University of Chicago with a degree in journalism. My college years were rather drab so I thought to see a bit of the world before settling down. A girlfriend and I flew to Paris, the City of Lights, you know."

"Very romantic city," Mark said. "Did you have a nice time?"

"Yes, but we thought to see it all, so after two weeks we left for Rome. And from there we went to Madrid, Athens, Amsterdam, Copenhagen, Stockholm and maybe other places, too, but definitely Oslo. This is where I met and fell in love with Baron Harstaad. By then, my friend was bored and homesick so she returned to the states, but I stayed on."

Martha watched as Mark cracked the seal on a bottle of sparkling water and empty the contents into a Waterford cut crystal tumbler. She waited for Mark to turn from the sideboard and made a show of looking at the face of her e-device before she continued.

"It was a fast and furious courtship. You see, we fell in love and within three weeks were married."

Returning to the seating area, Mark placed the tumbler on a coaster within Martha's easy reach. Martha looked at the water with little interest and waited a second or two before she took up the tumbler and slowly brought it to her lips. She had paused her storytelling and watched Mark as he resumed his position on the sofa. He retrieved his e-device from his coat pocket and continued his typing. She continued to look at him as his thumbs flew across his tiny e-device keyboard and started to wonder what he was typing. She then took another sip from her tumbler and let her gaze slide to the windows.

Mark stopped typing on his little keyboard and sat back against the sofa cushions to watch Martha. A small interlude of silence transpired before Martha coolly brought her gaze back to Mark. Looking at him steadily, she spoke.

"The Baron passed away after a short illness. That was two years ago last May. Since then I have been a bit lost but I believe I've found my calling now."

Watching Mark for any sign that would give away what he may be thinking, Martha slowed her voice for effect and said, "I'm going to enter U.S. politics. I would like to be a Senator."

Mark uncrossed his legs and shifted his weight to the front of the sofa cushion. Martha thought that he looked like a cat poised to strike. "Mrs. Harstaad, anything is possible in this wide wonderful world, and The Hartfield Connection is here to almost guarantee it."

◆　◆　◆

Successful negotiations with legal resulted in a contract chock full of all her demands including twenty-four-hour access in case she had questions, daily electronic updates from her new staff of handlers, and weekly summaries of the progress The Hartfield was making on her behalf. Martha Gainsbrook, as the widow Mrs. Jennifer Harstaad then found herself on the fifty-sixth floor of The Hartfield Connection.

The fifty-sixth floor is where Hartfield's large staff of client handlers are settled. As Martha was being shown through the area to a private meeting room, she noticed that all of the workstations had been equipped with state of the art means of information retrieval and communication. They entered a private meeting room that was tastefully furnished with comfortable chairs, original art, refreshments and organic snacks.

Mark introduced her to the two Hartfield handlers that had been appointed to her contract. "Mrs. Harstaad, this is Jess and Diane. Jess is your liaison and is here for you whenever you need him. Diane is his assistant. Now, if you'll excuse me, I have business elsewhere. If you have any questions or concerns, please don't hesitate to call me anytime."

Mark took Martha's hand and smiled at her before quietly leaving the room.

Martha, Jess and Diane sat down to begin building her new profile.

Jess, spoke first, "Mrs. Harstaad, we would like to begin by asking you a few questions that would help us to better understand you, your goals and your expectations. It would serve to build a foundation and to alert us to any areas that may need special attention."

Martha tried to look pensive and lightly tapped her finger on the tabletop to suggest she was wrestling with a thought. Then she spoke, "I've not mentioned this to anyone before. I was involved in a situation while in Athens with a girlfriend."

Jess looked up from his laptop and slowly relaxed his hands away from the keyboard while sharpening his attention on Martha.

"On our first day in Athens, we stumbled across a small back-street shop selling couture dresses by Givenchy for a steal! I found a beautiful black dress that was low cut across the shoulders with just a hint of lacy ruffle at the bodice. I was in love with it. My friend found a little red number that made her look absolutely gorgeous. We were so thrilled with our purchases that we decided we had to show them off by going out nightclubbing that evening. Around midnight, we found ourselves in a trendy bar on Andronikou Street. Within minutes we had attracted the attention of two very tall and very cute men who proceeded to ply us with ouzo and hovered around us, flirting and making small talk. The more ouzo we drank, the more we talked and before we knew it, we had practically told our life stories."

Martha hesitated for a second, seeming to organize her thoughts and noticed that the two handlers sat silently, politely waiting for her to continue.

"Their names were Alexandros and Nikolaos. Alex and Nicky. They said they were brothers from a very prominent family in the city. We told them our names, that we were American citizens on vacation and that we were staying at the Hotel Grande Bretagne. Basically, we told them everything."

Martha got up from her chair, moved slowly to the windows, and gazed out across the skyline.

"After two hours of drinking, my girlfriend claimed a splitting headache and we piled her into a cab back to the hotel. I stayed at the bar with Alex and Nicky. We laughed and danced and drank ouzo with honey for another hour or so when I realized that I had had enough fun and alcohol. I decided to leave. Alex and Nicky walked me out and waited with me at the curb for a taxi. We were very drunk, laughing and cutting up. Alex had to relieve himself and instead of going back inside the club, decided to use a nearby alleyway."

Martha turned from the windows and faced her handlers. "May I have a glass of juice? Cranberry, please."

Jess went to the sideboard and busied himself with icing a tumbler and pouring the juice.

He handed the glass to Martha.

"Mrs. Harstaad, you've only just described a night out on the town. Is there something more specific about this evening that we should know about?"

Martha lifted the glass to her lips but before taking a sip, said, "Oh, yes. There's something specific." For a moment, the only sound in the room was the tinkling of ice in Martha's glass as she stepped to a chair and sat down. She placed the glass on a coaster next to her and continued.

"Alex had just stepped into the alley when we heard loud voices and Alex hollering 'No, No, Don't!' just before two gunshots rang out. I could see the bright flashes both times the gun fired. Nicky started to hurry toward his brother when two men came running out of the alley. One ran the opposite way down the street into the darkness and the other came running toward me, knocking Nicky to the ground."

Martha stopped for a moment and touched her forehead with two fingers as if to clarify the memory. She took another sip of juice.

"This man came within five feet of me and hesitated for the briefest of seconds before sprinting off down the street. But I saw his face. I saw it very clearly. I think that when he hesitated and was staring directly at me, he was trying to decide whether to kill me or not because I had been a witness to his crime."

Shifting slightly to cross her legs, Martha looked at the screen of her e-device, lightly touched a button and said, "My girlfriend and I left Athens the next day and within five hours we found ourselves in Amsterdam. A world away from Greece."

During Martha's retelling of the account, Jess had resumed typing on his laptop. He looked up at Martha when she fell quiet. "I don't think you need to worry. These types of circumstances are helpful for us to know about. If anything else, any other situations like this one occur to you, be sure to tell us."

Martha thought that the story would raise a red flag with a government investigatory committee or at the very least with a European agency of some sort, and wondered if Jess had found her story objectionable. She observed his face but he displayed no emotion that she could detect.

Martha wanted to draw him out. "I'm afraid that I may have acted a bit frightfully in the time intervening between college and my marriage. I've led a somewhat fast-paced lifestyle since the death of my husband, Baron Harstaad of Norway, two years ago."

Jess spoke. "Your activities during the time period that preceded your marriage may only be a small obstacle but we'll have to look into it further before formulating a strategy."

Martha asked, "And concerning my high profile lifestyle of the past two years?"

Jess' assistant, Diane, spoke up.

"Mrs. Harstaad, no media counter-measures can be proposed without first conducting a thorough background check for all relevant facts. This will take several days and involve staff not currently assigned to your management team. There may be matters of protocol that require special consideration that should be referred to our Security Department."

"Are you saying that your company security can handle these matters? I would think that it would take a much more powerful entity than your company security to effectively deal with situations that may involve several European countries."

Jess answered, "Oh, company security is fully equipped to manage any situation whether it involves domestic or international associations. Don't worry. Our departments have successfully handled more sensitive situations than this. All you need to do is to leave it in our very capable hands."

And as Martha glanced at the knowing smile and raised eyebrows on Jess' smug little face, she knew she was looking at a man with a secret.

◆   ◆   ◆

The hour it took to download Pete Malloy's pseudo-references and bake up an access badge seemed to take forever. Pete was starting to wonder why in a world of F-G network speeds and instant robotic recognitions – what the hell was taking so long? Waiting was a bit of an annoyance since Miss Ebbert would not brief him to the job at hand, but instead filled the minutes with a version of Hartfield's corporate history that could have played on most kiddy channels.

As they waited in the outer office, Pete noticed how stark the décor was in contrast to the outrageous lobby with its handcrafted tiles and 2-foot gold letters, the plush velvet carpets and the exotic woods. The Security Department had an air of military precision about it and a discipline among the staff that Pete had only witnessed once before during his enlistment with the Air Rangers. This had the same feel about it. The feel of something almost maniacal. And with those thoughts, the hairs on the back of his neck stood straight up.

As if in response, the outer hallway door lock snapped and the handle twisted its half-circle arc that unlatched the mechanism allowing the door to swing in with a soft whooshing sound. Miss Ebbert was startled by the noise and stopped her slow commentary. Both she and Pete turned their heads to see a young man of about twenty-five enter. He addressed himself to Miss Ebbert, not bothering to look at Pete until he was finished speaking and then only to stare at him. "Miss Ebbert, Lieutenant Abers has instructed me to deliver this to you. It's Mr. Malloy's access code badge, encoded with access level Zed."

"Thank you, agent. I have all that I need."

Standing up and smoothing the front of her dress and turning to face Pete, Miss Ebbert smiled and said, "Now. Shall we begin?"

As Pete was conducted through the inner hallway of level S1, Miss Ebbert briefed him as to why he had been hired. "There has been some sort of information drop-outs that had been detected in System Station 9. Operations have been running diagnostics on System 9 but have been unable to locate exactly what has dropped out. The rate of drop-outs exceeded the accepted level thereby triggering an alert."

At this point, they reached the outer door to "Station 9 Ops" where Malloy was to test his access code badge and follow the commands to establish ownership with the system. Inserting his new badge into the red-lighted slot caused the panel to backlight and a voice from the panel started to instruct him, "Welcome Mr. Malloy. Please place your chin on the plastic brace and focus on the object at the back of the view. Press your right thumb on the designated pad and count to three."

Pete started the count, "One. Two." And with a sudden gentle popping sound, a pressurized puff of air hit him right in the left eye. Startled, he jumped back but before he could verbalize a response, the pleasant panel voice continued.

"Thank you, Mr. Malloy. You have been successfully integrated and may now use all tools and access available to your level Zed security."

The panel dimmed and the badge slot snapped to green. Malloy pulled his badge out, pocketed it and turned to Miss Ebbert, "Next time, a small warning, if you would, please."

With a small smirk, Miss Ebbert responded, "It is a one time initiation and start-up and won't necessarily be repeated during your employ with us. We'll enter when you're ready, Mr. Malloy."

What followed next was a tour of Station 9 Operations with a full briefing of the lost dropouts. As Pete drank in as much intel as he could, Miss Ebbert talked on about the system alerts and how two remote desk computers up on the 21st floor had become suspect. Completing the tour of Operations, Pete asked to be shown the two remotes so that his analysis could begin in earnest.

Stepping off the vertical on the 21st floor, Miss Ebbert directed Pete to their left and led the way down the wide hallway and around to the left again to the Director of Finance's office suite. Pete's bug detector, embedded in his wristwatch, had been sending small electronic shocks to his wrist at even intervals since stepping off the vertical. It had been detecting numerous hidden surveillance devices embedded in the frames of original art pieces and most of the fresh flower arrangements along his path. It seemed to Pete that The Hartfield didn't trust any of its employees, preferring instead to observe their every move.

They arrived at the hall door and Miss Ebbert motioned for Pete to use his access code badge again. He did, but this time there was no pleasant greeting and thankfully, no air blast to the eye. He positioned his face within the two and one half inch required distance and endured a brief eye scan and, with an audible click, the door popped open.

Pushing through, Pete observed a wide, brightly lit outer office with several overstuffed suede chairs for waiting clients and a neat desk where, presumably, a good looking receptionist would smile and greet those clients and welcome them to Finance. Another badge/scan apparatus leading to the inner workings of Hartfield's Financial Department was just beyond the desk. One more shock indicated one more bug device and Pete idly wondered if he would have any hairs left on his wrist left by the end of the day.

Once inside, Pete noticed, first, the overly expensive furnishings that made the workspace seem like something that leapt off the pages of a furniture boutique magazine. He was momentarily amazed at the wealth that had been spent in the name of office equipment. After his bug detector fired seven warnings, his training took over.

Noting to himself that there were two accountants busily pounding keys, he noticed the small desktop computers and other electronic accoutrements necessary to run the financials of a company like The Hartfield. He counted about twenty such stations between the entry and the doors to the executive CFO's office, whose two massive oak doors were located in the center of the wall at the rear of these open offices. Large windows flanked these doors but were currently shuttered closed.

Advancing forward, with Miss Ebbert in tow, Pete unsecured the doors and entered the office of Tom Ashton, VP of Hartfield's finances. He quickly spotted a small, well-appointed workspace set up off to the right and a massive Bubinga wood desk situated in front of a bank of windows that ran the entire length of the office suite.

Miss Ebbert's e-device chimed softly and after removing it from her pocket and glancing at the screen, turned to Pete and said, "I'm sorry, Mr. Malloy, but there is a matter that I must take care of."

Pointing to the smaller workspace, she said, "This is the secondary port to log drop-outs". She motioned to the laptop on Ashton's desk, "The main errors were tracked to this computer. I'm sure you'll find everything you need here. You can make your way back to level S1 Security when you're through." She let herself out, quietly closing the door behind her.

Pete took off his overcoat and laid it across the back of a leather chair in front of the large desk and crossed the room to the shutters. Peeking through a slight crack, he saw that one of the two accountants had already left and that the other had packed up his things and was on his way to the hallway door, about to leave. When the outer office door closed completely, Pete hesitated a second or two longer to make sure that neither returned for some forgotten item, before returning to his task at hand.

Powering up the computer at the small desk, Pete quickly mined his way through the top layers of files to the area most likely to hold data and files of a more personal nature. After several minutes of searching, he located a folder titled "AW1014.3", opened it and saw hundreds of large files. *Damn, they're all encrypted and using an unfamiliar coding protocol.*

Betting that the "AW" in the folders title stood for "Anne Whitman", Pete jacked a sidecar drive into the back of the screen and began the time-consuming job of copying files.

The laptop proved to be more transparent than the desk computer and Pete wondered how much information had been removed before the cry went out for help. Working deftly, he removed the base and flipped the back of the case open, careful not to crimp the motherboard cable. The virtual memory was sure to have ghost images of the last 500GB of use, so Pete popped it out and placed it on the desk. From his overcoat pocket, he produced a small gizmo, extended a clip-wire from its base and attached it to the memory chip. Turning the unit on, it whirred to life and a green LED started blinking – a signal that the unit was busy with its copy function.

Pete retrieved the sidecar drive from the small desktop computer. He then loaded and launched a homespun piece of software that would produce reams of encrypted junk data that was sure to impress the Security boys monitoring his progress. He returned to the laptop just as it had completed copying the virtual memory and reassembled the computer. After securing the small screws along the bottom of the case and inserting a clean sidecar drive into the I/O port, Pete dragged the hard-drive icon to the sidecar and dropped it on. When all the copying had been completed, he loaded his gobble-de-gook program onto the hard drive and launched it.

A close survey of the office and a quick search of the desk drawers assured Pete that he had left nothing to chance. Once he was satisfied, he gathered his belongings and left the office pretty much as he found it.

◆　　◆　　◆

After two hours of storytelling and several fast sessions of Question and Answer, Martha Gainsbrook decided to call it a day. When her e-device chimed with another incoming call, she excused herself and stepped to the windows before answering. "Yes. Almost. Thank you for the information. I'll talk with you again soon."

Turning back to her Hartfield handlers, Martha announced that she had given them all she could for that meeting, and added, "I hope that you've found my candor to be of some help but I find I'm late for another appointment and must leave. If there's nothing further, perhaps we can meet again tomorrow morning?"

Jess asked how might they get in touch with her and Martha answered, "I'll contact you, after all, I've been assured 24-hour access and my schedule is generally pretty full." She tapped out a fast message on her e-device and picked up her personal belongings. As she turned to her handlers, she noted the looks of slight confusion with just a hint of annoyance, but before anyone could say anything, Martha said good evening and was out the door.

Walking with slight purpose toward the verticals, Martha fully expected that one of her handlers would snap out of their shock at her sudden departure and catch up with her, insisting on showing her out. To her delight, that did not happen.

Martha's careful but deliberate walk to the verticals gave her Gazelle encoder plenty of time to locate and tap any surveillance ports she passed and transmit the data back to her office. When she reached the verticals, she noticed that one of them had been designated for "Executive Use" only, so naturally pressed the thumb-scan pad to see if the lift would come. Which it did not. Feigning surprise, in case she was being observed by a camera, she signaled for the other vertical, which responded immediately with the quiet noise of far-away gears.

As the vertical started its decent, a call light on the panel lit up and the button for the 21ˢ floor suddenly glowed orange. The vertical reduced its speed and gently came to a stop. The doors quietly opened and revealed a nice-looking man in a clean-cut suit with an overcoat over his arm standing easily a couple of feet from the open doors. As he stepped onto the vertical, he shifted the coat from his right arm to his left and smiled a good evening to Martha before pressing the button marked S1. And wouldn't you know it, the bug finder on his wrist was firing like crazy.

The vertical quickly reached the ground floor lobby and Pete held the doors open as Martha stepped out. With a nod and a glance in Malloy's general direction, Martha strode through the lobby doors and into her Rolls Royce already at the curb.

♦　　♦　　♦

Back in Station 9 Operations, Pete Malloy asked that a rookie be assigned to him and commandeered a workspace. After a minute of tapping keys and opening screen windows, Malloy sat the fresh-faced rookie down and told him to monitor the data stream for this exact sequence: O1P.71-8E5V3N. When he found it, he was to tag the coordinates.

"When you have tagged the number, you are to continue to search for the next logical occurrence of the sequence, and that is 8 to the E6, and so on. After three hours, you are to find a replacement for the work. This is too important to be compromised by eyestrain or fatigue. Is that understood?"

With a look of serious concentration, the rookie responded, "Yes, sir, just as you request."

Pete found the Security Personnel and Operations Manger,

Lieutenant Abers and briefed him to the protocols that Pete had just set up and to mention a few suspicions that he had fabricated regarding the security sweep of the system so far.

Lieutenant Abers was a man of about sixty. He stood just over six feet tall and wore his hair cropped in typical military fashion. He rarely smiled. Pete imagined him being one of those grizzled old boot camp drill sergeants that got sadistic thrills trying to break new recruits. Abers had thought to glide into his old age with military honors but that didn't quite materialize. After thirty two years as a non-commissioned officer, it was strongly suggested to him that he retire from the military. Several months later, he secured a job with The Hartfield Connection as the head of their Security Department Personnel. He felt that he was back.

Addressing Abers, Pete said, "I've loaded and am running the latest version of v-tracker, well, really it's my version of v-tracker because I have modified it to fit my needs."

Lieutenant Abers' eyes opened a bit wider at this statement and appeared ready to make a comment but Pete stopped him by holding up his hand and continuing, "I assure you that nothing has been compromised and I'm certified Level 7 so am fully capable. Anyway. The two suspect systems up on the 21ˢᵗ floor are not to be disturbed by anyone but myself. That's a strict request. I've set up a monitoring station here and have given instructions as to what to look for and how to log it. This algorithm will take some time to complete, so I'll leave you to it and be back in the morning to review the results."

Pete shifted his weight and relaxed his posture, in contrast to Abers who stood rigid, almost at attention. Pete asked, "Are there any other compromised systems I should look at?"

Abers barked out, "No."

Pete asked, "Do you have any questions for me at this time?"

In his brusque style, Abers said, "No Mr. Malloy, the two systems up on floor twenty one were the only ones our detectors found compromised and, at this moment, I have no questions for you."

Satisfied that he had stirred up security around Station 9 Ops, enough to keep them busy for at least two days, Pete repeated that he would be back in the morning to review the findings. He thanked Abers for all his help, complimented him on the professionalism of the outfit he ran and left. As Malloy made his way down the hallway to the outer doors, he flipped open his e-device and was a bit dismayed but not surprised to see that it was getting no reception whatsoever. But his wrist was popping like there was a Jacob's Ladder attached to it.

Outside the building, Pete made his way to his vehicle totally lost in thought. He wondered just what exactly did Security suspect, since they seemed to already know that the two remotes used by Anne Whitman and her boss had been compromised? Pete thought it might be safe to guess that Security didn't have the means to dig out computer ip addresses outside of the company's network. It might also be safe to also guess that Hartfield hadn't made a solid connection between the computers and Anne Whitman's disappearance. Pete was pretty sure that they might be hoping to locate the missing information and bury the mistakes before it was picked up by anyone else. Tonight's activities had added a few more interesting pieces to Pete's investigative puzzle. And as he walked down the street to his car, breathing in fresh air, Pete spoke out loud to himself, "I've got a long night ahead of me."

THE INNOCENCE OF POWER

8
New Puzzle Pieces

Pete Malloy's sleek black Senelli glided around the corner of the street his private office was located on. As his mind refocused from his evening at The Hartfield to the small annoyance of trying to find a parking space along the curb, he noticed something glaringly obvious: that beautiful cobalt blue vintage 1936 Rolls Royce that he had just seen minutes before in front of The Hartfield was now parked in front of his building.

As he drove slowly past, the tinted windows prevented him from viewing the occupants, but he glimpsed the dark silhouettes of the driver and one other man sitting in the passenger side of the front seat. From the parking space up the block, Pete hesitated before getting out, spending a bit of time observing the Rolls and its occupants. Seeing no activity, he got out of his vehicle and walked directly down the center of the sidewalk. Pete deliberated with himself whether or not to confront the situation.

Should I address this head-on or try to ignore it and enter my building as if nothing…let's say…nothing close to a huge, obvious cobalt blue auto…is parked on this street at night. Yeah. I'll ignore it and make the first move theirs. Walking at his normal gait, Pete came within five paces of the auto without any recognition or contact by the occupants. He climbed the steps to the front door of his office building and still nothing happened.

Okay, if that's how this is going to be played, may the better team have it. He keyed the door open, stepped into the foyer, closed the door and secured the bolt. *Well, that went just fine.*

Three flights of stairs up and the story had changed. As Pete drew closer to the hallway door of his office suite, his bug finder zapped him so hard, he thought he actually heard the bolt of electricity make a snapping noise. He froze in his tracks and removed the PA-48 from its holster while taking the safety off. In the same fluid motion of bringing the weapon out from under his jacket, he slid the lever from single shot to cluster fire after assessing the need for close range damage if he encountered more than one intruder in his office.

Silently opening the hall door to the outer office, Pete noticed, through the gap of the now ajar door, that his desk lamp was lit. Quickly checking to his left and to his right, he was satisfied that the outer office was clear. He stealthily made his way to the inner office door. Hesitating to listen for any sounds, Pete heard only the steady rhythm of his own heart mingled with the barely audible hum emanating from the PA-48 in his hand. Slowly reaching out with his free hand, he ever so slightly nudged the door. It slid easily and silently open under his gentle touch. Further, further, further the door opened slowly revealing the silhouette of a woman bathed in the blue hazy glow of a laptop screen she had perched on her lap.

"Good evening, Mr. Malloy. Do come in and make yourself comfortable. We have a lot to discuss." On that note, Martha shifted a bit in her seat to face Malloy, who was still standing at the ready in the doorway, weapon steadily pointed at her head. Martha made a slight movement of her hand to indicate she was looking at the furnishings around her.

"You have a very nice office, I hope you don't mind that I've made myself comfortable?"

"You're the woman from the vertical at Hartfield's."

Martha smiled a thoroughly disarming smile and said, "Yes,

thank you for noticing. I hope you don't mind my letting myself in? I know you're working on a missing persons complaint having to do with The Hartfield Connection. I've done a bit of research on you and can see that you have an impressive background. You seem to be one of the good guys."

"Yes, that's all well and good, but who are you and, please, feel free to impress me with *your* background."

Martha said, "I've been in touch with the police captain at the 401 Precinct, downtown. He talks very highly of you." Martha sat quietly, giving Pete a moment to absorb her statement, then said, "Won't you join me for dinner? I've brought most everything we'll need."

Relaxing his body just a bit and holstering his PA-48, Pete was reminded that he hadn't eaten since breakfast, so he agreed, almost too quickly, to share a meal. Martha flipped open her e-device, pressed a speed-dial sequence and said, "Alan, would you bring up the basket and boxes, now? Thank you."

Turning her gaze back to Pete, Martha invited him to take the seat opposite her and continued the introduction of herself including a brief explanation of what she was doing in his office. She had already decided that the best approach to gaining Pete's confidence was to let him in on the deception.

"My name is Martha Gainsbrook. I work for the CIA. My team has been tasked with investigating The Hartfield Connection for possible treasonous acts against the government." Martha paused for a moment and watched Pete's expression, noting that his face did not betray any thoughts or emotions he might have been experiencing.

Continuing, Martha said, "The government feels that The Hartfield is involved with shady business practices and other affairs that are not in the best interests of this country. My job is to find irrefutable evidence that either supports or dismisses their claim." Glancing at Pete, Martha saw a flicker of concentration cross his face.

"I'm a little surprised and yet, not," said Pete. "In the two days that I've been closely involved with The Hartfield, there are several things that don't add up."

Martha drew a slow breath and continued, "When you saw me tonight at The Hartfield, I was posing as a new client by the name of Jennifer Harstaad. I had just left a meeting with my two handlers who are going to make me more presentable to the public, but more importantly for Jennifer Harstaad, very presentable to the U.S. government."

Martha took Pete's pause in their conversation as a hint that she should continue. "We know you're investigating the disappearance of Anne Whitman and, with the help of your PD contacts, you've taken the job of Security Auditor at Hartfield's. As Security Auditor, you've no doubt noticed the incredible number of surveillance devices embedded in that building, as well as the varied levels of security on every door."

At this, Pete retrieved his access code badge from his shirt pocket and showed it to Martha while slowly twirling it until it came to rest between his index and middle fingers.

"My first impression was that Hartfield has a huge security machine in place for what in all appearances is an office building. It's run like a novice paramilitary camp."

Martha nodded in consent and continued, "As for myself, let me try to impress you…I started building my résumé just after college when I decided that a career with the CIA was exactly what I needed. It offered me a combination of physical and mental exercise that I thought would serve to keep me agile." Pausing for a moment to close her laptop and move it from her lap to the tabletop, Martha said, "And I was right, I've managed to sprint my way to new heights."

Pete looked at Martha and thought that she was either very good at deception or was telling the truth. He remembered the phone call to Ed, his PD friend that morning. Ed had mentioned that two CIA big shots had met with brass. Was that Martha? It would explain how she knew several unpublished facts about him.

He studied her face and after a few seconds said, "I agree that there's something bigger here than we know of."

Martha nodded her head in agreement and continued, "Please accept the fact that I'm here at the behest of persons at the highest levels of our government and that I believe that we can work together to our mutual interests. I also think that time is of the essence for both of us." Martha paused, giving Pete a moment to respond.

Pete shifted a bit to stretch his legs and moved forward on the cushion in order to stand up. Gaining his feet, he stepped to his desk and turned to face Martha. "I hope you won't take offense if I confirm the details of your story. Or as much of it as I can. Would you allow me a moment and a phone call?"

Martha smiled and said, "Of course," and reached for her laptop.

Pete stepped behind his large oak desk to the picture window and pulled his e-device out of his front pocket and dialed a series of numbers. After a moment he spoke in a hushed tone to his PD friend and listened to the information that was given. In all of two minutes, Pete had heard as much detail about the CIA visit to police headquarters as his friend could offer. What he heard made him think that Martha's story had some merit. It also made him aware that his involvement in Martha's investigations was about to become something very serious for him.

Turning back to Martha, and squaring his shoulders, Pete said, "I'm interested in working with you only if we work as equals. No personal agendas and nothing held back. Those are my only conditions."

Smiling and extending her hand for a gentleman's agreement, Martha said, "I wouldn't have it any other way."

♦   ♦   ♦

Both Pete and Martha had resumed their positions facing each other in the twin leather chairs positioned between Pete's oak desk and the door to the outer office. Pete had just lowered himself on to the seat cushion slightly facing Martha, thinking that he would observe her more closely. As Martha settled back, she turned a little more toward Pete and said, "We have something in common, you and I. We seem to be working the same case, although from different angles."

A soft tap on the door caused Pete to tense back to an alert posture and he automatically started to rise from his seat, but with a gentle motion of her hand, Martha calmed the moment, and said, "Yes, Alan, please come in."

Alan entered the office carrying a large basket by its two side handles and Pete recognized his uniform as that of a chauffeur. Behind him was a well-dressed man of medium build, carrying two filing boxes and steadying an overstuffed manila envelope on top. He placed the two boxes next to Pete's oak desk and handed the envelope to Martha, then quietly left the office. Meanwhile, Alan cleared the coffee table that stood between the chairs where Martha and Pete sat. Pete watched every move as Alan opened the basket and started setting plates, silverware and glasses for two at the end of the table closest to Martha. As Pete observed Alan's fluid movements, he was aware that Martha was watching him. When Alan had finished bringing out the meal containers and two chilled bottles of sparkling water, he turned to Martha and asked if there was anything further she required.

"No thank you, Alan, this looks fine."

Alan glanced over at Pete, nodded his head and left the office as quietly as he entered.

Pete asked, "Are those men part of your team or were they hired for the evening?"

Leaning forward on her cushion, Martha started opening food containers and moving them about on the table. The aroma of warm food started to fill the room. After a second or two, she spoke, "Those men are part of my team." Martha began to serve the food. "Alan, Alan Murphy, is my right-hand man. He was an Air Force Military Attaché for General Arnold for several years before joining my team. The other gentleman is Bruce Edwards. Bruce was a Navy Lieutenant for ten years. His last command was aboard the USNS Bowditch. Don't let their apparent demeanor fool you, they are highly trained specialized agents and are on-the-job 24/7." Martha handed the bottles of water to Pete and began serving dinner from the containers.

The aromatic smell of roasted vegetables reached Pete's nose and as he deeply inhaled, he was able to identify two separate herbs: rosemary and thyme.

Martha spoke, "We have black bean and quinoa stuffed bell peppers. There's a hint of jalapeño heat just to bring out the flavor. There's roasted early carrots and asparagus with aged parmesan, and these little things," she indicated by showing Pete a little crispy brown ball speared on the tongs of a fork, "...are crunchy goat cheese bites. And there's a sliced nectarine."

Martha handed Pete a plate and placed a cloth napkin across

his knee and placed a fork and knife on the table just in front of him. She balanced her own plate on her lap as she deftly sliced a few bites from the bell pepper. Smiling at Pete, she said, "Bon appétit."

They ate quietly for a few minutes, enjoying the silence, their own thoughts about The Hartfield, and the amazing food.

Pete was the first to break the silence. "I haven't eaten since early this morning. I hadn't realized how hungry I was."

Martha smiled and said, "It's important to recharge your batteries once in awhile. This *is* good. I'll have to thank Alan for his culinary choices."

After they had eaten, Martha cleared the food containers and seeing that Pete was a bit more relaxed with the situation, continued with her briefing. She opened the overstuffed envelope and handed a few pages to Pete.

For a minute all that could be heard was the rustling of pages while Pete quickly scanned the reports and briefly looked at data charts. After picking up the report's highlights, Pete stopped turning pages and looked up at Martha, his mind racing with what he had just read.

Martha was holding papers in one hand and thumbing through her e-device screens with the other. Realizing that Pete had stopped reading, she said, "Suspicion has been building for several months that The Hartfield Connection is deeply involved with activities aimed at defrauding the U.S. government. There's also evidence that The Hartfield is defrauding one or two of our European friends, by way of masking or hiding the truth about Hartfield clients wanting to do business with them."

Pete said, "That's dangerous ground to take. It's one thing to face criminal charges here but to face European or Asian courts can be very risky. You could spend many years in prison without the benefit of a trial. Why would Azekiel Hartfield risk such a thing?"

Martha replied, "Money. Power. Possibly lots of both." She put her e-device down next to her on the chair cushion and leafed through the papers until she found what she was looking for. Continuing, she said, "You may be aware of the 'American Fairness in Government' legislation that was passed into law several years back by a clear majority of both the House and the Senate. It states that all persons wishing to be elected to a federal office must first pass a rigid set of government tests conducted to determine each candidate's suitability to hold the office they're running for. Even the slightest hint of scandal or questionable behavior is enough to eliminate them as candidates. It's the government's way of cleaning itself up and making itself truly a …government of the people, by the people, for the people."

Martha noticed that Pete was listening intently and wondered what his thoughts were at that moment. As if in reply, Pete asked a question, "Okay. So, Hartfield is suspected of duping the government and several European contacts by perpetrating fraud in the form of well-coached persons?"

Martha said, "Yes. But our suspicions are based on more than mere fabrication of personal histories and associations. It goes to a much deeper level than that. My team and I have acquired intel that tells us there are three secret laboratories in the lower levels of the Hartfield building. We know that these labs are equipped with state-of-the-art equipment."

Martha shifted in her seat to more comfortably sit facing Pete. She lifted her laptop screen bringing it back to life and as it continued its screen updates, Martha typed a series of keys, bringing up another folder to the desktop. Turning the screen so that Pete could see it, Martha continued, "The labs contain advanced versions of current medical apparatus that we believe are being used to conduct some kind of advanced experimentation. We're getting closer to knowing the exact nature of what goes on in the labs but we need more time and information before we can say exactly what it is." The file that Pete was looking at contained references to billing documents and invoice ledgers from several major medical equipment suppliers.

Reaching for a water bottle and refreshing both their glasses, Pete said, "As I was being led around Security, I noticed the lab buttons on the vertical panel but they required a level of clearance they didn't grant me. And by the way, how are you acquiring your intel?" Having finished sipping his water and setting the glass down, Pete sat back in his chair and waited to hear a few new pieces to his evolving puzzle. "I have to tell you that my bug finder went a little intense when we shared the vertical."

Martha retrieved her Rabbit Encoder from her purse and held its face so that Pete could see it. It was barely three inches long and two inches wide and was rapidly streaming data, periodically interrupted by highlighted messages that paused momentarily before being swept away by the deluge of buffered data.

"By posing as a rich society woman bored with my current lifestyle and wanting to conquer new heights, I became a Hartfield client. It was surprisingly easy. However, I was only inside the building for four hours but once inside, this device," she lifted the Rabbit Encoder to indicate its value, "transmitted my conversations and movements, and this device," she produced a smaller object, her Trapper, resembling a woman's compact, "tagged every e-device along my path. Our encounter in the vertical was where you were tagged and I had your bio streaming to me as I crossed the lobby floor to the front doors."

Martha could see by the look of subdued astonishment on

Pete's face that he was impressed with the level of electronic sophistication she was unveiling. She wondered what he would think when she brought out the rest of the gear. If Martha could have read Pete's mind at the moment, she would have been a bit surprised to know that he was miffed that her Rabbit Encoder had so rapidly brought up his personal information. His thoughts were contrary, though. He also felt a bit excited about the level of technology and the possible associated worth to his business.

As if she was reading his mind, Martha got up from her place and crossed the office to the two file boxes next to Pete's desk. Glancing back at Pete, she said, "Please clear the table for us, we'll need a bit of workspace."

From the first box, Martha brought out two portable flat screen monitors and four wireless transceivers/receivers that she placed in a specific order on the newly cleared table. It took her less than one minute to connect everything to a power source and bring up the stations as well as the laptop she was using when Pete first encountered her in his office.

With no hint of derision in her voice and speaking with more of a teaching tone, Martha continued, "It's not just my two handhelds working here. I have a full team of specialists and analysts that are looking through and sorting data streaming from several hundred sources."

Tapping a few keys, the monitors changed to display feed points ranging from many locations inside the Hartfield building to dozens of Hartfield employee e-devices trapped during Martha's excursion that day, along with many points between that included street cams and routers. It was almost overwhelming, if it hadn't been so fascinating. Pete couldn't take his eyes off the stations, but nevertheless, he asked for the most current conclusions that Martha's experts were revealing.

Reading her laptop screen, Martha said, "The chatter from the floors above the Security Operations level are mostly irrelevant with the exception of two or three. Mr. Sturgess and Mr. Hartfield are closely monitored and have been in contact several times throughout this evening. I'll send that stream to the station on your right hand, now." Martha's fingers flew across the keyboard keys and within seconds, Pete's screen displayed another desktop window. Martha continued, "The security breach that you were called in for really has them concerned."

As Pete got up from his chair, he said, "I don't doubt it," and moved to where his overcoat had been hung on the coat-rack by the door. Rummaging through the inside pocket, he retrieved the two sidecars and returned to the now converted coffee table where he held them out in his right hand. "I did a bit of shopping while I was there this evening. Let's load these up and see where they'll take us." Resuming his seat, Pete popped one of the sidecars into the monitor closest to him and handed the other one to Martha who did the same with hers.

Both monitors whirred to attention as the sidecars were detected and their contents sorted. Immediately, several folders appeared on each screen and Pete said, "This sidecar contains the files I took from a VP's laptop in finance. I've got files from Anne Whitman's dedicated line but they will need to be de-encrypted."

At this, Martha typed and entered two or three command lines that set off a fifteen second explosion of activity resulting in all the folders and files from both sidecars being displayed in plain prose and arranged neatly on the screens – in chronological order.

Pete looked at Martha, "Is it possible for me to get a copy of that?"

Martha smiled and said, "Let me see." She typed a few software sequences and hit the send button. "You'll find it on your personal laptop next time you bring it up."

Several long moments passed while both Pete and Martha intently studied their respective screens. Martha's e-device broke the trance with its soft chime. She picked it up and said, "Yes. Are you getting this? Good." She listened, still scanning the screen in front of her, then continued, "Deploy team Alpha to the suggested coordinates. Yes. I want them fully outfitted but stealthy. Keep me apprised and thank you."

She turned to Pete, "Two of the communiqué found on Anne's system seem to suggest that she went into hiding somewhere in the Canadian outback and a check of border crossings in the past week confirmed her entering Canada at a remote station on the Saskatchewan border at about the same time her parents reported her missing. I've dispatched a team to find her and to keep her safe."

"Here's a memo I found stashed in an obscure folder on Anne's system. It's from Hartfield's CFO, Ashton, to Hartfield himself." Pete's eyes were moving swiftly across the page, now enlarged on his monitor, "It clearly states that there are discrepancies in Lab Three's expenditures for synthetic human genome that Ashton was asking Hartfield to approve."

Both Martha and Pete sat in silence reading through many of the files, memos, data sheets and letters that the sidecars contained. The minutes passed and became an hour. Martha looked over at Pete who then looked over at her. Both had faint looks of disbelief written across their faces. They held eye contact for a second before Martha said, "Would you like a cup of coffee?"

♦　　♦　　♦

The Hartfield Connection had always striven to be a model

business in the community. Azekiel Hartfield insisted that all up front operations meet the demands of any business model: customers first, efficiency in actions, and build revenue. Simple enough. But this was all on the surface. The shiny face that made its way into news articles and photo opportunities. Underneath, hidden away from only a select few, was the real face of The Hartfield Connection. The face that Azekiel preferred.

In her first week of employment at The Hartfield, Anne Whitman became aware that something was not right. The quarterly accounting numbers for several of the departments had not balanced to what she, herself, had calculated. She had checked those figures three times and each time they did not add up. She had brought this up to her boss, Hartfield's Chief Financial Officer, Mr. Tom Ashton. He had looked at the figures but had waved them off and explained to Anne that the departments may have reported out of date figures from their ledgers and she was not to worry about it. Mr. Ashton assured her that he would take care if it.

During the next two days, Anne Whitman found additional information that pointed to a completely different kind of business being conducted at The Hartfield. There were bills for the purchase of medical equipment and accounting ledgers that stated that these bills, and others, had been paid through the Financial Department. She noted that Tom Ashton had signed the checks. Anne was uncomfortable with the few unreported memos and receipts that she had found tucked away in Ashton's computer files and had become highly suspicious of Tom Ashton and his motives.

Her suspicions quickly turned to distrust when Ashton told her that the unreported accounting was of another matter that she need not concern herself with and had asked that the matter be dropped. It was at this point that Anne's distrust turned to fear.

♦　♦　♦

Martha pulled a thermos of coffee and two cups from the basket and proceeded to pour them full. Handing one to Pete, she said, "This is almost unbelievable. The files and records that I've skimmed so far are truly a fantastic account of the darker side of a corporation."

Taking the cup from Martha's hand, Pete said, "Yeah. Look here." Pete turned his screen so that Martha could get a better look at what he was pointing at. The desktop displayed two neat columns of smaller windows arranged side by side. Pete had brought up both Anne Whitman's and Tom Ashton's computer files that had been unloaded from the sidecars that he had boosted from the two Financial Department systems at The Hartfield.

Pointing to the column on the left, Pete said, "These are files from Ashton's computer," and pointing to the right side, "...and these are from Whitman's. The duplicate files are highlighted and after a fast read, they look to be fairly incriminating." Shifting the screen back to his vantage, Pete continued. "I'm betting that Anne Whitman found and copied several pieces of incriminating information about Hartfield's gray business practices, got frightened about what she was seeing and fled."

Sitting back in his chair and stretching out his left leg, Pete continued, "This gives us limited proof that Hartfield is most likely conducting very secret and highly risky human experiments with questionable medical methods. Hartfield seems to be extremely serious about keeping that bit of news from getting out, which may explain the extraordinary security methods used throughout their building."

Martha added, "We've sent a search team to find Anne

Whitman, but so has Hartfield so it's a race to see who finds her first." Martha watched Pete's face as he studied the contents of his computer screen. She thought he looked very serious but in such a way as not to wrinkle up his face with frown lines. His eyes moved along in a measured fashion across the virtual pages and seemed to dance with excitement in the blue glow from the screen.

With a slight chuckle, Pete raised his eyes to look at Martha and said, "Fortunately for us, their security methods are more brawn than brains or neither of us would have been allowed to leave after our visits." And raising his eyebrows a bit in question, asked, "Have you found any interesting bits?"

Nodding, Martha said, "Yes, I have. My analysts have concluded, from several saved e-comm messages and various memos taken from the sidecars, that Hartfield's labs are conducting several types of experiments. None of which have been clearly written about in any text, or talked about in any level of detail as recorded on any of the devices we've encountered. This is all we've got so far but keep in mind that we're only a few hours into this."

Martha leaned forward to reach the coffee thermos and said, "The 'how' and 'why' of it can't accurately be determined from this source of information alone. We'll need to round out the picture with a bit more information before anything conclusive comes to light."

"I do have something else to tell you." Martha sat forward in her chair and poured hot coffee into the two cups. Pete watched her intently as she got up from her place and stepped around to the other side of the table where they had been working to place the now empty thermos back in its basket. As he watched her and waited for her to speak, Pete noticed her long legs and how she stepped lithely around power cords and the half emptied boxes that littered the floor. He noted to himself that she was a strikingly pretty woman. Not beautiful in the same way as a fashion model, all made up and glittery. But pretty in the sense of calm beauty, like an inner beauty that can be seen on the outside. His thoughts were interrupted when Martha had resumed her seat and began to speak.

"My patrons have procured Hartfield's bank records and it revealed several very large cash deposits that were credited within the past week. One of the deposits was the money I had wired to them when I signed a contract just this evening as Jennifer Harstaad. It's how they do business; once in agreement of terms and conditions and a contract is drawn up, you sign on the dotted line with one hand and punch up money transfer passwords with the other. It all moves very fast." Looking at her monitor, Martha clicked on a window or two before continuing, "Bank records show two other sizable transfers into Hartfield's accounts and then, within minutes, large sums were transferred out to an offshore. It's suspected that Hartfield is using a pseudo-bank aboard his two hundred thirty five foot luxury yacht that has been anchored just outside U.S. waters for several weeks. If that's true, we think he'll wire the funds to another bank somewhere unknown. But it's being looked into as we speak."

Holding her coffee cup up to her lips, Martha first inhaled the rich aroma drifting up on the steam before tipping the cup and tasting the hot liquid. Losing herself in the moment, she thought abstractly of a small outdoor café she had visited while in Italy several years earlier and a feeling of calm overcame her. As she brought herself back to the current minute, her eyes scanned the flat screen closest to her and caught a glimpse of highlighted conversation that was scrolling slowly past. She reached out and tapped the pause button to halt the marching sentences and took a second to read the dialogue more closely. "Pete? You may want to take a look at this."

Pete leaned closer to Martha to see her screen and noted that she smelled faintly of fresh flowers. Focusing on the data now stopped on the screen, Pete scanned the text and then said, "Looks like a somewhat cryptic conversation between Sturgess and Hartfield. It took place recently by the look of the timestamp. Their communication style is interesting. They are not quite saying everything. It's as if they have developed a way of talking without really talking. Half sentences and innuendo. It's strongly suggesting that they are hiding something."

Martha nodded and said, "We know that Hartfield is in charge of all business as it affects the bottom line and it appears that Sturgess is his number one man, in charge of almost everything else. Do you think that they are hiding things from each other?" Smiling, Martha added, "That's a rhetorical question."

Pete smiled in return and said, "And, it would seem, from their peers and subordinates. I suppose if anyone else had any idea how much money was flowing through that company, they would ask for a raise."

Taking another sip from her cup, Martha said, "They are definitely embroiled in a scheme that may have the potential to frighten their investors away in droves. I suppose that if any of this were to leak out, Hartfield's worth on the world market would plummet."

Pete and Martha sat quietly for several more minutes scanning data and absorbing the myriad of information flowing past the screens. The soft blue-white light from the screens gave the office an otherworldly glow. The furnishings and the surrounding walls appeared in a mirage-like rippling effect making objects appear to dance. The only sound was the soft rhythmic ticking coming from a small desk clock situated on Pete's large oak desk and the occasional click of a keyboard key.

♦   ♦   ♦

Another hour had passed almost unnoticed before Pete cleared his throat and said, "By the way. As Security Auditor, I've tasked Hartfield's systems with generating random data that will keep several of their rookies very busy at their monitors. Since it's clear that they don't suspect that they're doing a good imitation of squirrels running on a wheel, it's possible I can re-enter security for a bit more shopping."

Pete watched as Martha got up from her position in front of her screen and stretched her back by standing up tall on the balls of her feet and reaching her hands up to the ceiling. After sitting back down, she said, "That felt good!" and scooting back on the chair cushion, looked over at Pete and said, "My patrons have supplied my team with lots of information gathered over the past many months. One interesting piece of info has to do with one central character in particular and is the primary reason my patrons became involved." Martha located and opened for display, the status sheet for a junior senator from a southern state, his freshly scrubbed face dominating the upper-left corner of the page. "Meet the well-heeled senator, Mr. Frank Torres. Elected by a majority after a well-run campaign last year. Curiously, his campaign took a decidedly different approach after he became a Hartfield client. My patrons have had Mr. Torres under close observation for some while but everything they've learned about the good senator always leads them back to the Hartfield and to security blocks."

Turning back toward Pete, Martha continued, "With their curiosity piqued and their suspicions mounting, they set up a small surveillance on Hartfield's newer clients. They hoped to capture enough information from these surveillances to spot trends and map discrepancies but were largely unsuccessful. And this is where I was brought in. To round out the picture by filling in the gaps and I'm doing so by posing as the widow Jennifer Harstaad."

Her fingers flying across the keyboard, Martha continued, "In addition to myself, two new clients were signed under contract today: Elizabeth Preston and Travis Stratton. Their status sheets are on your desktop, as well as our intel. Both of these persons are of special interest to my patrons and represent hundreds of millions of dollars outright and possibly more in hidden and backdoor costs. With the U.S. government budget talks underway and appropriations looming on the horizon *and* senatorial elections just six months away, my patrons are highly interested in getting to the bottom of this rather quickly."

Giving Pete a moment to absorb what she had just been telling him and watching his facial expression closely, Martha noted that he had a strikingly boyish look about his eyes. She wondered if he had a sly sense of humor or if he liked lighthearted joking better. Then he looked up at her and said, "As I'm glancing through bits of surveillance data from your trapped e-devices, street cams and bugged bugs...sorry about that pun." At which Martha gave a small laugh and smiled in amusement, thinking, *yes...lighthearted joking.*

Smiling in return, Pete continued, "I've noticed very little awareness on the part of most employees that Hartfield is engaged in anything other than PR work. However, one conversation that took place just after you left your meeting with your handlers looks promising. One Jess Parks made a call to Sturgess to tell him that the meeting went well enough and that he had assured you that Hartfield could handle any situation it encountered in its efforts to…'correct your errant history and to fabricate a new path for you to follow in future.' That's a pretty big statement, don't you agree?"

Martha located and brought up the transcript of her meeting with her handlers. Reading it through for a few seconds, she broke her concentration with, "Yes, and more so since they had said nothing like that directly to Jennifer Harstaad. You'd think 'she' would have liked to hear that kind of news. Jess Park was the lead handler. I remember the look on his face. He looked too hungry. We should look at him closer."

♦　　♦　　♦

It was well past 1AM when Pete's e-device chimed breaking his concentration from reading everything he could from the screen in front of him and off the displays he shared with Martha. He could see by the announcement on his e-device screen that the call was from Sid Hutchins, one of his friends at the PD. Engaging the call button, Pete answered, "This is Malloy. Yes. No. Send everything you have on Hartfield. Yes, the company and its founder. Also, do you have anything on a Mark Sturgess? He may have operated under an alias up to his working for Hartfield. Thanks, Sid. I'll call you tomorrow. Good night."

Changing his e-device to "no sounds", Pete set it down next to his empty coffee cup, turned to Martha, and after a deep breath followed by a short yawn, said, "My associates at PD will send what they find, but it'll take a few hours for that to happen. Martha, my head is reeling with all this information and I have an early meeting with Hartfield's security team. I'm afraid I'll have to call it a night."

Looking up from her laptop, Martha said, "Thank you. Listen,

I know this is a lot of information in such a short amount of time, but time is something that is at a premium for us right now. I think we would do better with clear minds."

Martha handed her wire device to Pete, saying, "Take my Trapper with you on your security visit tomorrow."

She picked up her e-device and tapped a sequence of buttons, then held the device to her ear. "Hello, Alan. We're calling it an evening." Within a few seconds, Alan and the second agent quietly arrived and started to disassemble the computer set-up and collect all the loose papers that Pete and Martha had managed to spread out over almost every surface of Pete's office.

Martha stood up from her place at the end of the couch and stretched her arms out and flexed her back with a slight twist to the right and then to the left before turning to face Pete. "We'll have the current transcripts of my conversations with various Hartfield employees and any other noteworthy items, first thing. May I suggest we meet at my business office tomorrow? When will your morning meeting be over?"

"I should be clear by 11AM."

"Perfect. I'll send the office address and my contact information to your e-device."

With the nights work neatly boxed, and Pete's office returned to normal, Alan followed the other agent out the door to the outer office but hung back to wait for Martha, who was standing talking with Pete.

Martha cocked her head and looked at Pete slightly askance. A smile started to form as she said, "See. I knew we would work well together."

"Yes. It's been a very pleasant evening." And smiling broadly, Pete reached for Martha's hand. After a slight squeeze, he gently turned her hand palm-side up and slipped the two sidecars into her palm and closed her fingers around them.

"Good night."

Still smiling, Martha turned to follow Alan out into the hallway, down the stairs and into the Rolls Royce idling at the curb.

THE INNOCENCE OF POWER

9
Harmless Threats

The morning was not quite in full swing, yet numbers of Hartfield employees had been steadily filing in and were taking their places behind desks or in front of computer screens.

From the hallway of the 87th floor, barely a sound could be heard coming from the closed doorway of the Office of Operations and Client Interests. As Mark Sturgess was on his way back to his office from an early morning meeting with Travis Stratton's legal team leader, a finance secretary was on her way out of Operations to return to her station on the 21st floor. The heavy oak door slowly began its half-arc swing just as Mark reached for the ornate brass handle. Helping it along, he stepped back to let the person exiting his outer offices come through. Smiling his nicest smile, Mark nodded his acknowledgement of the girl's greeting as she thanked him for holding the door for her. He then stepped inside. The young woman at reception looked up as he approached and with a smile, handed him several small pieces of paper, each representing a message that she had recorded during his brief absence.

Mark's e-device chimed and glancing at the screen, he read that his presence was requested back in Legal. The message read that Miss Preston had just arrived, unannounced, and was telling her team that she was not satisfied with the latest version of her contract terms and was asking that Mark be summoned into a meeting as soon as possible. Mark glanced at the message and pressed the "file" on its screen thereby removing it from his view. Miss Preston. She was quickly turning into a liability and it was

Mark's job to turn her into an asset. He needed several moments of careful thought before making any decisions that would perturb Elizabeth Preston any further.

His recent visit to Legal was to obtain a briefing on the current status of Travis Stratton's initial visit of last evening. The handlers assigned to Travis made it clear that they had sufficiently pumped Stratton's ego and although he appeared to be more than a bit high on champagne, signed an iron-clad contract and transferred a year's worth of operating cash into one of Hartfield's client accounts. After making a few personal calls, Travis Stratton had been escorted down to the lobby where he met several friends and, laughing loudly, left the building and hailed two cabs to spirit the group away, presumably into the rousing club scene of the city.

As Sturgess entered his office, his e-device chimed again but this time it was old man Hartfield.

Setting his jaw and letting the device go to a second ring, Mark answered, "Good morning Mr. Hartfield. And how are you this fine day?"

The device buzzed with Hartfield's commanding tone, "Mr. Sturgess, good morning. I'd like to meet with you on a matter of some import. I understand that we have two new promising clients and would like a thorough briefing on their status and your project plans."

Mark, not surprised that the old man knew about the latest client acquisitions, spoke confidently, "Two very good gains for the company. I'm sure you'll be happy with the acquisition. And I'm more than sure you will agree with the process and the final outcomes we have planned."

Azekiel Hartfield spoke with little feeling or tone, "Let's meet over dinner in my office tonight. 6PM."

Mark glanced at his watch for the time and replied, "Yes sir. I would be happy to. 6PM." And heard the click indicating that Hartfield had hung up.

After he pressed a couple of buttons on his e-device Mark spoke, "Evvie. Please order two dinners from the executive kitchen and have them delivered, hot, to Mr. Hartfield's suite at precisely six this evening. Thank you."

◆　◆　◆

At school, young Marek Stern was excited to find that he liked science and had been very proud of the fact that he was also very good at it. He completed assignments early, doing extra credit and volunteering in the classroom. He breezed the basics and excelled in the more advanced sciences, finally discovering biology and, more specifically, biophysics.

In his high school sophomore year, his science project, The Effect of Electro-magnetic Energy on Hybrid Cell Production, won first prize. He was awarded a trophy and a one hundred dollar savings bond that his father advised him to keep in a safe place. Marek had worked hard to put his cell production theory into practice. It took him weeks to get the nine-volt battery to properly charge his copper coiled container and he searched for days along the town's creek bed for a newly deceased rat...whose purpose was to contribute bone marrow stem cells. During the award ceremony, Marek's science teacher had announced to everyone attending that Marek would go far in the field of scientific discovery and that he was a young man with a bright future.

After high school, Marek applied to one college, Yale. His transcripts were in good order, far above average but it was his letter of introduction that impressed the admissions faculty. It contained an eloquent missive on why they, Yale, should accept him for enrollment. This carefully worded letter was followed by an explanation of a theory that Marek had been formulating for the past two years. He was curious about how biophysics and nanotechnology might be combined and he theorized that it was possible to automate several physical responses to molecular excitations. This theory so impressed the admissions faculty that they asked one of their advanced chemistry instructors to read it. The feedback from the professor was simple: enroll Mr. Marek Stern. He will prove to be a valuable asset to Yale's already highly accredited status.

Marek's first two years at Yale were beyond exciting. He applied himself to study and in his spare time worked in a borrowed lab, on advancing his theory. But as he moved into his fourth year, he started to realize that he was working toward a life in a laboratory among beakers and electron microscopes and notebooks and like-minded people. His only hope of becoming noteworthy and more valuable was to win the Nobel Prize in Chemistry. Wasn't this exactly the kind of life he was trying to escape? A life in one place, doing one thing...forever? He continued forward to his degree but as these thoughts weighed down on him, another thought started to consume him: get out. Four months after his graduation from Yale, Marek Stern left.

◆　◆　◆

Mark supposed that this time was as good as any to join the meeting with Miss Preston down in Legal so he turned on his heel and headed out, again. Reaching Legal was easy enough, it was answering or ignoring his e-device that took most of his attention. Sometimes he wondered why taking control of matters seemed like such a task. When he had a second or two, he was going to look into some kind of software that would replace several of his irritants, and then maybe he could walk fifteen feet without an interruption.

Fixing his well-practiced smile upon his smooth and stony face, Mark pushed open the conference room door and greeted Elizabeth Preston with an out stretched hand.

Ignoring it, Miss Preston started in on her main complaint, "Mr. Sturgess, my requests to have performance details, pertaining to the level of service that I'm contracting for, were not included in the most recent draft of my contract agreement. I would like to see it included along with a timetable of milestones. I think it only fair that a schedule include these deliverables as I would like to know if any of the staff that will be assigned to me are falling behind in performance and would need to be...upgraded."

Mark held his smile and arched his eyebrows to underscore his concern for Preston's harangue, but his mind was racing...*This is going to be far more trouble than anticipated. Her top-flight friends don't need to hear that she's unhappy with The Hartfield.*

Addressing Elizabeth, Mark said, "I think we can safely include whatever contingencies you desire in your contract."

And thinking to himself...*because I'm confident that, if necessary, we can break it or seal your doom later, whichever is called for.*

Turning to one of Elizabeth's handlers, Mark said, "Please include any language in Miss Preston's contract that she desires, all within legal bounds, of course." Shifting his stance back toward Elizabeth, he added, "Will that make you happy?"

She nodded her consent. Mark then ordered that a small tray of refreshments be provided and that a funds transfer apparatus be brought in so that Elizabeth Preston could transfer her final contract obligation payment immediately after signing the revised, and agreed to, contract statement.

◆　　◆　　◆

Within days of his leaving Yale, Marek decided to throw off everything having to do with his "previous" life. He would reject the academic dogma that praised hard work with appropriate rewards and would walk away from a life stuck in the middle-class grind until he died. No. Instead, he would seize opportunities, attain success and, if needed, be inappropriate. He would live rich, he would have influence, he would be powerful, he would be new...and with this, Marek Stern was recreated as Mark Sturgess.

The first liberating thing Mark Sturgess did was to give himself a make over. With a new haircut and a stylish new wardrobe, Mark decided that he needed to take a break from everything and visit Europe. With his last one thousand dollars, he bought a one-way ticket to Paris and boarded the plane with no regrets. The eight-hour flight gave Mark time to consider a plan. He would need more money, much more money, if he were going to stay longer than his few dollars would carry him. He refused to engage in base blue-collar employment such as being part of a wait-staff in some dirty little café. And he knew he didn't possess the skills or contacts to walk into a white-collar position in banking or industry. His thoughts rolled on and around the subject of money and how to get it until he drifted off into a fitful sleep filled with doubts and airplane turbulence.

When he awoke, it was decided. Mark would find a nice, inexpensive, but well appointed, room to let, spend at least two weeks familiarizing himself with his new city and write a felicitous letter of introduction to the French Centre d'Etude de Polymorphisms Humain Research Institute. The Center for the

Study of Human Polymorphisms. The Institute was the premier center for international genetic research and known throughout Europe for their groundbreaking advancements in locating and cloning major genes of human DNA. Mark had no doubt but that they would accept him into their programs and he had no doubt whatsoever that he would soon be working his way up the ladder of scientific management success. And indeed, four weeks later the Institute had signed Marek Stern, under his new name of Mark Sturgess to a three-year contract, complete with a bonus and an advancement schedule.

◆　　◆　　◆

Mark's day was sizing up about as expected. Constant interruptions. Fussy rich clients. Small fires to put out in various departments. Reporting to the old man. *Always a pain.*

With his well-practiced smile firmly in place, Mark took his leave of Elizabeth Preston, left Legal and headed to the verticals.

Meanwhile, up on the top floor, old man Hartfield was making several calls to friends in high places to keep up on the current state of their progress or to arrange introductions or deliveries. Two calls were placed to brokerage handlers and buy/sell orders had been given. An investment group associated with the European markets made a surprise video call to introduce their newest rumor and ask if there might be any interest on Hartfield's part to the tune of half a billion Euros. Minimum. Being a bit vague, the old man rang off with a "We'll see", and left it at that. After one more call, to a private jewelry designer to check on the status of last week's order, Hartfield concluded that his morning business was done and left, by way of his private doors, for an early lunch.

10
No Boundaries

Pete Malloy had been awake and up for an hour before his alarm came to life at 6AM, shattering the silence of his third story flat and disturbing his train of thought. Mechanically going through the motions of preparing his breakfast of poached eggs, dry organic seed bread, sliced pears, juice and coffee, Pete returned to his thoughts.

What seemed to be a routine missing persons case had turned out to be a completely different situation. Pete thought that his case would follow simple protocol: compile a background story, conduct interviews, collect clues and follow the evidence to the desired outcome. Case solved. Everyone happy.

No.

The case of this missing girl, Anne Whitman, had developed into an almost unimaginable story of a shady company doing secret experiments, government intervention, secret agents, bizarre deceptions and a level of electronic trickery that far outpaced anything offered for sale in the public market. Pete's police department friends were not able to shed any light on the global aspects of this situation, but he had no doubt that Martha would be able to fast-track all of that and uncover any number of additional, and most likely to be, inconceivable details.

It was also becoming apparent to Pete that his regard for Martha was slowly but surely turning into something deeper than the simple regard for a coworker. He believed that his feelings were based on trust and respect but there was something deeper.

Something he couldn't quite put his finger on but knew beyond a doubt was present. He felt it when she was near, when she smiled at him and he knew that when he smiled back at her, he felt genuine affection toward her. Pete also felt that it would be brash to push this conversation to Martha at this point. He acknowledged his feelings and knew them to be real but decided to give it a bit of time before trying to define it with words.

Pete's first instinct about Martha, following their tense introduction the night before, was one of guarded trust. But Martha's willingness to bring Pete into the Hartfield conspiracy theory, seemingly without hesitation, spoke volumes. She had a myriad of resources at her fingertips and a team of crack operatives working for her on the case. In spite of Martha's inclination to include him in the case, Pete knew that there was room for concern about his role in all of it. He did not yet have an understanding of the bigger picture. A picture that included "patrons", kidnapping, conspiracy, fraud, international collusion, and three laboratories conducting dark and secret things. And that could all just be the tip of a very large and unwieldy iceberg.

Looking up at the antique analog clock just above the kitchen sideboard, a gift from his grandmother's household, and taking note of the low rhythmic ticking sounds it made, Pete figured that he had about two hours to make his morning meeting with Lieutenant Abers and his band of merry peons.

While slowly making his way through his breakfast, Pete scrolled through headlines as reported by three publishers, one National Rag and one International Bulletin. Finding nothing unusual, or for that matter, anything interesting, he shutdown his laptop, but not before noting that a copy of Martha's de-encryption software was parked on the desktop, as she had promised. Pete became aware of a small grin that had crept onto his features and as he locked up his laptop in the sideboard, he thought...*The one thing I find most interesting this morning is...Martha Gainsbrook.* And on that thought, with a short laugh to himself, Pete continued getting ready for his day.

Showered and relaxed, Pete shaved and dressed, but before donning his jacket, he lifted the PA-48 from its charger and checked its readiness. Satisfied that it was fully loaded, he slipped it into its holster and nudged it into place next to his ribcage. As he slipped his overcoat off the hanger and made small adjustments to its drape over his jacket, Pete made a mental inventory...*Okay, I've got thirty minutes to make the appointment, got my keys, the access code badge, spare sidecars and Martha's Trapper. I'm good to go.*

Pete left his flat and after making his way to his Senelli and warming up the engine for a moment, pulled out into the last of the morning's commute traffic.

◆　　◆　　◆

The audible snap of the Station 9 Ops door latch announced Pete Malloy's arrival on site in the Department of Security Operations. Both the rookie sitting at a terminal, and Lieutenant Abers, who had been hovering just behind him, turned their heads, in perfect unison, to see who had entered. Pete was put in mind of two barn owls as he observed their swift neck movements and unblinking stares. He almost laughed out loud. Recognizing Pete, the rookie went back to work without a hint of greeting, but Abers straightened out and made the five paces between them in about three seconds.

Flashing a somewhat flat and obviously practiced smile, Abers greeted Pete in a clipped manner, "Good morning. My staff has been extremely efficient in monitoring your streaming data and have identified several instances of the sequences you had requested. I must say, Malloy, this all seems a bit esoteric and I would feel better about spending my manpower on this effort if it didn't seem like such a fool's errand. Perhaps if you were to explain it to me so that I might understand exactly what it is you're doing?"

Expecting exactly this level of posturing from a man of Abers' type, Pete smoothly, and without hesitation, answered his thinly veiled demand with, "This is very advanced methodology for detecting even the slightest trace of an invasive piece of software or a foreign source of ingress." And with a slight, barely noticeable tone of derision in his voice, Pete continued, "It takes a practiced eye to catch the anomalies, as every one is unique to its initial point of contact. I'm afraid that we don't have the time to conduct on-the-job training right now. Maybe another time?"

Abers made a little noise as he exhaled sharply through his nose, thereby making it perfectly clear that he was not happy with that response. Realizing that he wasn't going to gain anything by insisting, he relinquished with, "Very well. Another time." But Abers eyed Pete steadily for some moments before breaking off and turning away.

Glancing past Abers to where the rookie was staring intently at the columns of numbers scrolling by, Pete asked, "So what have you got for me?" and took a step past Abers.

The rookie paused the screen and reached for a small sheaf of papers. "Yes sir. During the last sixteen hours, these two dozen instances of the requested numerical sequences were found." Handing the neatly labeled pages to Malloy, the rookie continued, "Our monitoring was, and is, very thorough. We're positive we've noted every one."

"I'm sure you have. Good work. Please continue to survey the data, and I like this…" Pete lifted the pages, smiled and nodded his head to indicate to the rookie what he was referring to, then said "…it makes my job easier."

"Yes sir. Thank you, sir." The rookie's eyes returned to the screen and with a flick of his finger, the data columns resumed their course.

Pete turned to Abers and, still glancing through the pages, asked, "May I have a printout of all company laptops and computer station IDs, please?"

Abers waved his hand at another rookie, indicating with a nod that he was to generate the requested information. Pete took the opportunity to stroll around Station 9 Ops but while acting nonchalant, had been looking at screen displays and terminal identification labels along the way. Once he had caught sight of Abers and noted, with humor, that Abers had been glaring at Pete every step of the way. It took about five minutes to generate the laptop and station ID information and once it was in hand, Pete made a study of both prints, all the while building an affected attitude of concern for what he was culling from the pages. It was important to Pete that Abers believed that something very concerning had happened.

After several minutes of rustling pages, rechecking entries and circling random things, Pete looked up from his scribbling with a thoughtful but slightly worried look on his face and said, "Lieutenant Abers, I need full access to all computers on the 87th floor as well as clearance for those on the top floor. I would like to verify these findings before making any kind of report and I'll need a quiet workspace. I might be some time so would you provide a cold glass of water, a pen or two, a fully authorized laptop and a highlighter?"

♦   ♦   ♦

Two hours later, from the relative comfort of a quiet meeting room off of the main hallway of Security Level S1, Pete Malloy had managed to access Mark Sturgess' company desk-top, his laptop, Hartfield's laptop, and three systems in the Personnel Department. Most of the files floating on these systems had been successfully copied to Pete's sidecars and he was busy installing sniffers and watch devices that would transmit newer entries from Hartfield's and Sturgess' private and company computer systems to remotes stationed in the area and staffed by Martha's people. Nothing blatant. Everything very subtle so as not to arouse unwanted attention.

Pete organized the various sheaves of paper into two neat stacks, carefully placing blank pages on top to prevent prying eyes from seeing any of the elaborate subterfuge contained below. He then secured the sidecars in a tight pocket inside his jacket and began to compose what resembled a handwritten report using a blank page of printer paper.

These particular activities always made Pete smile. It provided him with two minutes of amusement as he used his imagination to create the most unbelievable fabrications. Taking pen in hand, he wrote...'*Incidents over the past 16 hours, while inconclusive, are deeply concerning. A preliminary test has shown these interruptions to be symptomatic of typical intrusions but may mask other activities that could be of a more severe nature.*' (*Yadda, yadda, yadda.*) '*At this time, further tests and a more in-depth analysis are advised.*' (*Blah, blah blah.*) '*I will proceed with all haste. Signed, Global Security Analyst, P. Malloy*' *Hah! That was fun.*

Packing up his pile of papers and placing the handwritten page on top in a fairly obvious, but half-hidden manner, Pete stood up and stretched his frame up to its full height. Leaving his water glass in a ring of liquid and several highlighter markers strewn about the table, he stepped to the door and opened it.

Lieutenant Abers was hovering in the hallway several paces away talking to one of his rookies. Upon seeing Pete, Abers, without taking his eyes off of Pete, handed a loose page of paper to the rookie, thereby dismissing him and, in one fluid motion, turned and stepped toward Pete. As Abers closed the distance between them, Pete noticed that his eyes were glued to the papers Pete had been holding as if trying to use X-ray vision to discern their message. Greeting him with a polite smile, Pete said, "A very successful, if somewhat incomplete, hunt."

Taking the top page, his handwritten missive, from the pile, Pete quickly thrust the remaining pages toward Abers, who reached for them without hesitation.

"These are to be kept in a secure location. I'm assuming that can be easily accomplished. Lock and key preferred, of course. This," Pete continued, rustling the single page to indicate what he was referring to, "...comes with me. I'm compiling my report for Mr. Hartfield and it's for his eyes only."

Abers jaw slackened and he stood speechless for a second or two. With a touch of humor Pete noted that while Abers' eyes darted slightly back and forth, some of the color had drained from his face.

Quickly recovering, Abers said, "Of course but if there's any information my department should be aware of at this time, you may have an obligation to brief me to it."

"I understand your concern, Lieutenant Abers but I am not at liberty to share my findings with you at this time. I'm afraid Mr.

Hartfield would not be pleased if I did that."

They stood for a brief moment before Abers replied, "Yes. Protocol must be observed." Stepping aside, Pete walked straight ahead to the verticals with the unmistakable feeling that Abers was drilling holes into the back of his head with his steely staring eyes. And this made him smile. Abers had been so quick to anger that Pete couldn't help but to push him. The vertical's doors opened at the touch of the call button and as he stepped into the small capsule, Pete composed his face before turning to see Abers, still standing in the hallway holding the few hundred pages of useless gobble-de-gook. Touching the Ground Floor button, Pete stood stone-faced looking at Abers and waited for the doors to slide silently closed. When the doors had closed to a scant two-foot opening, Pete raised the handwritten page and gave it a little wave in Abers' direction. The doors then quietly shut and the vertical started its smooth journey up.

◆   ◆   ◆

A soft chime announced the vertical's arrival at the lobby and as the doors whispered open, Pete was a bit startled to see, standing not two feet away from the opening, Mark Sturgess. He was standing stock still with an efficacious grin across his face.

"Good morning, Mr. Malloy. May I have a word with you, in private, if you don't mind?" Sturgess indicated the way and both men fell into step as they crossed the lobby to one of the two spacious meeting rooms reserved for Hartfield visitors.

Once inside the spacious room and with the door softly closed behind them, Pete took a leisurely stroll around the room to look at the original oil paintings displayed along the walls that were illuminated by very advanced lighting embedded in the frames. As he pretended to look closely at the art, his bug finder zapped his wrist three times.

"Very impressive collection, Mr. Sturgess. Originals, I presume?"

"Yes. We extend our search for original artists throughout the world. Mr. Hartfield is quite a lover of beautiful things. Please, let's sit for a moment."

Both men moved to take a seat but Pete took the chair with the clear view of the door. *No unexpected surprises, thank you.*

Sturgess began, "Lieutenant Abers has informed me that you've completed a preliminary analysis of our security breach. May I know what you've found?"

"It's too early to tell. I've run only one sequence of detectors and while they corroborate your suspicions of system ingress, speculation at this time would only skew the results, leaving us with a false positive. I'm going to wait for additional test results before making final operational correction recommendations to Mr. Hartfield."

Sturgess shifted uncomfortably in his seat. His agitation was almost palatable "I fear Mr. Hartfield is a very busy man, what with our growing clientele and all that that means for the business. And I'm adamant in my request that you do not discuss any findings with Lieutenant Abers. He can be somewhat rash in his decision-making. No. It would be in everyone's best interest if you delivered updates and results to me directly. Don't you agree, Mr. Malloy?"

Pete tried to look thoughtful as if he was weighing out Sturgess' proposal, although his thoughts were racing. *Okay. Sturgess is either flexing his corporate muscles or making a power play. Either way it will suit my needs to play along with him.*

"I'm perfectly willing to provide you with copies of my

findings as my analysis progresses. However, my final report will be delivered to Mr. Hartfield, as well as yourself. I hope that this is acceptable to you, Mr. Sturgess, as it will fulfill my contract obligations and would make everyone happy. Especially Azekiel Hartfield."

Rising from his place and fixing that now familiar smile on his face and extending his hand for their gentleman's agreement, Mark said, "Perfectly acceptable and thank you for your time."

◆　　◆　　◆

It was 10:30AM and as Pete steered his Senelli toward downtown, he dialed Anne Whitman's parent's contact number. Mr. Whitman picked up on the fourth ring and after short pleasantries were exchanged, Pete briefed him to his progress.

"I've cast my net and am starting to gather information about your daughter's actions and contacts since starting her job at The Hartfield. I have associates working with me and expect something more concrete within a day or two." Pete absentmindedly reached out to power up the car's GPS but his hand froze in mid-air when he heard what Mr. Whitman said next.

"Mr. Malloy, two men were here this morning asking questions about Anne. I managed, I think, to convince them that I didn't know what they were talking about – that Anne was fine and busy working at The Hartfield. They left but I had a funny feeling about them. Would they be associates of yours?"

Momentarily surprised at the statement, Pete said, "No. I've not asked any of my contacts to talk with you. Can you describe them to me?"

"Yes, I think I can." A short silence filled the void, then Mr. Whitman spoke, "One was close to my height, maybe six-foot with dark hair and fair skin, light eyes, the other one was shorter and rather stocky. Maybe five foot seven, darker skin, like from the Mediterranean. Black hair, dark eyes. Both were about in their mid-thirties and wearing dark suits."

Pete had switched on his car phone's audio to record the descriptions and had set the phone to speaker so he could hear Mr. Whitman better and with less distraction. "Could you tell me what kind of car they were driving? Were there others with them? That kind of thing?"

Mr. Whitman said, "Well...I think they were driving a big SUV kind of vehicle, dark blue, almost black. The windows were darkened so I couldn't tell if there were any other men in it. I'm sorry, Mr. Malone, I didn't get a look at the license plate. It all happened so fast."

Pete wasn't surprised that Whitman didn't get the plate information. People rarely did when they thought that everything was simple. By the time they figured out that the situation had turned serious, it was over and the vehicle was usually long gone. "That's okay."

After a moment of thought, Pete asked, "What would you and Mrs. Whitman think about a short vacation? Say about one week, maybe two, in a nice crowded sunny location?"

"If you think it would help, and we could use a change of view. My wife is just now starting to settle down and we're both feeling dazed from all of this."

Pete formulated a plan and ran it past Whitman, "I have a friend that owns a beautiful condo overlooking the ocean. I'll arrange for you to stay with him, that way you will have a restful location and I will have peace of mind that you're in a protected place. My friend's name is Joe. Joe Rosen. He's a good man and a hell of a card player. I'll have him call you later this afternoon.

In the meantime, pack enough clothes for two weeks, and don't worry Mr. Whitman. Everything is going to be fine."

After ringing off, Pete made three more calls and was just finishing up when his Senelli eased to a stop in a side street parking space, three doors from the loft office address Martha had provided.

11
What Goes In Must Eventually Come Out

Stepping off the industrial lift, Pete Malloy was greeted by a fresh faced young woman who said, "Good morning Mr. Malloy. Ms. Gainsbrook is expecting you. Won't you follow me?"

The young woman came around from her position behind the elevated reception desk and indicated to Pete that he was to follow her through the heavy frosted glass doors just beyond.

The sight of several busy work areas that were separated by wide walkways and large potted plants pleasantly surprised Pete. The girl stood aside and waited by the doors with Pete, who was calmly scanning the loft office space taking in all the details. Each work area had a half dozen persons stationed in front of screens, talking on phones or talking in small groups. The systems were very much high tech, bordering on future tech, and glowing their results in a wide array of colors and symbols. Not every work area was set up the same but everyone on the floor looked competent and about their business. As Pete turned his gaze forward again he spotted Martha at the far end of the room, walking toward him. It was then that Pete again noticed her smile. It made her eyes dance with a hint of...playful mischief?

The young woman politely smiled, nodded and went back out through the glass doors to her position in the outer reception area.

"Pete," smiled Martha, "welcome to my lair." She reached out her hand and Pete's natural instinct was to take it with a slight squeeze. He leaned forward to take note of the color of her eyes and to remind himself, again, that Martha was an absolutely stunning woman.

"As you can see, we're busy building a better picture of The Hartfield Connection and most of what they're connected to." Martha turned and they did a slow walk back up the wide aisle in the direction she had originally come from. Along the way, she briefly explained the focus of each work group.

"Here we have 'Communication' which is our largest on-site team. They handle the incoming signals from everything we've trapped, tapped and scanned. That data is sorted and packaged, a cursory analysis is done and it's delivered to me and to our Advanced Analysts, over there. That group then creates a real-time storyboard to build a timeline, which gives us a better feel for what's going on. We need to separate the 'business as usual' activities from the more sinister 'behind the scenes' activities before deciding short term actions or creating more involved plans. 'Strategy and Planning' is over there and this is my area."

Pete noted to himself that just walking through the loft office had left him feeling energized and expectant. Martha's area had been set up in two distinct spaces. In one space sat a large oak table about six feet long with two monitor screens on top. The webbed office chair marked this area as Martha's desk. Separated by a wide-open space of about twenty feet was a second area with two small mid-century modern couches facing each other over a long Lucite coffee table that was flanked on either end by two straight-backed padded chairs. Both Pete and Martha took seats in her lounge area where Pete noticed a few neat piles of paper had been placed at the end of the coffee table and that several small e-systems were powered up and humming away. As they were settling in, Martha said, "This laptop is for your use. Please feel free."

As Pete relaxed into one of the chairs located in Martha's work area, he took a moment to gaze around the loft office. He wanted to soak in the atmosphere and to get a sense of the activities being performed by the three main groups. To get the lay of the land, so to speak. Everyone looked professional and everyone looked busy.

Turning back to Martha, he said, "This is an amazing space. Very well thought out and well organized. Visually, it's very appealing, very centered."

In response, Martha slowly looked around the office at her team, as if looking at them through Pete's eyes. And with a sincere smile on her face, turned to Pete and said, "Thank you." Pausing for a moment to organize her thoughts into a succinct and coherent statement, she continued, "This is the culmination of successes from several logistical setups I've done in the past. I've found this design to be both efficient and stimulating. It seems to work the best for everyone and it's good for business."

Martha reached for the top most pages from a stack of papers and scanned the text and data displayed there and Pete leaned forward in his chair to look at the screen setup on the laptop in front of him.

After a few seconds, Pete broke the silence with, "I've had an interesting morning over at Hartfield's."

Martha, looked up from her papers and, raising her eyebrows in mock surprise, said, "Was it all you had hoped it would be?"

"Some, yes and some, no." Pete sat back in the chair to make himself a bit more comfortable while speaking. "I had expected a certain amount of militarism and discipline among the security personnel and I believed that my directions would have been followed to the letter. In fact, I was counting on it. However, Abers surprised me a little in the way he handled me. He's not one for moderation, even in his attitude. He tried to bully me into reporting exactly what I was doing and what I had hoped to gain. I'm sure he's bothered with my use of his people without him knowing the full plan and eventual outcome and he may be concerned about his future as the head of Security Operations. More likely than not his attitude has probably gotten him into trouble before this and he may have stepped on a few toes along the way." Looking around the loft office, Pete asked, "Is there a cup of coffee here with my name on it?"

Martha said, "Yes as a matter of fact, there is." and pointed to an insulated serving pot and several cups sitting on the small credenza by her desk.

Pete said, "Thanks!" and helped himself to a cup of coffee.

Returning to his seat with the coffee pot in tow, Pete continued, "When I left, Abers caught me in the hallway. Or, better put, he stalked me in the hallway. He was quite upset that I had put another twenty four hours of work onto his men and had demanded that I brief him to whatever I was doing and what outcome I was expecting."

Taking a sip of his coffee, Pete nodded his head with the satisfaction of the moment. He took a second to appreciate the aroma of the coffee blend and the hot steam that rose to his nostrils. He loved the taste of a well-brewed cuppa joe and the momentary feeling of well-being it could deliver.

Pete slid back in his chair and continued, "Abers was so upset that he called Sturgess, who practically ambushed me as I was stepping off the vertical in the lobby. We had a short conversation whereby he also tried to bully information out of me, albeit politely." Shaking his head, Pete gave a little snort of laughter before finishing his story.

"I understand that no one wants the 'boss' to know what's going on in their particular department but these guys are acting on the verge of paranoia and desperation. They are barely controlling their anxiety levels on this matter. Anyway, While I was there I managed to access additional systems and spirited away more information that may help us further."

Pete reached into his pocket and produced the sidecars and the borrowed Trapper. Martha took them from Pete's outstretched hand and looked about for a second, scanning for a familiar face, and upon seeing him, motioned for him to step over.

"Alan, please take these to Comm, high priority. Thank you," and turned back to Pete.

"We've had some real progress since last night. Here, let me show you." Martha leaned forward on the couch and tapped a few lines into her laptop and several files popped open on the desktop. Opening the topmost folder and popping open the first file, she started to talk, "Through mobile surveillance, we were able to intercept chatter from the Hartfield scouts that are tracking Anne Whitman. They've crossed into Canada. We decided that it would be prudent to deploy another mobile team of trackers…to track the trackers…so to speak." Smiling, she was looking at Pete and noted that his reaction was immediate and friendly.

"Good one!"

Nodding her head and innocently smiling in agreement, Martha said, "I thought so!" Then continued, "Our first team is still searching for Anne Whitman and they report that they're getting closer; our second team will tail the Hartfield scouts. And on another point, Hartfield's employees sure are talkative, most of it inane sales pitches, some legal wrangling and small talk between coworkers. It's taken a bit of sifting but we think we have picked up on a thread."

Martha leaned forward, reached for Pete's cup and poured him another half cup of strong dark coffee before passing it over to Pete, who thanked her with a smile. She then walked to the sideboard and poured herself a cup of tea from another insulated pot, added a slice of lemon and returned to her place by the low worktable.

"Take a look at this." Martha handed three pages to Pete and continued, "Last night when we talked about the cryptic manner in which Hartfield and Sturgess communicated with each other, we lacked content. Well, I believe we now have some. When we look at their communiqué between 6:15PM and 3AM, this begins to emerge."

Martha tapped a few keys on her laptop and one of the overhead screens in her area came alive with a display of tightly spaced sentences – the total exchange between Hartfield and Sturgess – with highlighted words that appeared random but upon a closer look, read like a sentence: Lab Three Must Deliver By The End Of This Week.

"Analysis of Hartfield's tonal inflections revealed that there is tension relating to urgency whereas Sturgess' tones, comparatively speaking, are much more controlled. This may indicate that the two are not as conspiratorial as we first thought."

This bit of news caused Pete to reflect on how it all fit together with his puzzle and he absentmindedly put his fingers to his face and stroked his chin in deep thought. A new description of the bigger picture started to form in Pete's mind and with it, an observation, "Sturgess took me aside this morning and asked that I start reporting to him, unofficially, that is. I left him thinking that I would but also let drop that my contract says otherwise. Hopefully he will interpret this as a grift – and possibly offer me more money or something bigger."

And after a moment, Pete asked Martha, "Do you think the labs have anything to do with the security breach created by Anne Whitman?"

"Basically, yes "

Martha's nails clicked across her keypad and as data streamed past on the right hand side of her laptop screen, four small video displays were starting up vertically on the left. "We've also got this."

When the displays went active, they each appeared to be playing in a ten-second loop and when they all appeared to be stable, Martha said, "You remember that my foray into the 'lion's den' was under the cover of a rich widow named Jennifer Harstaad. As Harstaad, I transferred a huge sum of money to The Hartfield and subsequently, it was transferred offshore somewhere. Well, on the day the Harstaad funds were transferred, two other large sums were transferred and we've tracked those two transfers back to these two characters."

Sitting back in her chair, Martha picked up her cup and held it steady for a moment before continuing, "We've knitted together the feeds from two street cams and have identified the two new Hartfield clients of special concern: Travis Stratton and Elizabeth Preston – in the top two displays – both of whom are extremely moneyed and lacking in character. But the better find here is that the person in the third video feed is Anne Whitman."

Pete sat back in his chair and absentmindedly put his fingers to his chin again and momentarily lost himself in thought. *No surprise there, but it brings up the question of 'Why'. Why the cover-up? Why not just say that she quit over a pay dispute or some other trivial excuse? They've obviously assessed her as a threat. A threat they feel should be eliminated.*

Discretely watching Pete, Martha gave him a few seconds with his private thoughts before continuing, "We are now watching Preston and Stratton, using them, in addition to Jennifer Harstaad, to build a solid picture of Hartfield's process of spinning straw into gold. And, according to a background check, with these two, they'll need lots of spinning. There's another character we're looking at, too."

Martha took a sip of her tea, set the cup down on the table and leaned into her laptop. A few seconds later, another window of data was displayed neatly on the large screen above the workspace. Looking up, Martha indicated to Pete that she was referencing the large screen as she continued, "My patrons are interested in a particular subject. I've been brought in mainly because of him. He's a junior senator from a southern state, Frank Torres. His résumé reads like a typical small-time radical turned politician, except that he wasn't a very successful one. After a few years of organizing and participating in anti-government rallies, and who, after three visits to The Hartfield Connection, sauntered through a pre-election campaign straight into a six-year Senate term. We'd like to know how that was done."

Seeing that Pete had finished his coffee, Martha picked up both their cups and the insulated pot and returned them to the credenza.

"Pete, the data from your sidecars and preliminary data from the observations of Preston and Stratton won't be ready for at least an hour. In the meantime, how about you and I get a bite to eat. I know a great place in the downtown area that serves a wonderful organic blue plate special."

Pete closed his borrowed laptop and smiled. "I'll drive."

◆　◆　◆

The restaurant was quiet and the booths comfy. There was enough space between the rounded tables to give the impression of privacy without sacrificing too much on the number of persons that could be seated at one time. The décor was tasteful and not too overdone. The lighting coming from the niches and down from recesses in the ceiling added an almost perfect balance to the natural daylight filtering through the gauzy curtains covering the windows. During the day, the restaurant catered to the local business crowd and strove to be upscale without being pretentious.

Martha and Pete had been shown to a booth next to the windows facing the main street in front of the restaurant. The noontime traffic had picked up and the sidewalks were getting crowded as well. The view was softened by the wide median with its mature trees and flowering shrubs, which made the booth by the windows a nice place to be.

Looking through the menu, Pete said, "What are you thinking of having today?"

Martha's eyes had lit upon the list of salads offered and had almost made up her mind. Looking up from her menu, she said, "I'm thinking about the warm beet and Brussels salad with feta cheese. How about you?"

Pete flipped the menu pages and said, "The cold mixed greens salad with poached wild salmon sounds good."

After the waiter had taken their order, Martha and Pete made themselves more comfortable, sitting back and adjusting wide cloth napkins on their laps.

Pete watched Martha as she gazed out the window, looking at the leaves of the trees in the median move in the light mid-noon breeze. He waited a moment then said, "Martha, mind if I ask you a personal question?"

Martha smiled at him and said, "No. Not at all."

Suddenly, Pete realized he was about to ask Martha something very personal and although he had already asked permission to do so, he wondered if it was the right thing to do at this time. After checking his thoughts, Pete asked again, "Are you sure you wouldn't mind? I don't want to make you uncomfortable and am willing to keep things above board, if you prefer."

Martha looked at Pete for a second then answered, "I appreciate that, thank you, but I don't mind at all so…ask anything you like." Then smiled expectantly.

Pete's curiosity had gotten the better of him. He did want to know more about Martha so asked her, "Well, I was wondering if you are married, do you have a family?" Pete's question was friendly and curious.

Martha tilted her head and looked over at Pete and said, "No. I'm not married, although I was in love once. Deeply in love. With my best friend. We were together for two years before he was deployed to the Middle East as an attaché. We talked about how our romance would play out with him in the Middle East and me here stateside. After a bit of discussion and a lot of soul searching, we decided that being friends was more important to both of us, so we parted as best friends." Smiling, she continued, "No kids. My mother passed away several years before I went off to college. My dad's retired and lives in eastern Maine, on the cliffs above Starboard Cove. A little rough, but he loves it."

Just then, the waiter appeared with their entrées. As he set their plates in front of them, he motioned for another server to bring fresh glasses of iced water and another Tetsubin teapot of black tea. Satisfied that the table was in order and smiling to both Pete and Martha, he took a half step back and in one smooth movement, turned and stepped away.

Martha picked up her fork and said, "This looks wonderful. I hope you'll enjoy your lunch. They always do such a nice presentation, I almost hate to mess it up."

"Yes, this does look appetizing – let's see how it tastes." Pete took a bite and said, "Very nice and thank you for suggesting this restaurant. It's nicely appointed and very comfortable."

Taking a bite of her salad and then a sip of hot tea, Martha asked Pete the same question, "How about you, Pete. Are you married?"

Pete had been listening to Martha talk and had absentmindedly moved his salad around the plate in an effort to mix in the dressing. He took a moment to taste the results and said, "My wife passed away ten years ago. I've been a single dad to two wonderful sons since then. My eldest is a lawyer, although he prefers to be called an attorney." Smiling with the thought of his lawyer son, Pete continued, "My youngest is a writer. He's published two original books: one of poetry and a work of fiction." Taking another bite of lunch, Pete said, "I'm very proud of them both."

A quiet moment passed and Martha, looking at Pete noticed faint streaks of gray at his temples and, as he looked over at her, the dark green of his eyes. She asked, "Did you like your college years? What was your major?"

Pete thought for a second and said, "I liked them well enough. I earned a degree in criminal justice with a minor in law. Just after college, as I was thinking about my career and my life and law books and courtrooms and it all started to look a bit dull. The more I thought about a life among criminals and judges, the more I wondered about my ability to stay perched on top of the fence separating them."

"And did you find your balance?"

"No. The more I considered it, the more apprehension I had about a life of law. After a short amount of time, I think it was just after the summer I graduated, I enlisted as an officer in the Marines. After training, I joined Black Ops. That sort of thing. The rest is history." Smiling a sort of "isn't-that-obvious" kind of smile, Pete waited for Martha to react before he reached for the bread plate and proffered a helping.

Her reaction was exactly what Pete had guessed it would be. Martha, shaking her head "no" to the offered bread, and sitting back slightly in an attitude of mock disbelief, said, "And that history led all the way to tracking a missing girl from Hartfield's. That's a pretty long history."

Pete, looking surprised with a sly smile on his face, said, "Yeah, probably a story for another time."

They ate in silence for a minute or two before Pete asked Martha what she thought was really going on at The Hartfield.

"That's a very good question but I think I can only answer part of it at this point." Martha took a sip of her tea and continued, "From my personal experience, limited as that is, Hartfield has definitely put itself next to the country's wealthiest population and caters only to that demographic. You can almost hear their excitement levels go up when they've completed their background checks on a rich client's financial status. They're very greedy. Now, is that because their service and overhead warrant such high prices or is it because they need vast amounts of cash to fund various concealed enterprises. That's part of why we're here. We still have to answer several major questions – how are they circumventing the government's regulations pertaining to the American Fairness in Government Law and what is going on in those secret labs?"

Pete buttered a slice of dark brown bread and laid his butter knife down across the top of his plate. "Let's not forget about Anne Whitman. My guess is that Anne may have stumbled onto the answer to that, and possibly other answers, as well," Pete had put his fork down for a moment and was regarding Martha with thoughtful attention, "which is why she felt she had to run."

Leaning slightly forward in an unconscious attitude of seriousness, Pete continued, "I believe something fantastic is going on in those labs. Something so unbelievable that if Anne had gone to the police, they wouldn't have bought her story. I think that only a small number of Hartfield employees are in on whatever is happening in the labs, and I think most of the department VPs have some level of awareness of it."

Martha picked up the thread, "The two key persons in all of this are Hartfield and Sturgess. We're not minimizing the involvement of other persons like Abers or the now absent CFO, Tom Ashton. They're as culpable as any, however, it's obvious that they're focused only on their small parts, not the complete picture. For that, we are led back to Hartfield and Sturgess."

In response, Pete said, "And after my meeting with Sturgess this morning, I'm sure he's in deeper than even Hartfield may realize."

Both Pete and Martha sat for a moment contemplating what they had just talked about. Pete spoke first, "The labs may be tasked with manufacturing illegal drugs that are being sold to out of country buyers and whose monies are supporting the lavish lifestyles of top Hartfield executives. Their silence is being bought. However, there may be more money coming in than can be spent or hidden and that's become a problem. The CFO became complacent which made him sloppy and that caused him to be transferred. I think that's a euphemism for 'properly dealt with'."

Martha, nodding in agreement said, "You may be right."

The waiter came up to the table to enquire if everything was satisfactory and could he have the table cleared. After the plates were removed and the teacups refilled, a small assortment of cookies and sweets were placed between Martha and Pete, with the bill discreetly tucked underneath. With a smile, the waiter said, "A sweet bite to finish your meal. Have a wonderful afternoon," and left them to sip their tea and grab a brief moment before returning to their business.

A soft, barely audible chime from Martha's e-device brought them back from their individual thoughts. Glancing at the e-device's screen and looking up at Pete, Martha said, "Your sidecars have been downloaded and analyzed and are waiting for us. Shall we go?"

Pete tossed a couple bills on the table and followed Martha out the front doors. His Senelli was parked a few steps down the street and the ride back to the loft office was smooth and uneventful. In the intervening silence, Martha thought to herself about the quiet times that occurred between her and Pete and how she was so very comfortable in his company. She had not felt that way in a very long time and that made her smile.

◆　　◆　　◆

Alan was waiting with the data extracted from Pete's sidecars and the latest up-to-date intel from several established sources. Group leaders were already assembled in Martha's area and after she and Pete had joined them, Alan began his informal briefing.

Alan spent his cadet year with the CIA training and five additional years deployed to various situations. He joined Martha's team two years ago and it hadn't taken long for him to be recognized as a top analyst and a good lead person. He excelled in analytic methodology, developing and applying precision to intelligence and analysis. He loved stats, math and design. Martha took special note of Alan's ability for anticipating and preparing for eventual situations and rightfully guessed that it was his military background that originally sparked his enthusiasm. Alan had found the military's penchant for organization very useful and the forays into unstable international situations rousing, finding that, as more trouble was brewing up, he would become more focused and alive. It was a natural move from military service to government service with the CIA.

Alan took his place in front of the group and began, "Several bits of pertinent information were located on the sidecars that Mr. Malloy brought in earlier this morning. References to Anne Whitman were found in an obscure email sent from Personnel to Ashton shortly after her on-site interview. It recommended her for the executive secretary position in his department. We think this, along with the street cam video, may be fairly solid evidence that she did work there. We've heard from Beta Team, which is following Hartfield's trackers, and they bought several hours for the Alpha Team by disabling the trackers vehicle. The trackers are affecting repairs so will be mobile again soon. Meanwhile, Alpha Team reports that they're getting closer to finding Ms. Whitman after inquiries at local food marts and similar establishments placed her in the area as late as two days ago."

Martha asked, "Have they requested additional support?"

Alan leaned back against Martha's desk and said, "No. They said that protecting Ms. Whitman wouldn't be a problem but if clashes with Hartfield's trackers occur, they would appreciate it if we would intercede with Canadian authorities."

"Easily done. Please continue."

Alan consulted his papers and turning a page or two let his eyes skim the notes before continuing, "There are current bank statements indicating large sums of company money is being transferred offshore. Within the last six weeks, over a quarter of a billion dollars has been seen moving across the wires. We're still following the transfers to locate the deposit point and any disbursements that would have happened."

Alan looked up from his papers and glanced across the faces of the group he was addressing. "I think we have the most recent intel on this next point." Referring to another page in his hand, Alan continued, "There were some very interesting invoices that came from an encrypted folder found among several seemingly benign folders relating to the legal department. Apparently numerous deliveries of medical apparatus have been made dating back to when the Hartfield building was originally constructed. At first the equipment was of a type normally used when first outfitting a new lab: beakers, tubes, vials. That sort of thing. Eventually, the invoices started listing more advanced kinds of lab equipment, like monitors, needle systems and ventilators as well as imaging systems. These types of systems suggest something more to do with human support and research."

One of the team leaders, Jessica Roberts, spoke up, "Have you derived a supposition from this?"

"Nothing solid." Alan twisted around to reach a remote control unit on Martha's desk and poked two buttons, one after the other. The large screen above Martha's desk came alive. The top of the screen was displaying the current activity being fed from the various departments in the loft office. Alan directed everyone's attention to the bottom half of the screen, where several lines of text were displayed. "As we looked at the more recent invoices, the picture changed again. Here we see flow cells, actuators and interestingly enough, linear devices. Our theory, to date, is that Hartfield's labs are working independently. One is focused on biochemistry and one is involved with robotics, although without further data, it's impossible to say how deep either of these disciplines go."

Martha leaned forward in her seat. She could feel her back muscles contract in response to her mounting anticipation and prompted Alan with, "And the third lab?"

Alan spoke, "We don't have a clear picture of lab three because there has been a distinct lack of data concerning it. I think it's safe to assume that lab three has not been idle. The more likely story is that it has bigger secrets and is kept quieter because of it."

Martha scanned the faces in the group and asked, "What's the story-board on labs one and two?"

The team leader, Thomas Perry, from the Advanced Analysis group was the first to speak up. "It's possible that the biochem lab, lab one, is researching and experimenting with DNA and protein chemistry. They have a huge independent data retrieval system that would be necessary to store all the information associated with basic human DNA sequencing and to accommodate additional data brought forth by their research. The amount of monitoring equipment indicated by the invoices suggests that they may be using live models in their experimentations, not limiting themselves to theoretic models. We're supposing that there could be up to eight scientists, at the PhD level and above, needed to operate our scenario at its most efficient." He nodded to an associate, Jerry Brink, who gave an overview of lab two.

Jerry was sitting toward the back of the group and rather than speak to the back of their heads, stood up and stepped to the side of the group before answering. "We've concluded that lab two is concentrating on robotics. This is based on several invoices that list a myriad of electronic components and linear devices, as well as apparatus associated with laser studies. We're still analyzing the sidecar data and intel from other sources and should have a more clear picture of lab two's mission by early this evening."

Pete noticed a look of retrospect come over Martha's face before she spoke to the group. "We have a corporation whose affluent clients manage to procure positions in very high places throughout businesses and governments worldwide. We have a frightened young woman who may know something that has put her life in jeopardy. And we have three secret and highly protected labs. Given this information…I'd like to hear your thoughts on how this may play out."

The round-robin began with Jessica Roberts, "The money obtained from rich clients is funding not only Hartfield's and Sturgess' lifestyles, it's underwriting the labs. It's possible that through its international contacts, The Hartfield is researching some type of chemical weaponry to be combined with robotic drone delivery systems. The highly placed clients are insurance toward success for sales or staging."

Another voice sounded, that of Thomas Perry. "The biochemical lab may be creating smart-drugs in order to achieve domination in the field of pharmacology. The robotics lab may be in support of the biochem lab or it may be a separate enterprise focused on many things: security, aviation, surveillance, space."

Pete spoke up. "I can't help but to think that all three labs are tied up with each other. The truth is, the labs are not only being funded by wealthy clients, there has to be a direct benefit to them. We've seen Hartfield clients assume positions in the highest of places after undergoing a few months of training and management. I'm not convinced that these individuals possess enough discipline to hold to their training after even a few weeks." Taking a deep breath in and letting it back out, Pete continued, "Anne Whitman knows something or is in possession of some very incriminating information. Hartfield wouldn't go to the expense of an all out manhunt if she didn't. They wouldn't risk international discovery over a trifle."

Martha had gathered her thoughts and nodded in agreement. She stood up from her place and turned to face the group as a whole. "Stratton and Preston will be our sortie into the front-end operations. My alias as Mrs. Jennifer Harstaad has been successful in providing an in-depth look at the kind of character Mark Sturgess is and a glimpse of what Hartfield is capable of. If lab three were to deliver their product by the end of the week, we need to know what that is and we should limit our 'discovery phase' to just a day or two. Any longer would be too late." Looking around at the concerned faces of the group, Martha concluded, "However we look at it, we need more information and we need it fast."

THE INNOCENCE OF POWER

12
Deception and Trickery

The next day was busy for everyone working in the loft office. Several additional members had been brought in and put to work in the Communication and Advanced Analysis areas and the office had taken on an air of electricity. The overheads in the Comm area were a blur as data whizzed by from a myriad of sources including the mobile tracking devices that had been tucked into Sturgess' Mercedes SLR Stirling Moss and Hartfield's bulletproof corporate limo, as well as the sniffers that Pete had attached to their electric devices and the continuous feeds from their mobile phones.

The street cams provided further intel on Elizabeth Preston, showing that she had arrived and had left The Hartfield twice within the same morning. A quick sync with the e-comms in the legal department reported that she was not happy with a three to four month process lead-time; she wanted results within two weeks and wouldn't be happy with anything other than what she wanted. She had made it very clear that she would pull her financial capital outlay if Hartfield didn't see it her way. The legal department was currently wrangling with this issue while trying to buy time by promising her a meeting with Mr. Hartfield as soon as his schedule had an opening. They had no intention of refunding her money – already deposited off shore – or of letting her meet with Hartfield. They were desperately trying to figure out how to handle Miss Preston.

Travis Stratton was back, too. Taps of Legal had shown that Mr. Stratton had advanced two sizable sums of money since his original meeting with Sturgess. All indications were that he was happy with whatever Hartfield had provided and was paying forward on another level of service. E-comms on the 56th floor, where the little armies of PR fix-it people were officed, showed that Mr. Stratton was currently being taught etiquette 101. Previous clips of Travis Stratton's social behaviors indicated that this class might be more difficult than not for both the teacher and the student.

The graphic depictions being produced by the Advanced Analysts were by far the most interesting. This group liked to avoid the rigidity of a single scenario; instead, they built multiple possibilities in order to see how the majority of their data could fit together.

The master screen, duplicated on redundant screens along the walls throughout the loft office, currently had three real-time storyboards. All three streaming data lines evolved as additional information was received and deemed reliable enough to be folded in.

One scenario had Hartfield involved with illicit drug trade with foreign countries where current clients were known to reside and had real or subliminal influence or control of several possible distribution channels. Through Hartfield, these clients were able to step into leading roles throughout several governments and more than a few corporations and had evolved changes in the regulations aimed at controlling imports and exports. Either through disarming the import regulations or by reducing inspections staff numbers, several key entry points had been made available. Drugs could easily flow in and out without much notice. This would represent a multi-billion dollar profit worldwide. A very lucrative trade.

The focus of the second scenario was the development and transfer of various technologies ranging from communication platforms to weapons grade laser systems. In this scheme, Hartfield aimed to dominate, nay, command the field of technology development and sales. The business of war was the biggest global business currently operating and Hartfield aimed to own it. U.S. policy strictly forbade private corporations to engage in technology transfers to any foreign country at any level of development. However, once again, previous and current clients placed in strategic positions on U.S. soil and in foreign locations were influencing transfer possibilities.

A third scenario was also being formed around the idea that somehow the cutting-edge robotics technology, being glimpsed at through Lab Two's inventory rosters, was responsible for a combination of the first two theories. That is, robotic machinery was the best place to hide weapons grade technology and could be used for smuggling experimental drugs – something most governments don't allow their own pharmaceutical corporations to use on human subjects until well after years of clinical experiments and published reports. Hartfield might be fast-tracking these things.

What these three theories all had in common were the Hartfield clients. The well placed, highly influential Hartfield clients. The question that the Advanced Analysis team was tasked with answering was: What is The Hartfield Connection really doing?

As the morning wore on, the pace seemed to quicken. The homing devices placed on Hartfield's and Sturgess' automobiles had shown that Sturgess had been primarily at the uptown office location while old man Hartfield's limo had been tracked around the city to several locations before returning to its berth in The Hartfield Connection's VIP valet parking space. Hartfield's e-taps had provided a snapshot of what he had been looking at: mostly stocks that were currently trading on the world markets, the commodities exchange rates of domestic holdings and a thorough reading of foreign affairs reports. While he was out and about, Hartfield had made one phone call to Sturgess. Martha's comm team had used the pseudo-code key developed earlier to glean one tantalizing bit of information from the mobile phone conversation that transpired between Hartfield and Sturgess: Hartfield had promised a constituent that results would be delivered before the weekend was over and had informed Sturgess to ensure the deadline.

Sturgess, on the other hand, was almost fully occupied with the security breach facilitated by Anne Whitman. He was in almost constant communication with Lieutenant Abers and was receiving updates as to what progress the Hartfield team, assigned to locate Ms. Whitman, had made. His angst was almost palpable through his e-devices. And as every good hunter knows…a nervous prey will almost always do something uncalculated, and that's the best time for the hunter to pounce.

Martha's team was ready.

♦   ♦   ♦

What little time Mark Sturgess had not been spending on security was being given to the care and special handling of Elizabeth Preston. It seemed that Miss Preston's personal schedule for success was not quite synchronized with that of Hartfield's. Her team of handlers had informed her that the timeline should allow for the proper procedures to follow departmentally proven steps that were necessary for a successful outcome. Legal had tried to buy time by "studying the matrix" and having "departmental discussions" on her matter, but Miss Preston remained unhappy.

Arriving precisely one minute before their semi-impromptu

meeting, Mark entered the plush meeting room and greeted Elizabeth in a personable style. He thought that the smile on his face would pass for friendly and serve to defuse any tensions that Miss Preston had been building up as she waited for him to arrive. He was wrong.

At the sound of the door opening Elizabeth turned from the windows to face Mark. He noticed her cold, hard eyes as she glared at him. "Good afternoon, Miss Preston."

Taking two steps toward him, Elizabeth Preston seemed to take in an exasperated breath and then began, "Mr. Sturgess. I have been very patient with you and with the firm. However, I am beginning to think that this company does not understand what 'client satisfaction' really means. From the treatment that I have received and the run-around I'm now getting from your so-called legal department, I am almost at my end." Elizabeth stood with her feet planted firmly to her spot, almost daring Mark to speak.

Mark, smiled his trademark smile and motioned for Elizabeth to take a seat.

"Please, Miss Preston, let's sit and talk for a moment. Would you like something to drink? A water, perhaps?"

"No, thank you." Taking a seat in a large leather chair by the windows, Elizabeth folded her arms across her bosom and stared at Mark.

Mark took the chair next to hers and sat back in an effort to appear calm and in control of the situation. He said, "I'm so sorry that you aren't completely happy with the service that you have received from The Hartfield. Tell me what seems to be the problem."

Mark knew what the problem was. Elizabeth had met with him twice within as many days and at one point, had leveled thinly disguised threats of lawsuits and accusations of fraud aimed at him as well as Hartfield. At the meeting, two days ago, where Mark spent a lot of energy trying to calm the situation, he had called Legal to have a new contract drawn up that included Elizabeth's revised timeline. He then called her PR team lead to inform him of the new requirements and how they were to proceed from that point forward – meaning, kid gloves for Miss Preston and full accounts to himself. The last meeting with Jack Abourn, VP of Hartfield's Security, culminated with Sturgess informing him that Miss Preston was to be processed through their system to Level II and to await further instructions.

Now, as Mark listened to Elizabeth's deliberate harangue, he wondered if she was the kind of person who wouldn't be satisfied with any level of service given to her. He was starting to think that she would never be happy even if all his attention were to be paid strictly to her. He doubted even that would be enough.

When Elizabeth had completed her more than thorough explanation of what it was she wanted written in her contract, Mark leaned forward in his seat so that she would be very clear that he was paying attention to her. "I believe that The Hartfield will be able to accommodate all of your requests, Miss Preston and I'm so sorry for any miscommunication that might have happened in your dealings with any of our personnel. I'll make the necessary calls and direct Legal to have a revised contract ready for signature by tomorrow morning. Would that satisfy you?"

Elizabeth got up from her chair and walked to the door. As she reached for the door latch, she turned halfway around to look over her shoulder at Mark, who had stood up and was waiting for her reply. "Yes, Mr. Sturgess. That would satisfy me." And with that, she opened the door and left.

Mark made a phone call to old man Hartfield, but his line was unavailable and Mark was shunted to voicemail. He left a clipped statement about the decision to move Elizabeth Preston's timeline up and ended the message. Mark's mind was racing. It would be easier to control Miss Preston if she were enmeshed further into the system, and the further in she was, the more reluctant she would be to discuss her progress with non-Hartfield persons. It was all a matter of insurance.

♦　　♦　　♦

Mark Sturgess was no stranger to the navigation of business hierarchy or of client relations. He had learned his craft early in his career.

Mark's first inclinations, after joining the Centre d'Etude de Polymorphisms Humain Research Institute in Paris, were to make a mental note of the top five power players in the hierarchy. These people were the ones to impress and to influence and were positioned well beyond lab directors and low-level managers. The power players were the ones who could change goals and timelines as they saw fit. It took Mark all of a few months to make himself known to the Institute's executives, impress them with his knowledge and communication skills and to start to receive regular invitations to join them, either as small groups or individually, for lunch or drinks after hours.

Within one year, Mark was heading his own laboratory and was engaged in testing and proving the dynamic behavior of supramolecular structures within the adrenal system. Interesting enough work but not Mark's main goal. He had received several monetary awards for papers he had written and for several research suggestions he had made. Mark regularly found himself in the company of the Institute's executives and more prominent scientists, among them, Doctor Benjamin Deverell Hera who had been at that time engrossed in a highly confidential project that few people inside or outside the Institute were aware had even existed.

Mark used his income to move into a flashy apartment on the Rue de Rivoli. He had leased a Citroen S-class automobile and became available for high society engagements where he regularly met and mingled with many of Europe's fast trackers.

Everything moved along pretty much the same for about two years but when Mark's life started to even out, when the new friends and acquaintances became old and cliché, Mark found himself bored and restless and losing patience with those around him. It was time for another change.

Not all of the fast trackers that Mark Sturgess met during his party nights in Paris were on the up and up. Success comes in many packages: from old money that allowed automatic succession to power and fame, from new money that allowed the purchase of power and fame, the appointment to power and fame, and the seizing of power and fame by any means available. Most of Mark's acquaintances had employed some level of ruse to obtain their position: a brother, father, money, friends, their wits, and lacking that, information or some degree of blackmail.

The longer Mark associated with the Institute's circle of power and their connections, the more clear it became to him that it would be very difficult for him to become one of the inner group as an equal. No matter what he could bring to the table he could not break the barrier that kept his ultimate goal at bay. He would converse with them on their intellectual level and exchange familiarities but there was never any level of trust offered to him. And he felt it. And he knew it. And he didn't like it.

Gradually, Mark became dissatisfied with his business commission and his social standing. His research had reached a point where viable results were coming slower and slower and this directly affected the rate at which his discretionary bonus monies were being awarded to him. His social standing seemed to plateau and he no longer found amusement among the persons he regularly associated with. He found party conversations rote and small-minded and started to turn down invitations or just failed to appear at their gatherings.

Mark did not throw himself into his work. His work had taken on the mantle of an all consuming and burdensome beast that would, if it could, take all of Mark's time and drain his energy to the last life-sustaining ounce. Instead, he set his mind to thinking of how he was going to change his circumstances to his benefit.

In moderate and measured degrees, Mark developed a new plan for his life that did not include his joining an existing power structure. It outlined, almost too clearly, how he would be a player on the world stage. He would be a force unto his own; he would wield unimaginable power, command a vast fortune and garner an almost star-like fame. It was becoming more and more evident to Mark that he did not need to join the world. The world needed to join him. The picture of this new plan was for Mark to offer a unique service, collect clients, amass a small fortune and return to the states. The first step was to find venture capital and the next step was to begin.

♦　　♦　　♦

Mark Sturgess spent the next three years traveling throughout Europe skillfully developing his style, refining his taste for expensive luxuries and meeting all the right people. His charming personality and gift for quality speech served as his introduction to most of the European venture capitalists and his keen sense of these things allowed him to quickly discern how he would be of service to them.

Mark found that his connections made it rather simple for him to establish and realize contracts of obligation. All of his clients needed some level of service outside of the legal or ethical bounds of their businesses and Mark was adept at completing negotiations, exerting influence, explaining repercussions and bringing the job to a close. No matter what type of job it was or what it might take to make that happen. He would collect extravagant amounts of cash from his happy clients and when he perceived that his stay, in his current city, had just about reached its limits, that is to say, Mark had collected all the ready cash available, he would move on.

As his Swiss bank account became sizable, Mark started to consider his transition back to the states. In his leisure time, he researched specific companies, reading their prospectuses and weighing their futures against his. When his investigations were concluded and his mind had been made up, Mark Sturgess bought a first-class airline ticket and left Europe for the Eastern Seaboard.

◆　　◆　　◆

The mission was urgent: seek, retrieve and protect. Martha's Alpha Team was tracking its one target, Anne Whitman, with a brilliant mix of skill and experience. All four men were experts in their fields. The team leader, Rogers was responsible for his men and the mission and a superb tactician; the driver, Dayton was experienced in tactical and defensive driving techniques and all things mechanical; the technical specialist, Peters was an expert in all things electronic; and the operations specialist, Ruiz was experienced in explosives including several curious methods of deploying them. All had earned recognition from the highest places of government. Singularly, these four men were formidable, but combined they were a force to be reckoned with.

On Martha's direction for immediate deployment, they had conducted a short briefing and within one hour, had collected and packed everything they would need to successfully complete their mission. Along with the gadgetry and weapons, Rogers ordered enough survival gear to last seven days, and extra ammunition to be stowed aboard the large black civilian SUV that would be their command center and base for as long as necessary.

Each man was aware that the mission was going to be played out among the general population of a foreign country and out of sight of the authorities. This would mean a low profile and covert operations tailored not to gather attention. They would simply be four men on a yearly fishing vacation.

The approach to the Canadian border, using highways and surface streets was swift enough but using satellite guidance, the team chose another route across: a seventy-five mile stretch of abandoned logging roads. That particular route appeared to be more direct, albeit a shorter distance than the two-lane highway that veered west for forty-five miles before returning to the appointed border crossing coordinates. The ride was rough and seemed longer than the two hours it took to make the distance. Between satellite updates and status chatter, each man was able to grab a moment to look out at a most beautiful but rugged terrain, to relax their minds and to breathe in the easiness of unpolluted air. Rogers was a believer in a calm before the storm. He encouraged small breaks and focusing techniques to re-center his team so that both mind and body would work as one when the initial adrenal rush of mission engagement occurred. And in situations such as this, it would occur.

The logging road disintegrated into a fire access road before turning into what resembled a well-worn dirt road that ran behind several horse ranches clustered along a small ridge of granite outcroppings. The vehicle made its way onto a rural access road and emerged from the side trip sixty miles from the border. Turning north on the main highway, they resumed their course at an increased speed to make up for a bit of clock-time they lost in the hills.

When Alpha Team had reached the Ogdensburg Border Crossing station, Dayton, the driver, struck up a friendly conversation with the border guard.

"Hello to you! Fine day for fishing, isn't it?"

The guard smiled and said, "Hello. Yes, a fine day for fishing. May I see your passports?"

As the guard looked at the documentation and checked the accompanying photos, Dayton pressed on, "My sister told me that the fish in Canada were bigger and smarter than the ones in the states. We've made a ten dollar bet on it!" Smiling, Dayton continued, "We're on our way to meet her and I'm hoping that we're on the right road. I think she passed this way about two days ago, maybe you remember her?"

The guard, looked pensive for a second and said, "I might. Ogdensburg doesn't get that many visitor crossings. Mostly trucks. People like to visit Montreal and use Highway 87 for that. What does your sister look like?"

Dayton described Anne Whitman and the guard thought for a second before answering, "There was a young lady that fits your description, she didn't mention 'smart' fish though, but I think I remember her taking the left fork in the road, just there." And pointing to an intersection in the road about one hundred yards past the guard shack, added, "That fork will take you out to Big Rideau Lake where the fishing is very good."

Before the guard raised the crossing grate, he leaned out of the large sliding window, looked the SUV over, slowly moving his eyes from the front bumper to the rear bumper and said, "I'm going to ask to see your sporting license, to be sure your fees are up to date."

Dayton smiled and pulled a small, ornate piece of paper from the vehicle's center console and gingerly handed it to the guard, who looked at it and handed it back with a grin and said, "Good luck, and throw the smart fish back!"

Dayton thanked the guard and eased the SUV forward. After making the turn and watching the guard station recede into the distance, Dayton picked up speed and continued with deliberation.

Using cell-tracking, the team identified the last verifiable location of Anne's escape from the threat of Hartfield. The pinpoint on their map indicated that she was travelling on a road headed into the rough lands surrounding a wildlife sanctuary.

Tech Specialist Peters assessed their immediate environment, looking for any road that may shorten their drive time. Most of the accessible roads were not paved and so proved to be a liability. After looking at maps for a minute, he spoke to Rogers, "Sir, it seems that we're on the most efficient path available. The next town is about 35 clicks ahead."

Rogers thought for a second and said, "My suggestion is that we stop there and ask a few discrete questions. Let's see if anyone remembers seeing Ms. Whitman. Dayton's story about her being his sister is a good cover."

Operations Specialist, Ruiz, spoke up, "We could inquire about the availability of recreation cabins or other such amenities in the area to see if Whitman might be local. It's more likely that she would choose a small town over a larger one to fade into."

Rogers addressed his team, "Talking with the locals may give us valuable information and from there, we can plan our next step."

Tech Specialist Peters spoke up, "All this will need to be accomplished rather quickly, as the last intel received on Hartfield's trackers has them 50 clicks behind us but closing."

◆   ◆   ◆

Martha's Beta Team was in stealth mode as they trailed close behind Hartfield's trackers. In constant contact with Alpha Team and relying on GPS to provide a blind visual, Beta Team held their position steady, just out of sight of the trackers' vehicle. From their position, they monitored the tracker's every move. The homing devices, that had been covertly peppered all over the tracker's vehicle, gave Beta Team a clear heads-up to any stops or turns the trackers made. Sat-communications and Martha's crack team of comm experts gave copious amounts of intel on the trackers. For instance, it was a three-man team made up of ex-military mercenaries. The driver was just a driver who could shoot a gun. The team lead was a grizzled war veteran who, at times, slipped into his "Question Authority" attitude and complained about lack of respect and low pay. This was probably a favorite harangue, a sort of go-to complaint, because he was very accomplished in his warcraft with untold number of kills to his credit. And since becoming a mercenary for The Hartfield, his personal worth had quadrupled. The third man was an easygoing person with a sick sense of humor with a keen knowledge of weapons and tactical methods. Overall, Hartfield's trackers seemed to lack the integrity of a well-formed team, but they should not be dismissed as bumpkins with guns. They were tough, seasoned opponents that Martha's Beta Team did not underestimate. Just the opposite. Beta Team was ready for the worst. And they would probably get it.

◆　　◆　　◆

Pete had moved from the stiff chair to the couch and from his laptop was studying the graphic feed that was constantly spewing streams of data across the large monitors. It was rather fascinating, and a bit mesmerizing, to watch the scenarios build, pause, add and revise storylines as quickly as intel was being applied from its hundreds of sources. The four sidebars that were reporting the whereabouts of Hartfield, Sturgess, Preston and Stratton, were a work of science. It was amazing that technology could be used to track a person's location even as they took a step. The little landmaps with their moving dots were as admirable as they were thought provoking.

One scenario seemed just as plausible as the next and that one gave rise to several more possibilities. All the intelligence gathered throughout the mission painted a picture of Azekiel Hartfield as a self-possessed man obsessed with power and riches. Not only was he interested in furthering his desires, he was also interested in taking riches away from those he perceived as his enemies. He was more than a bit deluded in his self-assessment and enemies may have been too strong of a term, but he was focused and driven and that made him a dangerous player in this little drama.

Hartfield was playing on a world stage with little regard for laws and regulations or the sovereignty of foreign nations. It seemed to Pete that Hartfield had several plans in various stages of progress. All of them aimed at thwarting anything he perceived as a limitation or interference to what he wanted to accomplish. So what is it that he really wanted to accomplish from the labs under his highrise building?   Robotics, laboratory studies, genomics, biotechnology. Were these disciplines inter-related or on separate tracks? It was obvious that Hartfield had evaluated the economic risks against the economic rewards and had concluded that his ventures held the promise of huge rewards. So he played on with dollar signs firmly planted in his eyes and power the ultimate reward for his efforts.

◆   ◆   ◆

Shortly after starting his company, Azekiel Hartfield had been invited to a social event, a black tie affair where he had met and established an immediate rapport with two of the attendees. Both men were from Italy and had recently come to the states to foster relationships with American businesses and to garner their favor in future and very possible commerce with Italian businessmen.

Allessandro Laconi was the son of a middle-class working father who had tried, unsuccessfully, to expand his olive oil business into Portugal where he thought to make his fortune. Allessandro took his father's plight to heart and after two years in a private school, left to become a political lobbyist in favor of establishing revised export laws. He established himself as the man who could affect changes to laws governing local businesses and for the betterment of his constituents.

Emilio Pesaro was a small town politician who wanted more than anything to be elected to the Parliament of Italy, specifically to the Senate of the Republic. He had been plying his trade for a number of years with limited success, but after several unsavory instances involving married women had been reported in local and national newspapers, Emilio needed to boost his popularity. He felt that a good way to go about it was to get the backing of several big American companies. It would give him credibility and raise his public status to be able to brag about his international connections.

After being introduced to Azekiel, Allessandro said in his best English, "How fortuitous that I should be introduced to the owner of The Hartfield Connection at such a fabulous event as this. I have heard of your reputation and you have been highly recommended."

Azekiel shook his hand warmly and replied, "It's my pleasure to meet you, Mr. Laconi." And turning to Mr. Pesaro, shook his hand saying, "I'm glad to meet you, too, Mr. Pesaro." And addressing both men, "Shall we sit and talk for a moment?"

Azekiel lost no time in setting up a private meeting with the two men for the next morning at his downtown office. Meanwhile his mind raced as he developed short and long term plans for both Laconi and Pesaro. By the time the two Italian dignitaries arrived at the appointed hour, Azekiel had two contracts put together that named what he would do for them, what was expected from them in return and what it would cost them. It took six hours for the large deposit sums to be transferred across time zones and once that detail was settled, Azekiel briefed them to the details of his proposal and set up a schedule that covered the first three months of their new association. After the contracts were signed and sealed, and after everyone was satisfied with the pending results, Azekiel arranged for the company limo to take the two men to the airport where they were to catch their plane home.

Moments after Allessandro Laconi had signed on the dotted line and his deposit had been logged, he received, to his phone device, a gift of five names of companies he could count on for support in his lobbying efforts of the Italian Parliament. The companies had been handpicked by Azekiel and were all interested in expanding their operations into Italy.

In contrast to how easy it was to provide service to Mr. Laconi, Azekiel found one small block to his plan for Emilio Pesaro. The only thing preventing Mr. Pesaro from occupying the political position he so desired had been identified as the lack of open vacancies within the Parliament House. By Azekiel's calculation, three empty positions were needed to ensure that his client was elected. The elections were fast approaching and there were still only two openings up for grabs and while his client was actively campaigning, he was running a near third.

Hartfield was not given to recklessness. His mind worked with precision as he calculated outcomes to his cause and effect strategies. He did not believe in chance, or in fate, or in luck. For Azekiel, the eventual outcome to virtually all of his plans were guaranteed because he saw the goal and moved toward it, steadily, stealthily, persistently, until it was his. Of course, at times, somewhere on the path to success, an alternate approach might be needed after an unpredictable issue had been encountered. And it was always human error that caused those brief blips in Azekiel's procedures. But he didn't think that would be an issue this time. Emilio Pesaro had shown such admiration for Azekiel that Azekiel was certain beyond a shadow of a doubt, that Emilio would do what was required of him without fail.

Immediately following the transfer and conversion of five hundred thousand Euros from Emilio Pesaro, Azekiel dispatched a team of four Hartfield security personnel who were to travel, undercover, to Italy where they were to check into the matter of Senator of the Republic, Vic Russo's current health and to enquire if they could be of any assistance.

Two days before the Italian nation wide elections were to be held, United Press International carried a top news item: A member of the Upper House, Senate of the Republic, the Honorable Mr. Victor Russo, had been found dead at his residence after what appeared to have been a botched robbery.

And there it was. A third seat had opened up. How fortuitous that there was a candidate already poised to fill the vacancy so recently realized. There was no denying the sadness felt by the dead Parliament member's family and friends. Colleagues took turns espousing the virtues and fidelity of their fallen co-worker. Newspapers and wire services were aflutter with breaking news and interviews with dignitaries and heart-rending stories of Mr. Russo's love of country and working class roots.

Amid all the turmoil, Hartfield's client slid into place, only too happy to have achieved his goal. That night, one final payment was wire transferred to The Hartfield Connection's European bank contact and the next morning, Azekiel dialed a series of numbers and congratulated Emilio Pesaro on his recent success and his new, very important role in international policy making.

◆　　◆　　◆

Pete Malloy was roused from his thoughts by the soft chiming of his e-device. It was one of his friends, Jim, at the police precinct. Answering the ring, Pete smiled and said, "Hello friend. Yes, I have a minute or two for you."

The voice on the line started his monologue. "You've no doubt been knee-deep in discovery about Azekiel Hartfield, but what you may not have found out is how his past is tied up into his present. Apparently Hartfield grew up in a middle-class family in a middle-class neighborhood in a middle-class state. His parents, wanting something better for him, sent him off to a private boarding school in Europe."

Pete was puzzled over that information and asked, "Where do you suppose they got the dollars to pay for a private European school?"

Jim said, "It looks like they floated a very large loan and put a second mortgage on their home."

Continuing the train of information, Jim said, "While in private school, Azekiel excelled in business strategy and decided to start up a small business venture on campus producing and selling an e-device application of algorithms whose purpose was the automated reasoning of any professor's exam questions and outputting the answers. After some measure of success and amassing a small fortune, his venture was shut down by the school directors, who decided he should not gain by his apparent lapse of ethics."

Pete commented, "And so it began."

And Jim responded, "Yes, and so it began. This is all part of Hartfield's official school record. They asked him to turn over the profits he had made off of the students. Azekiel refused and was summarily expelled. Undaunted, he returned to the states and using his ill-gotten gains, started a small consulting business that put him in contact with some of the top money makers of that time that were in the area. Consulting quickly became public relations and our star was born. Azekiel Hartfield's wealth and power have increased annually ever since then."

Having heard Jim's abbreviated version of Hartfield's history, Pete picked up the thread, and added, "Hartfield hasn't been content to just let his firm do PR for the rich and famous. He has a much larger plan and is only using his firm's revenue to bankroll it. I don't quite have a handle on exactly what that is, but it's big and it's sinister and it's getting closer. Besides the missing girl, Anne Whitman, there are many shady things in play here, but most of them may be small potatoes compared to a bit of intel I have become aware of recently. I'll know more before this weekend and will drop you a call when I'm more positive. What did you find out about Mark Sturgess?"

A small silence and the faint rustling of paper could be heard over the line and then Jim spoke, "Yes. Mark Sturgess. It took some digging and a bit of real detective work but we've come up with this. Mark Sturgess is an assumed name. He was born Marek Stern in Mifflin County Pennsylvania in a small town named Reedsville. Nothing notable about his childhood, but we found a blurb about his winning a scholarship to Yale in, of all things, molecular biophysics. Apparently he was pretty good at this because while he was at Yale, he authored several papers on the control of gene expressions. Pete, do you have any idea about what that means?"

Pete, raising his eyes to look vaguely out the windows across the expanse of the loft office and faintly nodding his head, said, "Yeah, I do. I was briefly interested in biochemistry in my first year of college. Took a class in DNA Advancement before switching majors." Bringing his gaze back to the workspace, Pete continued, "I can tell you this, Jim, basically biophysics is a gene regulation therapy giving cells control over function that in turn leads to an adaptability characteristic of any organism. In simpler terms: cellular-level nanostring technologies. If that's any more simplified." Then switching his voice to a focused and more serious tone, "This is all very new stuff and the possible applications boggle the mind."

Jim gave a snort of laughter, "Ha! Guess I'll be doing a bit of light reading on my break later today! Anyway. Stern, aka Sturgess, graduated from Yale and then pretty much disappeared until three years ago when he surfaced as Mark Sturgess in Hartfield's high-level executive management team as an extremely high paid chief executive officer. We have no idea what he was doing in the meantime. It's my guess that he was either operating under another assumed name or out of the country, although we can't find any record of his leaving or of his return. Does this help you out, Pete?"

"It certainly helps to build a better picture of who we're dealing with. It's clear that neither Hartfield nor Sturgess stumbled into their present situations. They have been working toward this for many years. Jim, have you heard any facts or fictions about Hartfield's security and why they have so much of it?"

Jim had the answer, "Most of the rumors I've heard have to do with corporate secrets and because they cater to the famous, there is a need to keep up the appearance that Hartfield is a safe place for secrets. They routinely turn down ex-cops for any open positions. We're convinced that the tight security is mostly for show, but you never know. There has been a constant suspicion that the level of security is a little much, since a good piece of gatekeeper software might be more necessary as well as cheaper and more convenient than the huge staff of uniforms they have. What did you turn up after your interview with them?"

Pete tried to find the most succinct explanation for what he saw and what he would allow himself to tell his friend at this time. "I saw an overstaffed department, bordering on paranoia with a tight grip on their domain and their budgets. I managed to secret out a bit of intel on our missing girl, Anne Whitman, but it's not definitive. I've used a little trickery on their computer systems and may return to dig deeper into their files to see what else I can bring out. I'll copy all of this to you when I'm closer to the finish line.

"I'm in your debt, Jim. Everything you've told me here is very valuable and I appreciate you taking the time to put it together for me."

Jim's voice had lost its serious edge and he said, "Well, you're welcome and my usual rate of a pint of lager and a good piece of gossip still applies. Anything else?"

There wasn't anything else so with a promise to call with further updates, Pete rang off and returned to the graphic depiction of Hartfield's many activities flashing across the loft office monitors.

♦　♦　♦

Just before noon, Martha Gainsbrook returned from her scheduled appointment uptown and called a meeting with all the team leads, asking them to bring with them their latest findings.

Smiling as she approached her work center, Martha called out to Pete, "How's it going?"

"It's going quite well. Everything on my end is moving along as it should and I've just heard from my PD friend."

Pete took a moment to brief Martha to the details of his phone conversation with Jim about Hartfield and Sturgess. Pete ended his mini-briefing by nodding toward his laptop screen, "I've got to mention how mesmerized I am with the land-sat maps. The tracking of the exact whereabouts of our main characters is a technological wonder."

Glancing at the large display screen directly adjacent to her workspace, Martha said, "It's a very useful technology. Not very complicated but it takes an 'act of congress' to possess the means and use it such as we are. Fortunately, we've been granted full use of it for this case."

Setting her note binder down, Martha said, "Bring your tea. We have a briefing scheduled in the main area and you might want to roll your chair over, too."

After the first fifteen minutes of the meeting, all departments had completed their updates. Business was rolling along as usual, there were no glitches or problems to report and all departments were clear on the direction they would take to progress their investigations.

Then it was Martha's turn to speak. "I've just come from a meeting with our patrons and they are very pleased with all of the progress we've made in such a short amount of time. They've been periodically monitoring the streaming graphic feed pertaining to The Hartfield and feel that all of the scenarios are quite feasible and are tight possibilities. They would like to add their empirical data for our consideration as they think it is valid and would add to the overall understanding of The Hartfield in spite of the fact that they have no solid evidence to support it."

Martha looked around at the faces of her team leads and said, "There's one other thing. Our patrons are claiming that they have been observing a junior senator from a southern state, Frank Torres, for quite some time and that his behavior is becoming somewhat erratic. On several occasions he has been observed saying unfortunate things in a raised voice. For instance, during a hallway conversation with three other persons, Senator Torres suddenly hollered, 'It serves them right to have their houses flooded by storm waters.' Taking note of the aghast faces of his present company, Mr. Torres retreated to his office refusing to see anyone for the rest of the day. The next morning, he acted as if nothing had happened and even denied the outburst when asked about it by a more senior person. This type of behavior has been observed several times over as many weeks and the frequency and the severity of the outbursts seem to be increasing."

Alan Murphy, Martha's right-hand man, spoke up, "In itself,

that type of behavior fits the description of a man under a lot of stress."

Martha responded, "Yes. And possibly more." She shifted in her chair, readjusting her back against its support. After a brief moment, she said, "Another note regarding Senator Torres is that he has been seen after hours meeting with persons of a dubious nature. At first, it was thought that Torres may have had gambling debts and was being contacted by persons he may have owed large sums of money to, but a check of these persons turned up an interesting note: two of them are past clients of Hartfield's and one is currently working as a low-level member of Mark Sturgess' staff. Our patrons have informed me that Senator Torres has taken a leave of absence claiming to be overworked and in need of some quiet time. They've asked if we could increase surveillance of the good Senator and that we keep them informed."

Leaning forward, Pete asked, "Are your patrons aware of the other facets of this mission, for instance, the situation concerning Anne Whitman?"

Martha nodded and said, "They have been fully briefed to our status and support our efforts. We have been given the green light to move when we are ready and to use whatever means we think is necessary to bring this project and all of its aspects to a successful conclusion."

Taking a fast sip of her tea, Martha added, "Just one more thing of note. In addition to Mr. Torres, our patrons suspect others in the Senate of questionable ties to The Hartfield so things may run a little deeper than we are currently aware of. Keep this in mind as you're reducing data and building scenarios. Are there any questions for me at this time?"

Having none, the briefing broke up and smaller team groups formed here and there to discuss how the latest intel would affect their efforts.

Martha joined Pete for the brief number of steps it took to return to her workspace. "Are you planning to return to Hartfield's security department again?"

Pete pushed his chair up to the desk and still holding it by the back, said, "There's really no reason to return, but I'm planning to make a call to Abers and possibly to Miss Ebbert to arouse a bit of suspicion about the system hacking. I may point them toward Ashton or maybe even Sturgess. In any case, I think we have all that can be found using my undercover actions. Anything deeper will have to be pried out with a court order."

13
Stratagem and Subterfuge

Afternoon had worn on with the noise levels among the groups reaching a sustained din and as new data was pushed into the three storyboard scenarios the screens across the loft office updated at an alarming pace.

Martha had become tethered to her e-device during a rapid succession of conversations with several callers. After she had connected with all the current calls and returned nearly all of her messages, she sat back in her chair and prepared herself for the next volley.

Pete sat opposite her, slumped back on the couch with his feet up on the worktable balancing his laptop across his knees at arms length. He had accessed his spyware, embedded in several systems throughout the Hartfield, and was deep in thought as he stared intently at the posted results. He had become aware that he had been absentmindedly stroking his chin, and finding it somewhat embarrassing, looked up at Martha. Their eyes locked. As a smile crept onto her face, his thoughts started to tumble out, "Martha, I've been watching the data streaming from my sys-bugs and there seems to be an air of anxiety starting to pick up pace among the various groups of employees and extraneous characters associated with our little drama. Security has moved to a higher alert level and the financial department has been told to 'clear the books' as soon as possible."

Martha rocked back in her chair and said, "Alpha Team is reporting that they are close to procuring the Whitman girl, and Beta Team is cautioning that Hartfield's trackers are closing the distance at an alarming pace. So. Things are getting more serious."

Pete added, "Sturgess has been in almost constant contact with his minions and has been busy trying to satisfy Elizabeth Preston. He has Abers reporting updates every fifteen minutes and Legal jumping through fiery hoops to find a way to hook Preston into a vow of silence. Given her public history and her penchant for arguing, the best he might be able to hope for is to ensure her silence through coercion."

◆　　◆　　◆

Martha's phone had not stopped. She took three more calls and spoke with Alan, who told her that one of the street cams showed Travis Stratton leaving The Hartfield and that surveillance on his phone logged two calls to friends to ask about dinner plans. Glancing at Pete, Martha decided to interrupt his train of thought. "Would you like to take a fifteen minute break? We can take a brisk walk along the watercourse that runs behind the building. The fresh air will do our thinking good."

Stretching out his legs, Pete closed his laptop and stood up. With a smile and a nod he said, "My thinking could definitely use some air right about now."

They used the exit door located toward the back of the lobby past the verticals and down a hallway that led to the rear of the building. Just outside the door was a small flagstone patio and three stone benches that had been built under two beautiful Summer Red Maples, whose expansive canopies provided a cooling, dappled shade to the patio. Set back into the landscape garden was a mature Purple Ash, stately in its appearance and at that very moment, full of chirping birds.

As they stepped outside into the late afternoon sun, Pete scanned the immediate surroundings to get his bearings. About one hundred and fifty yards in front of them lay the narrow watercourse, its banks dotted here and there by large Black Oaks and stately Willows, with their long leafy tendrils being pulled along in the flow of the water. Covering the opposite bank were drifts of Marionberries whose low canopy of thickly ridged leaves framed great clumps of shiny black fruit. Birds took turns dropping from the lower branches of the Black Oaks and swooping past berry clusters before returning to perch with their mouths full and their beaks stained dark blue. Their chatter took on the air of excited expectation as their day neared its end, when finding sanctuary and settling down for the night would become a priority. Beyond the trees on the opposite bank, Pete could glimpse the outlines of other office buildings, sedate in their appearance.

Martha stepped forward and headed for the narrow stone path that seemed to disappear as it receded through the low unkempt tufts of grass toward the watercourse. Pete fell into step behind her and momentarily found himself emerging a few steps later onto a wider pathway that followed the watercourse as far as he could see in either direction. They turned to the right and rapidly synchronized their steps, falling naturally into a brisk pace.

Gazing up and around at the sky, Pete said, "Today turned out to be a nice day, it must be about seventy-five degrees right now."

Martha added, "Feels closer to seventy though. I think tonight may be a bit chilly."

Pete said, "Martha, I've been meaning to tell you that I'm very impressed with your team's operations and very impressed with how you interact with everyone and manage the project."

Martha smiled modestly, almost to herself as Pete continued, "Tell me, what led you to this type of work?"

Martha smiled again and glanced at Pete before looking ahead at the path they were walking along. "I think it was the promise of adventure that piqued my interest. I just couldn't see myself in a nine-to-five job and after giving it some thought, spoke with a CIA recruiter. Soon after, I was accepted into the program." Adding with imitation mockery, "The rest is classified history."

After a dozen or more steps, Pete asked, "So, Martha, do you have any hobbies, anything special you like to spend your time on?"

"Well, I have a pilot's license and a couple times a year I fly out to see my dad. That's when I can afford to take a couple of weeks off at one time."

Smiling, Pete asked, "What kind of aircraft do you fly?"

Martha glanced at Pete wondering if his question was merely automatic or was he genuinely interested. Seeing sincerity in his eyes, Martha returned his smile and said, "I own a Beechcraft B200 King Air but am licensed for VLJ craft too."

They took a few more steps when Martha asked Pete the same question, "What do you do for personal fun?"

Pete took a brief moment to gather his thoughts and said, "I think I get the most enjoyment out of triathlon training. It gives me a nice workout but also a sense of accomplishment when I've met my goals."

Martha asked, "A triathlon is running, bikes and...what?"

"It's running, biking and swimming. I compete in the Hawaiian Ironman Triathlon every three years. My boys come with me when they can manage it. The next one is happening about a year from now. You should come with me!"

Nodding, Martha said, "Maybe I will."

The very next moment Martha's e-device chimed and after glancing at the screen, she decided to let that call go to message.

They walked along in silence, watching the ducks on the waterway and catching slight breezes as the wind rolled off the water through the reeds. The calls of starlings could be heard among the low shrubs and a few could be spotted in flight as they chased after their flying morsels.

Pete broke the quiet first, "This project seems to be picking up pace at an alarming rate. This morning it was business at its usual frantic pace, and now The Hartfield is showing signs of deliberate measures on several fronts. They are getting very serious about the breach in their security. I believe that they have cut network access for the majority of their personnel and have been making the initial moves in preparation for the delivery of something big."

"I had that feeling as well. Our intel has it that the 'something big' will move before the weekend is out. Hartfield has ordered several semi-trucks to be on site Saturday at 9PM."

Just then, Martha's e-device chimed. Looking at the screen, Martha decided that she should answer, "Yes Alan. I see. We'll be there in five minutes." Martha turned to Pete, "Hope you got enough air, we're needed back at the loft."

Stopping to look about him, Pete said, "It's just as well, I would like to meet with various team leads to start developing our strategy." Then looking directly at Martha and adding, but not before he noticed the fine smile-lines that had started to form around her mouth, "There won't be anything simple about this and there's nothing like a good plan to start the weekend off right."

◆   ◆   ◆

As soon as they pushed open the heavy glass doors past reception, Alan Murphy stepped forward and as he handed a piece of paper to Martha, said, "Tactical Team Leaders are assembled in your workspace. They're talking about readiness measures and what type of gear to assemble."

After everyone had moved their chairs into the gathering and had settled down, Martha, perched on the front edge of her worktable, began the briefing.

"I've been in contact with our patrons and they are in agreement that we have enough evidence to support the as yet to be proved theory that The Hartfield Connection and several of its associates are involved with criminal activities. The very least of which is their complacency in the Anne Whitman missing persons case, and there is evidence of tax evasion. Beyond that, our patrons strongly suspect wrongdoing here, on U.S. soil and abroad – possibly involving up to six foreign governments. We know of several officials and corporate leaders who have somewhat shady ties to Hartfield. Our patrons also suspect that specific persons in the U.S. Senate are involved in one way or another and have advised us that our project may uncover a myriad of wrongdoing that will certainly implicate high-ranking persons in many government and corporate positions. They are highly concerned with the latest intel that was provided to them this morning and have authorized whatever actions we see necessary. With this in mind, I would like to hear from each team. Tell me your ideas."

In round-robin fashion, the meeting members contributed to the discussion...

Alan spoke first, "Several layers of offense will be needed to stage an assault on a building such as The Hartfield in an urban environment. We will need First Assault teams to break the outer doors and secure elevators and exits. Sharpshooters should be ready and in clear view of all surrounding sectors. Second Assault teams will be needed to secure each floor, centralizing all personnel found in the building. These activities would be quickly followed by securing all electronics."

Pete then added, "The streets need to be controlled and local law enforcement are the best choice for that."

Bruce Edwards raised his hand and then spoke, "Fire and medical response should be stationed close and ready to go, maybe tucked away out of sight in a parking structure, two to three blocks away."

Martha said, "There are four floors below the building: Security and three laboratories. Special teams will be assigned with each floor."

Pete spoke up, "The team assigned to take the security level should be well armed. There are twenty to thirty security personnel on duty at any given time. They have a small armory but in my brief association with the Lieutenant in charge, I found him to be quite capable of actions bordering on those typical of a paramilitary. He demands obedience from his staff and is very psychotic about his position and the mission of the security department. Don't underestimate him...he will not go down easily."

Martha nodded, "On our signal, our patrons will cut Hartfield's communication access and freeze all bank and business assets. They are obtaining all the necessary warrants and paperwork so no need to work that issue. Operational timing will be very important."

The group's discussion continued...

Alan brought up a good point, "Access to upper floors can be accomplished through conventional means but to quickly secure the entire building in a timely manner it will be necessary to use Ingress Tactic 57, proposed for every fifth floor."

Thomas Perry, the group lead from the Advanced Analysis department spoke up, "Forensics, Engineering and Crisis

Management have all been brought in and are standing by."

Another hand was raised and Jerry Brink, a lead from the Communications group, spoke up, "The most optimal time for the initial tactical shift would be mid-morning. My thoughts are that it's most likely that more employees will be on site as well as key management and possible key clientele at that time than any other. Having all the players in one place makes it easier to interview them."

Martha, who had been leaning against the front edge of her worktable, shifted to a standing position and addressed the group leaders, "These are excellent ideas that have the full potential, and my support, to be turned into plans. I would add that two communication networks be established: one between team leaders and one between leaders and their groups, and that communication chatter be held to a minimum once the tactical shift has started. We will need a group of very diplomatic persons to act as liaison between all of us and the inevitable flood of media that will descend upon this operation. No spilling of the beans just yet!"

A muffled round of chuckles floated among the group, which made Martha smile in response.

Just then, her e-device gave off a soft chime and seeing the caller's ID displayed on the device's screen, Martha excused herself momentarily from the group to answer.

Pete watched her as she took several slow steps past her desk, just out of earshot of the group. He noticed that her posture was steady even as she listened intently to the call. Then, from the corner of his eye he thought he saw Martha straighten her spine and plant her feet in a way that suggested she had come to alert. Surely it was in response to something she had just heard.

After a few short moments, Martha returned to her meeting group with a slight look of serious concern on her face. Pete had been watching her and was admiring the apparent ease in which Martha had held herself in the many diverse situations that make up her daily business, but the subtle character of her expression, as she returned from her phone call put him on alert. He felt a small but distinct charge of adrenaline move through his muscles and instantaneously focused his mind.

Martha stood for a few seconds, seemingly lost in thought, before she spoke, "I've had an update from both Alpha and Beta Teams. It seems that, as Alpha Team felt they were getting close to securing Anne Whitman, a decision was made to have Beta Team close in and engage Hartfield's trackers. It was felt that the trackers were getting too close and a diversion would give Alpha a few additional moments to secure Ms. Whitman and fade into the landscape undetected. Beta Team engaged the trackers some five miles out from our mark. While they were only intending to delay the trackers, shots rang out and Beta returned fire. It seemed that their situation had turned a bit ugly."

Alan said, almost to himself, "That's disquieting."

Pete asked, "Do you have details?"

Martha, still standing at the front of the group, said, "Beta engaged the trackers along a deserted road, intending to limit contact with local civilians. The Hartfield trackers took an aggressive defense and fired medium caliber rounds back at them, crippling Beta's SUV. In response, Beta rushed the trackers, wounding one and chasing the other two into the woods. They're now on foot and in pursuit."

Pete spoke up and asked, "Did we sustain any casualties?"

Martha answered, "Thankfully, no."

Alan asked, "Any news from Alpha Team?"

Martha nodded her head and continued, "Alpha lost no time locating the small cabin where they were confident they would find

Ms. Whitman. Their tracking skills were correct and they now have Ms. Whitman in their care. However, as they were preparing to leave the area, they were ambushed by what they assumed was a second group of Hartfield trackers. I'm a bit perturbed that we did not see this in advance. At end of project, I would like an analysis of the situation and a process overview on how to avoid this in future. I'm told that Alpha is returning fire, with gusto, and they predict that they will be starting their return trip within the hour. Both teams report no casualties and only slight injuries and, most importantly, Anne Whitman is safe."

Pete watched as Martha fell silent. For a moment, she let her gaze stray across the busy loft office and past the large graphic displays to the bright row of windows framing the river walk along the back of the building. As she brought herself back to the group, she took a deep breath in, and slowly letting it back out, it became obvious to the group that she was forming her next volley of thoughts.

"Well folks, this situation has put a layer of speed and accuracy on our plans and actions that can not be denied. Is there any reason we can't be ready to move within the hour?"

◆　◆　◆

Martha Gainsbrook, Pete Malloy, First Lieutenant Alan Murphy, First Specialist Bruce Edwards, First Officer Sarah Pollock and Specialist Class Three Agent Jon Cho sat together in Martha's workspace, talking just above the heightened din of the loft office.

"Before we get too much further, introductions are in order." Martha looked around and said, "Everyone, this is Pete Malloy. Pete was working as an independent on the Anne Whitman case and since then has been working with us on the extended project.

He is a well-connected PI with an impressive career in Special Ops and law enforcement, especially in the area of investigation."

Pete smiled and nodded his greeting to the group and Martha continued, "Pete, this is Sarah Pollock, Bruce Edwards and Jon Cho. Sarah is a fifteen-year veteran with numerous awards and recognitions for valor, some of which have been received while running ops for me. She comes to us from an impressive background with the Army as a Lieutenant where she honed her skills and became an expert in quantum optics and field theory. She now excels in Quantum Electronics and is the logical choice for the Lab Two team leader. Sarah, this is Pete."

Pete smiled and nodded in appreciation of Sarah's impressive career and Sarah smiled and then raised her tea mug in a gesture of respect and polite recognition of Pete, "Welcome aboard."

Glancing at Jon, Martha said, "And this is Jon Cho. Jon graduated top of his class with a Masters Degree in Criminal Justice. He joined the CIA straight out of college and within his first five years, had worked his way up to Agent Class Three. Agent Cho excels in weapons and explosives and had worked with us on an earlier mission about a year ago. Jon has a reputation for speed and accuracy with almost any volatile substance and was a perfect choice for this mission."

Pete nodded hello to Agent Cho.

Turning to Pete, Martha added, "Bruce Edwards is a first rate tactical specialist and has been a valuable member of my team for about two years. You may remember him from our first encounter at your office. He spent ten years in the Navy achieving the rank of Lieutenant. His last post was that of Commanding Officer aboard the USNS Bowditch."

Pete extended his hand and leaned over toward Bruce with a, "Nice to meet you, I'm glad we're on the same team."

Bruce smiled, shook Pete's hand and said, "As am I, sir,"

Martha continued the group's discussion, "Building schematics, obtained from our patrons, show four floors below street level with initial access by way of one vertical. From Security, on level one, to all three labs, there are two verticals and we've seen a set of stairs that are designated for secure access only. I'll show you." Tapping a fast sequence on her laptop, an architect's drawing of the four subterranean floors popped into view on the overhead. Moving her cursor in little circles, Martha indicated the area she was talking about.

Alan, who had been studying the drawing, leaned back in his chair and said, "It doesn't look like there's access to the stairwell from street level."

Martha added, "Precisely. That's why we will have to provide our own. The stairwell connects the four levels but each level is secured by locking doors so casual traffic between them is not allowed. Agent Cho will lead a team into the stairwell." Martha took a brief second to look at the schematic displayed on the overhead and then continued, "Jon, You'll have to create a nice hole in the lobby floor that will allow you and your Epsilon team to safely enter the area below."

Jon said, "That should be easy enough. I'll use low-level explosives to keep the debris to a minimum, and then rappel down. Will need less that a minute to set up and another few seconds for everyone to descend and be ready to move."

Martha said, "Let's keep this as simple as we can. I would like five eight-person teams to be formed. One for each floor and one for the secure stairwell. Alan, you will lead Theta team and take Security. Bruce, you will lead Delta team on Lab One. Sarah, Gamma team to Lab Two. Pete, you and I will take Zeta team into Lab Three and Jon, you'll be leading Epsilon team in the stairwells."

Everyone nodded in agreement and seeing this, Martha gave them a few moments to organize their thoughts then said, "Once each floor is taken and secured, all team persons not needed for control of that floor will proceed with the ongoing teams. We'll keep our numbers up while we advance floor to floor. Questions? Concerns?"

Pete spoke up first, "I'd like to know more about what types of situations we may encounter once we're in there. I'm talking about situations beyond the ordinary expectations."

Alan contributed, "As you've noted, Security is projected to be the most difficult one to control but we should have the advantage within minutes of our arrival. Citizen control will need two persons at best. Once the remaining teams move forward, backup personnel can be brought down to assist with processing."

Just then, one of the persons from the Analysis Group stepped up with six mugs of tea. After handing them around, she smiled, gave a sideways glance to Alan, and stepped away.

"Very nice. Chamomile tea." Martha breathed in the heavy steam and then continued. "Our best intel has it that Lab One is chemical and medical. We're not exactly sure what that means, but Bruce, you will have to plan accordingly. Might want to consider taking a Haz Mat specialist as part of your team."

Bruce spoke in an easy tone, "We'll need filtering gear and maybe protective gloves. I'll talk with the other team members to see what they think. Otherwise, we're good to go."

Continuing, Martha told Bruce that there should be minimal resistance on Lab One level.

Bruce nodded and said, "Anyone entering Lab One, and this includes those going on to Labs Two and Three should wear a reactive screening suit under their fatigues. This will dramatically reduce the risk of exposure to any antigens or chemical particles we may encounter."

"Sarah," Martha continued, "you will lead Gamma team into Lab Two."

Sarah, addressing Martha said, "I understand Lab Two concentrates on robotics and laser engineering. The most logical conclusion to robotics technology and modern laser work would be weapons. Is there a possibility that there are working models staged in the lab? And if so, is there any intel indicating what these may be? We will prepare for a variety of scenarios but specifics would help tremendously."

"Alan, you have the most recent intel on Lab Two's status", Martha said, shifting her gaze to Alan, "Would you give us a fast update?"

"Absolutely. Recent taps on Lab Two support the theory that the ultimate purpose of Hartfield's robotics and laser engineering and development efforts are weapon based in nature, both separately and in combination. We think there are small working prototypes in the lab but only to demonstrate Proof of Concept. We suspect that this technology will be applied to larger working models in more remote locations so as to escape world notice. Sarah, if you can capture the lab without compromising the toys...we would certainly appreciate it."

Sarah gave a smile and nodded her head in agreement, and Martha continued.

"Zeta Team will move on to Lab Three." Turning to Pete, she added, "We expect a larger contingency of resistance from Lab Three, as it's the last of all places to run to but more importantly, because the staff levels have been noted as the largest."

Organizing her thoughts as she drew in a deep breath, Martha continued, "We know that Lab Three has been experimenting with human DNA nanoball sequencing. Intel does not support cloning but the advanced studies, hinted at by the reports and invoices we've collected, does. We've tapped conversations that Hartfield has had with several colleagues outside of the company and from that, we think they are rebuilding DNA with new programming or some sort of modified sequencing, replanting the modified DNA back into the original subject and expecting real, pre-programmed, changes to manifest in a relatively short time."

After a sip of her tea and a quick note of the surprised looks on her colleague's faces, Martha added, "This we know is not good. The implications are numerous and the applications could be countless, not to mention disastrous. Too many to speculate upon here. All Zeta Team members will be adding Nu-Skin as an additional protection along with their suit-ups and armor. We're not absolutely sure what it is we're up against and I want our protection well in hand."

Alan had distributed team lists and the latest data on the suspected activities in the Hartfield. "Does anyone think they'll need more than one hour to prepare?"

There was a soft rustling of papers and muffled questions and comments among a few of the meeting members but nothing percolated up to Martha, so she continued, "We'll need a huge contingency of post-assault personnel. As soon as we've secured the building, I would like a large team of medics to be brought in to treat all the injured: guilty and innocent alike. It's not our job to sort them out; we'll let the legal system do all that. Our job is to secure equipment and personnel and to hold them secured until we've processed them. After medical personnel have made a good start, crime scene folks and investigators will be allowed in. Finally, and I know you all know this...it's not over until the reports are filed. Team leads will debrief back here one hour after the shooting stops and you can safely leave your team in charge of your areas."

♦   ♦   ♦

The noise, the activity, the stress, the anxiety, the adrenalin, the nervous jokes and the ever present ticking clocks counting down the time gave the entire loft operation the appearance of tumult. It was anything but that.   And for Pete, it was soothing and reassuring to see the levels of precision being employed by the various teams as they coordinated with each other and with their team leads. It was like watching a large flock of birds performing their nightly murmuring before settling down as one gathering with one purpose. It was mesmerizing, and as the tension in his muscles started to recede, Pete let his mind drift back to a memory of an earlier project readiness when he was just a rookie with the Special Forces.

Those first surges of adrenalin were potent reminders of the high levels of alertness that were required when your mind asks your body to push its limits. In the heat of battle, you must keep your mind relaxed and focused on the job at hand.   To do otherwise would be a tumble down the rabbit hole into chaos and confusion.

Pete's first assignment had been a particularly tricky one. He had been stationed in Tamanrasset in the northwest edge of the African continent, in the dead of the Sahara Desert.   During midsummer, when daytime temperatures could reach 117° F on average, it wasn't uncommon to find that the locals had ceased commerce for several hours to retreat to the relative coolness of whatever shade they could find.   That summer there had been several skirmishes along the Sahara Trade Route involving highwaymen robbing local traders. These weren't simple robberies. They were more on par with outright mayhem and the locals were powerless to stop the continuing and increasingly more brazen attacks. As military guests of Algeria, Pete's unit had been asked to look into it as a goodwill gesture. The implication being: make it stop but do so with stealth and discretion.

Intel had it that the highwaymen were a nomadic bunch of misguided criminals who would rather steal than work and had been hiding in and around the high plateaus that bordered the trade route. Pete was assigned to a small team of men whose job it would be to locate said group, gather as much information as was necessary to get an accurate headcount and to extract them. Several drones had been launched to map the area and satellite data had been folded in to provide a series of highly reliable graphic data that gave exact locations of campsites and ad hoc roads used by the robbers for fast escapes and easy concealment.

The mission proved easy enough and the actual conflict was over just after it started, but it was the thrill of the speculation, planning and readiness actions that Pete remembered most vividly. The briefing meeting where the Commander introduced the mission, the brainstorming sessions where all ideas were considered and the best three scenarios built and fleshed out into contingencies and possible outcomes. When everyone was satisfied that all bases had been covered, team leaders would list basic transport and weaponry needed and trust the individual members with procuring all else needed, right down to the rations and water for each participant. This was when Pete realized that the execution of a mission was only as good as the plan and the team members that went into it. He also realized that he had a talent for problem solving and a desire to see a good plan carried out flawlessly.

◆　◆　◆

Less than forty-five minutes later, the din of the loft office had subsided into a low volume hum punctuated by voices calling out to one another with reminders or answers to questions. Everyone was on the move and more than several persons had already left the loft to form group teams in the underground parking below the structure.

Pete was passively observing the activities and checking his PA-48 for charge and number of rounds. He fingered the two additional fifty-round clips in his jacket pocket and thought to himself that he should have picked up two more before leaving his apartment that morning.

Alan, dressed in SWAT combat fatigues, approached Pete and said, "Hey, here's a set of protective wear...the Nu-Skin is to be worn next to the skin and the screening suit over that. Instructions are on the tags. Our support vehicles have an array of weapons and body armor and I'd be happy to give you some fast training on whatever weapon you choose."

Just then, Martha stepped up and said, "We're almost ready. Most teams are standing by and I would like to address the security and lab teams one last time to ensure we are all familiar with project particulars and to test our inter-team communication network. I'd like to let everyone know that we're taking separate vehicles and different routes through the city so as not to arouse any unnecessary suspicion."

◆　◆　◆

The underground parking structure was cool and dim. The air

seemed to be electric yet there wasn't a sound. The five teams of specialists stood in a loose group, all in full combat gear, holding fully loaded weapons, standing at ease facing Martha and waiting.

After a moment, she spoke. "We've done a good job preparing for this next project step. We can't see all possible contingencies but our experience and our trust in each other as experts and professionals will carry us through whatever unfolds." She looked around at the five teams and continued, "Center yourself for a moment."

Taking one breath in and letting it slowly out, she continued, "Let's move out."

◆　　◆　　◆

It was a few minutes before 6PM when Mark Sturgess stepped off the private vertical onto the top floor where Azekiel Hartfield ruled his empire. They were meeting for an early dinner and to discuss several small but pesky problems that had come up: Senator Frank Torres and his mini-meltdown in the halls of Congress, Elizabeth Preston and her increasingly absurd demands for highly personalized services and the delivery of their most recent "product" whose deadline was fast approaching.

Both men had taken seats in Akekiel's office lounge area and Mark had taken the liberty of pouring himself three fingers of Glen Garioch 1958 into a Waterford Huntly and had just made himself comfortable in one of the overstuffed leather chairs when his e-device gave a soft chime. He glanced at the display, noted that it was Legal with yet another question regarding Miss Preston, switched the chime off and tossed the device onto the table between their chairs. Watching Hartfield, Mark sipped a tiny drop of the bourbon and, as it slowly coated his tongue, organized his thoughts. He had already made all the necessary decisions, but didn't want it to appear that he didn't care to hear Hartfield's opinions or to seem impatient with his business philosophies or his oh-so-important ego stories. To Mark's way of thinking, he was already running The Hartfield Connection. All that was lacking was his name on the business and controlling interest of the stock.

Mark watched as Azekiel shifted in his chair and turned a bit more to face him as a force, not as a comrade. Mark felt that old man Hartfield was on the verge of becoming obsolete and as he stared at the old man, Mark almost felt sorry for him. Azekiel had waved off Mark's offer to pour him a drink and sat quietly looking at Mark with a passive seriousness that Mark was hardly aware of. Mark was feeling good and fancied that he moved with the grace and self-confidence of a cat in contrast with Azekiel who moved with age and disquiet. Mark quietly sipped his bourbon and waited.

Clearing his throat, Azekiel started it off, "There's no need to discuss Frank Torres. I've already taken care of that myself. However, I'm highly interested in the latest on our Miss Preston. She's sizing up to be quite a handful and I would rather we not end up as her partners when we come to the end of negotiations. Tell me, Mark, are we near the winning end of our contract with Elizabeth Preston?"

Mark hesitated for a second and took another sip from his glass before he answered, "Miss Preston is under the impression that she's in control of the situation and it pleases me to let her continue in that illusion. However, large amounts of her money have been transferred to our accounts and I have, on paper, tied some of the dollars to a foreign oil cartel with sympathies, and maybe a nephew or two, tied to radical interests. It's my intention to casually show this document to Miss Preston which will, I'm sure, compel her to sign the final version of our services contract and to think very seriously about any further pressures she may be considering to lob our way."

Azekiel considered this news and finally spoke, "I want that paper trail destroyed the minute she signs. There should be nothing anywhere in our records that indicate where money comes or goes. I'm not certain that your idea to create a document, false as it may be, was a wise decision and I would have liked to have heard of this predicament sooner as I probably could have resolved it in a more amiable way. To our advantage. Without paper." Azekiel uncrossed and re-crossed his legs and waited for Mark to respond.

But Mark's thoughts were running contrary to the conversation thread. He was thinking that Azekiel was a bigger fool than he had thought. What an ego he had, thinking that he could sweet talk Preston into complacency. Mark was becoming annoyed. Azekiel should know that Mark could handle this situation…Mark's the one actually speaking with her…Mark's the one who had all the experience…Mark's the one who calls the correct shots!

Then Mark spoke, "That may be true but I believe this situation has been appropriately handled and will not afford us any further trouble or concern. If another case as difficult as Miss Preston comes up, it will be brought to your attention immediately."

Just then Azekiel's watch emitted a soft beep and he glanced at it and started up from his chair. "I've got an important meeting coming up and can not be late. No, no. Sit and finish your drink. My apologies about dinner. We'll continue our discussion at a later time." Hartfield crossed his office and popped open a hidden door in the wall panel to reveal a closet. He removed a trench coat and a scarf and going to his desk, pressed a comm button nestled among a small array of lighted buttons and spoke, "I'll be with you in less than one minute and we are to take off immediately. Thank you." Turning to Mark, he said, "Contact me in the morning after you've had your coffee and we'll discuss my intentions for product delivery."

Mark raised his glass in a mock salute and returned to his position of repose, this time with his legs resting across the coffee table.

Hartfield donned his coat and picked up his briefcase and reached for the knob of the heavy glass door leading to his private gardens and flight deck. As he pushed the door open, the sounds of his private helio-jet winding up filled the office suite and sent a small spark of uncontrollable envy down Mark's spine.

Less then one minute later, the helio-jet could be heard winding its engines up to a deafening pitch and lifting up and away into the evening sky. Mark sat brooding in the silence that now enveloped him and let his thoughts drift.

14
The Fires of Gehenna

The timepiece on Pete Malloy's wrist ticked steadily on to the designated coordinates. Everything was ready. Everyone was in place. Nothing had been overlooked. The only sound he heard was the soft rustle of air as he breathed in and out and the steady rhythm of his heartbeat. The forward movement of the project was eminent and everyone going on the same signal was crucial. After that, movement would be fluid and each action would have a specific, yet undefined, reaction. It was all a matter of physics.

Pete stood at the ready next to Martha. They would follow Alan's team down to the remote parts of The Hartfield. He gazed at the faces of the personnel around him and noted to himself that there seemed to be quietude on almost all of them. It was reassuring to see this level of composure evident on those faces. Everyone was on the same page intent upon a singular purpose. This was quite different from most combat situations that took place in the heat of the moment where it's important to be over-pumped with adrenalin, aggressive and self-possessed as you charged forward. An absurd little picture came into Pete's mind...that of a horde of over-pumped men, screaming battle cries as they roared forward, waving their arms and weapons in threatening gestures hoping that it would scare their foes into submission. He chuckled to himself as he visualized a pumped up horde of men storming The Hartfield and the startled looks on the faces of the business people who populated the building.

Just as Pete refocused his thoughts, Martha touched her

timepiece and sent the signal to every team member involved with the Hartfield project that it was at that exact moment that their best laid plans were to begin in earnest.

As they stepped forward, the noise level in the street rose exponentially. All of a sudden, a dozen or more helios had surrounded the building and had lowered rappel ropes that were holding shielded and armed personnel who were creating ingress patterns at regular intervals up and down the building sides. A soft shower of safety glass shards rained down from above and formed a thin circle of brilliance around the base of the building. The illusion of soft, glittery snow was quickly broken by the abrupt crunching sound of boots smashing down over it as armed agents rushed forward to the building doors and lower windows.

The five sub-surface teams breached the unoccupied Reception area with little trouble and quickly jammed GetKeys into the call button receptacles for all five of the building's verticals. Punching a series of buttons and hearing the sounds of the lift gears, Technical Specialist Turner softly explained that the comm link between Hartfield personnel and the verticals had been severed and that all project leads had been notified that they now had total access by way of their GetKeys.

Pete nodded to Martha and said, "This one vertical is the only access to the Security floor. There are two other verticals just to the left of these doors that access the lower labs from there."

And on that, the doors softly opened and Martha spoke, "First, Epsilon Team will gain access to the Secure Utility Room through the coordinates in the Reception floor. This will allow them entry to the rear of Security by way of the utility room. Gamma Team will follow Epsilon and the rest of us will follow Alan's Theta Team by way of the vertical, but expect opposition the moment the doors glide open. We'll hold the doors at a few inches, enough to launch the smoke barrage, so masks on."

No one spoke but the soft sound of team members donning their face protectors could be heard. Each team member did a quick check of their fellow's gear and signaled that all was good by giving a thumbs-up sign.

"Second, Epsilon and Gamma, it may take a minute to clear our way out of the vertical so wait for my signal before bursting into the back corridor."

Agent Jon Cho, leader of the Epsilon team, had a "ring of fire" set up in the designated area just above the location where the Secure Utility Room was situated one floor below. The small bumps of explosives were covered with titanium Turtle Shells designed to direct the full extent of the blast downward through the floor, blowing a hole large enough for two or three men in full combat gear to drop through with little problem. Cho had completed the setup and was standing by with the detonator in his hand. He turned slightly toward Martha and nodded, then watched her steadily for the "go" signal.

The noise from the street was almost deafening. There were hundreds of personnel in various states of activity. The PD had cordoned off the area in a several block radius and had been systematically going floor by floor through the surrounding buildings, evacuating everyone and escorting them out and away from the on-going fray. Many support vehicles choked the road and personnel were busy deploying additional armaments and keeping watch on the foot traffic all around the Hartfield. Several command vehicles were present and easily identified by the muted glow of monitor screens and blinking comm lights emanating from access doors momentarily opening and then closing as personnel came and went.

Pete, standing close to Martha, heard her say, "Check your

weapons and your readiness." He watched Martha as she slid a round into the firing ramp of her customized Mac-10 and then give it a pat for reassurance. Hearing the clicks and clacks of weapons and launchers and looking from one expectant face to the next determined face, Martha smiled and said, "Giddyap."

◆　◆　◆

The smoke barrage deployed as planned and the signal was given to disembark the vertical and ingress from the Secure Utility Room. Blue-gray smoke choked the corridor, but what was missing put everyone on high attention…there were no dazed and coughing employees trying to get out.

Pete heard himself say, "The assault noises from above must have alerted them."

As the teams picked their way forward, and the smoke billowed up the walls and across the ceiling, obscuring the emergency lighting, a shot rang out. The muzzle flash looked like a dull blink of light further back in the cloud, but the sparks flaring off the wall as the bullet glanced its way past a team member's shoulder, was unmistakable.

Alan, taking his place at the front of his team and moving forward, yelled out "Go! Right! Top! Below! Nothing unturned!" Through his Infra-V face protector, Alan could clearly see his team advancing on the first door, checking its status before igniting the hinges with small explosives and pushing the door so that it fell inward. Two team members went in and several short bursts of fire were accentuated by muzzle flashes and terse commands from his men.

Alan's comm unit crackled to life, "All secure." With a wave of his hand, several team members moved forward to the next door and at the exact moment that the hinges were blown, a blood-curdling shriek was heard coming straight at them from further down the hallway. A lone figure emerged through the smoke, clutching an automatic weapon and firing wildly. As the man advanced, screaming "Semper fidelis", it became apparent that he was not wearing protective gear and was half-crazed with fear. Laughing wildly, he fired another burst of rounds before being picked off by a single shot. The man fell against the wall, dropped his gun from his hand and stumbled forward two steps before dropping to the floor.

Those three seconds of time unfolded like a slow-motion home movie and Pete, standing at the alert behind the advance teams, had barely taken the scene in when a spray of bullets came bursting through the smoke to strike against the wall behind him. Immediately fire was returned. The sound was earsplitting, and if not for the Infra-V masks, Pete was sure everyone would be choking on the lethal mixture of powder smoke and the blue-gray incendiary agents swirling around them.

As the team advanced, red laser target-finding beams sliced through the commotion to highlight their prey, guiding kill shots and briefly marking the hit before moving on. As each room was secured, civilians were grouped together and bound to halt their movement before the team progressed forward.

Epsilon Team reported that they made it through the lobby floor and the Secure Utility Room and had engaged the enemy at the rear of the Security floor. They had lost one man but had inflicted a heavy toll on Abers' forces that appeared, at first count, to be about twenty strong. These persons were fully equipped with masks and advanced weapons and displayed some knowledge of tactical behavior. However, after a brief skirmish, what remained of the original twenty, laid down their weapons and surrendered to the Epsilon Team without further incident.

Pete took two steps to Alan's side and yelled above the noise, "Abers is not here with this group!"

As Alan's team opened more doors, the noise levels and confusion escalated. Secretaries were frightened and screaming, cowering and clutching one another trying to distance themselves from the uproar. Small fires had broken out here and there when stray bullets had hit electrical outlets and computer hardware. Some fires had been deliberately set by the more astute office workers in an attempt to destroy papers and disks before being overrun, but the mixture of smokes was too toxic and they found themselves starved for air, choking and feeling faint.

Advancing down the corridor took all the skill and marksmanship that only experience could bring to the situation. Each team member had only a split second to determine if anyone spilling out through the unsecured areas was a combatant, a subversive or a misguided civilian and to respond accordingly. Behind them, the damage and the wounded were piling up. And the numbers of secured personnel were mounting.

Undaunted, both Alan's group and the Epsilon and Gamma teams moved forward with efficiency and a determination to secure the floor as fast as possible. The gap between them closed with every passing second and with every shot fired. By the time they had set up a cross-fire, Abers' security men, the ones lucky enough to still be alive, gave up, enmasse.

After a quick comm meeting, all teams made their way back the way they had come. Alan's group went back toward the verticals and the Epsilons along with Gamma Team went back toward the Secure Utility Room and the stairway connecting the labs, securing everything on their return path.

It was Delta Team's turn and on First Specialist Bruce

Edwards' command, the Medical/Chemical Lab One, on the next floor below them, would be taken.

♦   ♦   ♦

Azekiel Hartfield had developed his personal business strategy to include full control of several corporate endeavors and he intended to dominate production and sales of the goods and services most in demand. By the time he was nineteen years old, he knew exactly what this included and while his ambitions and business acumen had evolved and sharpened with the years, his goals had remained steadfast. One such goal was the control of the pharmaceutical industry on a global scale. Just thinking about it made old man Hartfield's heart sing. There weren't too many things that could come close to making him feel this way, unless, of course, it was the details involved in the process, the ideas, the development, the marketing, the big sales. In the course of realizing his dream, Lab One was born.

It was a thing of beauty. The best layout, the best scientists in the field, the best equipment. The best because anything less would not do.

There were several good-sized lab spaces set up in the center of the entire floor space. Offices and meeting rooms, a small medical library and two lounges were located along the hallways that surrounded the central labs. Three of the labs were involved with the reverse engineering of specific, previously released drug formulas and to find alternate chemicals that would do the same as the originals. One lab was tasked with the synthetic cloning of expensive chemical compounds and to produce a viable, renewable, and cheap source of drug additives and to conduct experiments in combining various compounds that would eventually replace expensive alternatives designed to set Hartfield first in the field.

The largest lab was one of Hartfield's favorites. It represented most of what the old man was working toward. The shiny stainless steel cabinets were cold and clean. The black granite work surfaces were hard and durable, resistant to chemicals or heat. A material that had endured the vast pressures of the earth over how many thousands of years before being formed and polished to what it was today. The state-of-the-art medical equipment that was no less beautiful. New, cutting-edge, sophisticated, complex. All the commodities that Hartfield attributed to himself he saw reflected back to him through the furnishings. His drive, his cunning and his foresight into the future were inextricably tangled up with the main lab's mission. The other labs on this floor were involved with a maintenance level of pharmacology...a sort of standard operating procedure, if you will. But the main lab was special, like Hartfield himself: unexpected, innovative, out-of-the-box, forward-thinking creativity whose results would cement Azekiel Hartfield's future as the world's most indisputable and foremost leader.

◆　　◆　　◆

The assault on Lab One went more smoothly although not without incident. The moment Bruce Edwards' team advanced from the verticals, shots rang out from a position down the hallway. Edwards could see four shooters in position in the last few doorways before the hallway led off to the left. On his signal, his team assumed a defensive stance by forming a shielded barricade in the front, thereby affording protection to themselves and those behind. They returned fire and as they passed each door, teams of two would blow the hinges and secure the rooms behind, finding an assortment of technicians and lab personnel huddled together and readily surrendering to Edwards' Delta Team.

The shooting in the hallway continued for some minutes, and as Delta advanced, the shooters down the hallway started to panic and fire wildly. With one man down, and one who had retreated back into his doorway and barricaded it shut, the remaining two made a break for the back hallway. Delta team wounded one, who dropped his gun but still ran. The signal was given and the forward team made the distance to the barricaded door and the end of the hallway in short time.

From the battle noises emanating from the back hall, it was evident that the fleeing security men had encountered the Epsilon and Gamma Teams coming from the rear of the floor. Edwards held up his hand, halting his team and taking position so as not to take hits by any stray bullets that might glance off the walls.

Small two-man teams continued to blast open locked doors and secure anybody encountered within. After blowing the hinges from the barricaded door, the team stood back to avoid being shot at by the crazed security guard who had taken refuge there. A short burst of bullets greeted the men when the smoke from the door explosives started to thin out, followed by the unmistakable hollow clicking noise that a gun makes when it is out of ammunition and the chamber is empty. Nodding to each other, Edwards' men went in and within six seconds had signaled that the room was secure and that the maniacal guard was cuffed wrists to ankles and going nowhere.

The firefight in the back hallway came to an end and Edwards could hear the Epsilon Team leader ordering the remaining guards to put their weapons down and to prostrate themselves...now! On his signal, Edwards and his team rounded the corner to assist in securing the remaining rooms along this back hall.

Most of the doors on the outer, northern side of the hall, led to offices and small meeting rooms. Most were void of employees with the exception of one or two office workers, who were taken into immediate custody and restrained until being fetched, later, by the authorities.

Working toward each other, Edwards' team and Epsilon's group made fast and efficient work of securing the rooms and, so far, three separate labs along the corridor. However, when they reached the last door, the last laboratory entrance on this floor, Edwards noted that the level of security protecting this door was much more complex than all the others.

"Wait a moment, Baker," Edwards said to his explosives tech.

"Before you light up the hinges, let's take a minute to have a look at this setup in detail." The tech stood back and Edwards eyed the security panel beside the doorframe and then looked at the scan panel next to the door's latching mechanism. Pressing a ready button on the keypad brought it to life and a query for the proper code was announced by a soft female voice emanating from the panel. The latch panel also lit up indicating that a thumbprint would be necessary. Edwards straightened up and the three men standing closest to him saw his furrowed brow and heard him audibly exhale in a sign of recognition.

Edwards took a breath in and let it out with a quiet shushing sound and said, "I believe what we have here is a VM3000 Locking Station. I'm sure there is another level of security just beyond this one, possibly in an antechamber designed to provide another means of keeping what's lying beyond from being seen by persons passing by this outer door after it's been opened. There's something else. If the proper codes along with the proper thumbprint aren't done in the proper sequence, an alarm sounds inside, and if you are very serious about the continued security of whatever it is you are housing in there, a destruct mechanism may be employed to destroy sensitive materials, or whatever secrets you don't want known."

Edwards turned and looked from one face to another. As he glanced at Tech Specialist Jones, he thought he saw the self-satisfied expression of a man who had just solved a puzzle.

"Jonsie, talk to me."

"Sir. I believe it's possible that we can easily defeat this hallway system by plugging in a cipher-code and re-wiring the back panel. It will buy us a few minutes in the antechamber and if this system was installed by the book, I should be able to breach it with a combo of keypad entries, low volume explosives and chewing gum."

Edwards asked, "How much time will you need on the second system?"

Jonsie replied, "Minute and a half should do it."

"Okay. Ready yourself." Turning to the other men standing by, some watching and others on alert, Edwards said, "Once the inside security is down, I'll want three men to stand post in the hallway and all others to be ready to rush the lab. Everyone, chem masks on. Be prepared for some resistance but secure all personnel as soon as possible while keeping lab contents intact. Or as much as you can." Touching his comm link, Edwards spoke to the Epsilon Team, "This operation may be a bit tricky so you may want to move your men back. Chem protection two is preferred."

Turning back to his team, Edwards nodded and said, "We're good?" Noting the returned nods, he secured his chem mask and said, "Jonsie. You're up." Jones moved to the panel and began to work.

Two minutes and several small bursts from the RDX poppers was all that was needed to open the two massive doors and provide the ingress through the antechamber and into the main lab as needed by Delta team.

As the team swarmed in and the smoke thinned out, the dimly lit interior of the lab came into view.

A large oak workstation with a thick, dark, granite top stood to the right of the antechamber doors. There were dozens of small drawers and places spacious enough for three people to work together on a project. An experiment had been set up on the granite surface and two glass beakers were situated over small open flames and bubbling away. Through the smoky haze, along the wall and further down the right-hand side of the room could be seen the murky dull blue lights of glass fronted refrigeration units, their glow casting an eerie effect around them. There were more workstations further into the room, each adorned with shiny bits of glass, vials of colored liquids or large petri dishes heaped with dry powders.

Tensed and alert with their weapons at the ready, Bruce Edwards led his team through the opening. Signaling for two members to go right and two members to go left, Edwards advanced up the center. Crouching and stepping as gingerly as they could, all were alert to anything that moved or made a sound and reacted with appropriate attention. As Edwards moved carefully forward, men fanned out to cover aisles to the left and right. Sensing something ahead, Edwards signaled for everyone to freeze and cover their backs. Peering into the shadowy depths of the lab, he saw it again. Catching his breath and feeling the hairs on the back of his neck prickle, Edwards caught the slightest glint of light reflected off of something shiny…which had definitely moved in his direction.

Instantly shouting for his team to take cover and firing one round to guide their focus to the immediate target, Edwards had barely made the distance to the floor when a loud whining noise started, followed by a huge pressure wave that sent everything in its path flying. A massive chunk of the concrete ceiling was torn free and moved by the pressure wave as if it were merely a child's toy. It was flung with such force and with unbelievable velocity straight toward the entry doorway and caught two men as they scrambled to take cover, crushing them immediately.

Edwards quickly called for advancement of his forward positioned men and provided cover fire for them as they advanced. Meanwhile, the audible whining sound started up again indicating that the weapon was going to be fired, this time maybe with more accuracy.

Having heard this sound once was all the warning needed to send the team for cover. Scrambling off to the sides out of the perceived path of the pressure wave, they stumbled over debris and dove under lab tables just as the second blast thundered through the room flinging glass beakers, lab equipment and stools toward the gaping hole that was once the entry doors. The force was so great that the heavy tempered glass doors fronting several storage refrigerators were shattered and pushed inward, knocking over glass containers that immediately formed small smoldering puddles of ooze and sending acrid heavy smoke into the room.

Before the weapon could be charged and fired a third time, Edwards climbed up on a table and from his vantage point, shot one of the gunmen dead and winged the other, sending him screaming to the floor. Immediately, his men made the distance and had the rogue cuffed and secured and stood alert in position next to the weapon. Edwards stepped forward and examined the cannon, which he could see had been hastily bolted to the lab table and was letting off light puffs of steam from the rear of the weapon from an area that appeared to be iced over.

"This is one curious mortar," said Bruce, and into his comm unit, "Delta...Epsilon...Lab One floor secure. Position, please."

Delta answered first, "Back hall secure. Present location: in position and awaiting 'Go'." Mark's comm crackled and Epsilon reported that they had secured the inter-lab stairway, had placed mini-explosives on the heavy pneumatic door at the bottom of the stairwell, leading to Lab Two and were in place waiting for the "Go".

First Officer Sarah Pollock, Gamma Team Leader, standing fast at what was left of the double secure doors leading to the hall, double-clicked her comm unit and spoke, "Gentlemen. On my mark." She gave a brief nod to Edwards, turned, and quickly strode back through the battered hallway to the verticals. As she went, she called out to a few of the men along her path. "Summers. Watson. Franklin. Mack." Each turned and stepped in behind her. Eight seconds later, Sarah and her team were assembled at the verticals. She touched her comm and announced, "Signal weapons check." Delta clicked, "Ready." Epsilon clicked, "Ready." She calmly looked from face to face of the Gamma Team members gathered around her and acknowledged their affirmative signals with a smile. Touching her comm, First Officer Sarah Pollock said, "All teams. Lab Two is ours. Go."

◆　◆　◆

Just after returning to the states, having been expelled from private education...*the fools*...Azekiel Hartfield invested some of his small fortune in government commodities, some in his new public relations business start-up, and a fair share into investing in M.I.T. with the express request that they build his automated reasoning algorithms into the next generation of artificial intelligence software...strictly confidential...and covered by iron-clad contracts full of non-disclosure statements and clauses stating that Hartfield retained all intellectual properties and patents and licenses and rights and whatever else was needed to secure all development outcomes or ideas...in perpetuity...virtually forever. For all of this, Hartfield would "donate" a vast sum of money, yearly, for a specified period of time. He chuckled to himself when he pictured the shocked expressions on the faces of the M.I.T. Board of Directors when he named the yearly sum and the period of time the "donations" would continue. In his haste to sign the proffered documents, the M.I.T. Regent dropped his $985.00 Mont Blanc fountain pen on the floor, shattering its ink well. With a shrug, he signed using a standard ballpoint offered by his assistant. And Azekiel knew he had them.

Slowly, the smile on Hartfield's face would recede, returning to his usual unemotional self-restraint when he would remember that the meeting with the M.I.T. Board of Directors was where he learned one of his first, really solid, lessons in business: everyone and everything had a price.

And price was something Hartfield would not have to worry about since his artificial intelligence algorithm had spawned hundreds of new patents from simple voice activated appliances to elementary thinking machines to pre-programmed free-walkers with learning capabilities. The patents kept coming and the money rolled in, was invested, and rolled in some more.

Within six months, Azekiel had purchased a $5.8 million dollar uptown loft and spent over $900k on a decorator to outfit it with the best of the best. Before the year was out, he owned the entire building.

Hartfield was filled with pride at the memories of starting his public relations business. His practice of recognizing the top five percent of business "players" and running background checks on them and their money always provided enough information for Hartfield to build a custom PR boost. He always found it easy to smile and politely sweet-talk his way past reception and secretaries into the large, well-appointed private offices, and once there, present his plan, shake a hand, sign a contract and leave with another top name on his ever growing and exceedingly impressive client list.

With his first $125,000.00 check, Azekiel bought a Jay Kos business suit, a pair of A. Testoni shoes, a celebratory bottle of 1993 Chateau D'Yquem Sauternes Bordeaux, and leased a Tesla Signature Performance. He quickly moved office addresses to the Upper West Side and within two months, had expanded his enviable client list and had hired ten more employees. And it was all getting easier as the months passed. It was exhilarating. It was like dancing in the fast lane.

The Hartfield Connection, LLC, expanded beyond its initial recognition and it wasn't long before Azekiel started shopping for international clients, specifically on the European continent. He considered it a real milestone to have signed Willem Adid Manoi, Europe's biggest and most visible, luxury hotel owner/operator, to his client list.

Part of The Hartfield dream included worldly accolades, unlimited sources of revenue (be it currency or the precious value of rarity) and the almost reverential air of respect that his business acumen would foster in virtually everyone he would meet and, of course, in everyone who would only know of him. These persistent and well-honed thoughts would come unbidden to Azekiel Hartfield at almost any time and he would smile and nod to himself and know that it was so.

♦　♦　♦

Lab Two was a thing of perfection with its efficient open-air concept. It had been set-up to specifically encourage cross-pollination of ideas and problem solving techniques and to support the on-going discussions of the advanced mathematics that were used and expanded upon as a matter of routine. It was the combinations, analysis and abstraction of mathematics that delighted Azekiel Hartfield. Right from the start the applications seemed boundless.

The space was very functional. Lab tables were arranged to provide efficient use of the space, but situated in such a way as to serve both open conversations and private desk-like areas where one could be away from the din of work-in-progress to privately consider ones own thoughts. There was an area for simple food preparation that Hartfield liked to keep stocked with high-protein, low-glycemic foods after he read that a diet high in complex proteins and low in processed grains and sugars was optimal for top performing brain energy. That and the fact that breaks outside the lab had almost been eliminated, culminating in additional work hours and faster development cycles for the techs and scientists employed there.

There were parts and gadgets and a good-sized workspace dedicated to fabricating any widget that may be conceived during the development of any one of the five projects normally underway at any given time.

Work surfaces were stainless steel, polished and clean. Tools were neatly arranged by size and use. And each station had task lighting that not only illuminated the work but had also been designed to focus the attention and reduce eyestrain by the use of the cool blue light spectrum. The overhead lighting provided a more natural type of illumination, providing the essential qualities of sunlight, along with the requisite amounts of vitamin D, so touted by the professionals.

Situated around the project workstations were a number of double-desks, enough space for a dozen individuals who could claim their own space and work on the conceptual beginnings of their projects or update their notes on the laptops provided expressly for this lab.

Storage cabinets, overhead monitors, shelves of tech books and manuals and the small, well-appointed meal prep area were situated along the outside walls.

Azekiel liked to visit Lab Two. He found quietness in the cold stainless surfaces and the organized sets of drop forged tools. It gave him a sense of being. But he lived for the excitement he felt when it all come together to produce a moving, thinking piece of robotics or the next generation of highly efficient laser optics. Then he felt like he was as light as air and would float effortlessly into his future...shielded by stainless steel and bright as the sun.

♦   ♦   ♦

The verticals, carrying two dozen Gamma team members, came to a soft landing on Lab Two's floor. First Officer Sarah Pollock set the GetKey mode to manual and opened the doors just wide enough to push a small camera through. Using the articulating cable arm to move the Spy Eye camera to "look" around the area, Sarah noted an enclosed chamber with a cipher locking mechanism. Opening both verticals' doors, the Gamma team members stepped out into the antechamber and a tech specialist quickly moved forward and was easing the front panel off of the cipher lock and had it defeated in less than ten seconds. This door swung open into a second antechamber with the same cipher lock as the first door. Within short order, the door security was routed and the team got their first look at Lab Two.

The interior was dim and Sarah, clicking her comm unit twice, had raised her hand, spreading her fingers wide in a gesture that signaled for her team to adjust their night vision visors and to heighten their alert profiles. Maintaining their stealthy silence, the team advanced into the space and started to fan out. The lights in the antechamber were extinguished so as not to backlight the advancing operation and to give Gamma team the advantage.

Almost at once, weird, clicking sounds started up all around them. Sarah's position in the lead gave her the first sighting and it almost took her breath away. Glowing in the green of her night vision visor, she watched as hundreds of small, multi-legged mechanical bugs the size of carpenter bees, swarmed along the floor and up the walls. These little devices would scurry along, stop, click a small red dot of light, and move away to repeat this action again and again. One stopped in front of her and she instinctively moved her foot to step on it, but it easily sidled away from harm, clicking in an almost indignant manner as it went. Deciding that the immediate threat-level of these objects was low, Sarah signaled for her team to continue their advance. Not known by her or her team, these mechanical "bees" were remote cameras, whose only function was to send visual data back to their controller, which, in this instance, was a technician huddled under a workstation at the far end of the lab. The visual from the "bees" was being retransmitted to two security specialists who were manning the lab's defenses, standing silently, in the dark, and monitoring Gamma's movements by way of the "bees" cameras as it was projected onto the inside of their night-vision goggles.

Meanwhile, Epsilon had gained ingress by way of the Secure

Utility Room and had joined the assault.

A scuffling noise came from their direction when an Epsilon team member flushed two technicians from their hiding place under a workstation. There were muffled cries and thumping sounds as the techs were forced to the ground and bound wrists-to-ankles, and subsequently knocked unconscious to keep them quiet.

Atop the workstation, where the techs had tried to conceal themselves, was an apparatus that resembled a small water cannon that was rotating around in small circles and slowly moving along a set of tracks secured to the tabletop. Sizing it up as a possible threat, it was put to rest with a swift brutal smash of a gun butt.

Everyone quickly became aware of the thin red laser beams that criss-crossed the floor in a sort of grid pattern. They were set about four-inches off the floor and seemed to be shooting out from under desks and from the kickboards along the walls. There was no way that anyone could traverse the floor and not break the light beams, so the only thing for Gamma and Epsilon to do was to move forward with caution.

As the first beam was broken, several round spheres, the size of cat's-eye marbles, came rolling out from all directions. As they slowed to a crawl, they exploded, sending small bits of metal shrapnel flying outward just over one foot in all directions from their centers. The thick leather uppers on the combat boots worn by Sarah and her team offered protection from the jagged shards, but some hit flesh, just above, sinking in up to one half-inch deep. While not exactly deadly, these nasty little marbles could hobble those hit, and if enough of the shards hit home, could cause lameness and could slow or halt the team's advance.

Fortunately for the team, there was only one round of the marbles, and after pulling two of the ragged shards out of her shin, Sarah ordered everyone to move up.

Suddenly, an intense slice of orange light shot across the space, grazing the upper arm of a Gamma team member who had just emerged from the antechamber doorway. Sparks flew as the beam cut into the shoulder pad of his flak-vest and a reluctant scream of pain escaped the Gamma member's lips before he was knocked backwards into the wall by the strange and invisible force accompanying the beam. His cries sent a new wave of adrenalin through everyone within earshot and those closest, crouched and dove away from the continuing glare of the orange beam, which had, for the two seconds it had continued to shine, sliced a three-foot gash several inches into the concrete wall behind them.

Several steps into the area, Sarah had seen the beam cut past her and had followed it back along its path to the source. She stepped forward to use a desk as a shield and fired a mini-burst of bullets at this new target. Three operatives behind and to her right followed suit, sending a spray of tracers and live rounds sailing to the orange laser's starting point.

Just then a blue-green light beam shot out of the opposite side of the room, effectively pinning four team members on the floor where they had taken cover. Amid the astonished cries of "Take cover!" were the chaotic sounds of guns discharging and damage to the infrastructure of the lab. The blue-green laser beam seemed to be melting everything it touched sending up toxic smells, fountains of sparks and arcing electricity, and smoke that choked the area, hampering everyone's vision.

Small caliber handgun fire mixed with the sounds of the combat already in play. Several of Abers' other security specialists had taken up positions throughout the lab and had now started their defensive assault in earnest.

The entire lab erupted into a frantic struggle with Gamma and Epsilon teams on one side and Abers' security personnel on the other. Gunfire rang out and live rounds whizzed past into the smoky depths. The noise levels rose to a deafening pitch and just when it had reached ear-splitting decibels, a huge explosion rocked the lab, knocking several fighters off their feet. Looking to the source, Sarah was half blinded by the shower of red-hot sparks flowing out of what had been the orange-beamed laser. Through the thick acrid smoke, she saw two Epsilon men and three of her team, move in and secure the area. They found two dead security men, one man mortally wounded, and two techs, bloodied but alive, with their hands in the air and fear in their eyes.

The explosion that put the orange laser out of business afforded a few moments when the blue-green laser stopped firing, probably because the operators had been knocked off their feet as well. Five Gamma team members, with Pete Malloy in their midst, moved swiftly across the lab to the far corner of the room. Sliding over tabletops, knocking over lab equipment and tools, they moved closer. Sarah, seeing that they were closing in on the laser's position, hollered 'Yo!" and lobbed an incendiary canister into the corner that exploded on impact, sending a chemical flash of light followed by thick blue-black smoke designed to temporarily blind those in its immediate vicinity.

The group flew the remaining distance and with shouts of "Drop it! Face Down! NOW!" quickly secured the laser cannon and disabled the security men found still alive.

Although small arms fire flared up here and there, followed by commands and short bursts of warning shots, Lab Two was virtually secure. Sarah ordered one final sweep of the area and asked that several canisters of charcoal "smoke-eaters" be opened and set to work cleaning the air. It was a few moments later that the canisters had filtered about seventy percent of the particulates out of the air allowing for better vision and the illumination from the portable lighting revealed the extent of the damage.

All that remained of the orange laser cannon was a melted, glowing hot pool of metal that was burning its way through the granite stone tabletop and sending a light mist of white smoke up to the ceiling and a red, oozing, sticky liquid down the side of the workstation to the floor.

All Hartfield employees who had survived the battle, were secured and were being grouped together in the center of the lab. The damage, now being seen clearly, was extensive. The laser cannons had wreaked havoc in the space, cutting and melting everything in their path. Where they had contacted flesh, a burning, gaping wound resulted and the pain that followed was likened to phosphorus burns. The blue-green laser cannon had been secured and remained in operable condition although it was belching a blue-gray smoke and was glowing hot along its firing barrel. Sarah stepped up next to Pete and watched him as he pushed his night vision visor back on his head so that he could see and breathe more freely. Both stood for a number of seconds, curiously looking the cannon over, wondering about its components and what its source of power was before Sarah spoke, "Did you see the damage this inflicted across the back wall? It cut into the concrete like a hot knife through soft butter. And the arcing electricity burnt huge gaping holes into all the metal that it came in contact with. Unbelievable."

Pete nodded and said, "One nasty little prototype. Too bad the orange one is gone, they were so different in their destructive power, I would be curious to know its full capabilities, too."

Sarah clicked her comm to life and said, "Lab Two secure and cleared. Med-Evac III and Captive Transport now cleared to enter." Her comm unit crackled in response, "Transport one-minute ETA." and, once again, another voice responded, "Med-

Evac Unit III on-site." She clicked her comm twice and said, "Job well done, Gamma. Job well done, Epsilon. Thank you all. We group in one minute at coordinates 1.0.1 x N.8.5."

◆　　◆　　◆

Like the crack of a bolt of lightning as it sends its static discharge to strike the earth, the sudden shock and noise of Martha Gainsbrook's operation involving The Hartfield Connection, jolted Mark Sturgess from his thoughts and sent him shooting to his feet. He turned to face the wide expanse of windows along the rear of Azekiel Hartfield's executive office and stood in shock at what was unfolding outside. Dozens of helios, lights blazing, were circling the building while others were landing on the roof, disgorging men, who appeared to be clad for a war.

Mark's fight or flight response kicked in and, at first, he chose flight and had taken two steps backward, but the small horde of battle-ready men had reached the heavy glass door by then, so he quickly switched to his third choice: surrender. He gulped the last of the Garioch '58 from his tumbler, set the glass down on the coffee table and raised his hands, fingers spread open, over his head and smiled his ever-so-hospitable smile as the first of the assault team members swarmed through the door.

◆　　◆　　◆

Martha Gainsbrook's voice crackled over the comm unit, "Zeta, to me, at Lab Two verticals." At once, several members from within the large group of persons combing through Lab Two's battle debris, either collecting specimens or tending to the wounded, started for the antechamber.

Pete Malloy turned to Sarah and said, "Well done, First Officer Pollock, I look forward to working with you again, some day."

Sarah smiled and said, "It's been a good day so far, hasn't it? Stay safe."

Pete picked his way through the mess created by the exploding cat's eye marbles and the broken equipment that was strewn, several inches deep, across the floor, his boots making audible crunching sounds as he moved along. Between him and the antechamber doors were several techs and security personnel, all bound and ready to be collected and stowed away to wait for their inevitable interrogation. As Pete stepped past the small group of detainees, he recognized one of the cadets as the specialist he had instructed to count the number of geese in the original game of chase, set up by his software patch on his first day in Security. This kid didn't look so gung-ho now that he was facing a more powerful authority than Lieutenant Abers. Tapping the kid's foot with his boot, Pete said, "Hey. Where's Abers?"

The kid looked up through his smoke burnt eyes and replied, "Lab Three, sir," and dropped his head in a fit of coughing.

Joining the growing number of team members assembled around Martha in the first antechamber, Pete smiled his greeting and stood among the group. Martha scanned the faces, and asked, "Has anyone seen Peters?"

Her question was answered by two team specialists who somberly shook their heads no. One of them replied, "He didn't make it. He went down after being shot by a small caliber weapon."

Martha nodded gravely and said, "I'm sorry. Peters was a good man."

Strengthening her resolve, Martha addressed the group. "Intel indicates that Hartfield's Security Department currently has a staff of over two hundred. We've not accounted for half of that number so far, so I'm expecting that a great many of them are holed up in Lab Three."

Pete spoke up, "One of the detainees indicated that Abers is in Lab Three."

Martha nodded and continued, "Ah, and we know what a zealot he is for Hartfield and for glory. We don't know exactly what to expect, so I'm ordering square bucklers to the front followed by incendiaries. Weapons ready, please." All members checked for fresh rounds and produced a small metal click, when they patted their readied weapon stocks against their flak-vests, as an affirmative. Pete checked his PA-48, holstered it and looked over his Mac-10 to make sure it had the maximum number of rounds loaded and ready and that the weapon was in working order.

Clicking her comm unit, Martha said, "Epsilon, are you with us?" The response came crackling back, "Yes we are. With a two-second lead-time for detonation, we're ready to dance."

"Perfect." Looking around at the faces turned her way, Martha said, "It's down into the belly of the beast. Stay sharp. Let's do this."

◆　　◆　　◆

Lab Three was the epitome of forward thinking by superior intellect. It was Azekiel Hartfield's pride and ultimate joy. He had achieved what no other person or group of persons in recent history could ever hope to have come close to. He was revolutionizing science, blazing new frontiers, reaching beyond the pinnacle of high science. In a word, he was having it all and having it now. He loved Lab Three. Three. His Holy Trinity, to his way of thinking. To the inexperienced eye, there was something a bit chaotic in the way the tools and machinery, with their accompanying tangle of chords and wires, were left laying about. But for the elite men and women who worked in Lab Three, everything was as it should be. All the monitoring devices were portable and could be rolled into position where needed. All the tools had their use and their place was wherever they were.

Besides the meal prep area, Lab Three had a wonderful library where one could sit and rest, regenerate one's energies, and clear one's mind. A vast array of technical manuals covering a multitude of scientific disciplines and theories were housed in electronic form and available on several e-tablets. The shelves of the library held original texts and rare printed books written by some of the greatest scientific minds and afforded Lab Three's personnel the non-replaceable tactile connection with the words of the masters.

Life in Lab Three was exhilarating because the possibilities were endless. More than once a doctor would tire and desire an hour or two of restful sleep before forging ahead on his project. There was a private sleeping area and beds provided for such times, so there was no need to leave for home.

The free space was divided into three distinct work areas for the three disciplines practiced there. Each space had adequate room for one study but was adjacent to the others when overlapping interests occurred.

The remainder of the space was dedicated to human studies and observation, and to surgery. It was equipped beautifully but would not have been necessary if not for the three disciplines: Molecular Biology, DNA-Templated Chemistry and Enzymology.

The polymerase chain reaction technique was extremely handy in the ongoing studies being conducted by Hartfield's lead doctor, Doctor Benjamin Deverell Hera, one of the most advanced researchers in molecular biology of the day. Doctor Hera had spent years trying to prove that the cloning of a DNA sequence need not degenerate after millions of copies, with the introduction of his specifically developed stabilizer serum. The Thermal Wave 2000, necessary to achieve extreme high and low temperatures, had been one of Hartfield's patented inventions, developed and built onsite in Lab Two. The machine had been conceived by Doctor Hera and was for his exclusive use. When he no longer required it, it would be rolled away for another time.

There was a marriage, or an attempted marriage, between the DNA-templated chemistry and cryogenics that interested Azekiel the most. Imagine...biologically active compounds being chemically sequenced within human cells within particular tissues, for instance, a thyroid, that could be released into the body when specific criterion were present...like stress or something more mundane like taking an aspirin. Cryogenics just added interest to the project. Could the biological compounds survive a little bit of cold and still retain their original vigor?

The third discipline of Lab Three was enzymology. Third, but not the least, enzymatic chemistry was a necessary piece of Lab Three's puzzle. Its ability to catalyze chemical process reactions within cells and its nature to "pave the way" for foreign biological controls, made it the perfect partner for DNA and molecular biology.

Lab Three might look messy and unkempt on the surface, but a wealth of discipline and desire roiled just below.

The doctors who staffed Lab Three were the best in their fields. They were seasoned by years of study with some of the most advanced research groups in the states and abroad. After laboring under the constant restrictions of government regulations and bowing to the criteria that came with grant money, working for

Azekiel Hartfield was a liberating experience. This was a private lab, not accountable to the government. Everything they needed was provided and anything they asked for was delivered. A researcher's dream. Hartfield's dream.

◆　　◆　　◆

The exact second that the verticals touched down on Lab Three's level, an immediate and continuing barrage of medium caliber firepower pummeled the doors. Little bumps formed a wild pattern on the inside door, indicating that the rounds being fired were penetrating the stainless steel room-side doors but slowed enough to only dent the vertical-side stainless steel. The dimples in the door indicated that there was a large antechamber, or no antechamber, but in either case...the battle had begun. Voices could be heard above the noise, commands to "Move up!" and "Ready!" Martha clicked her comm, "Epsilon, we're almost pinned in the verticals, provide cross-fire, please."

"Done," came the response.

Hearing the cover fire, and with bucklers in the front, the vertical doors were opened three inches, just enough to launch, in rapid succession, two incendiary canisters toward the muzzle flashes aimed in their direction. A misstep in the oncoming firing sequence was all the evidence Martha needed before ordering the doors fully opened, "Fan pattern, doors open!"

As the doors slid open, the noise level became deafening and hot, live rounds whizzed all around the Zeta Team. Martha could feel the thumps of the ricocheting rounds as they pelted her flak jacket. Epsilon had made it through the stairwell and into the front of the large lab area and had joined with Martha's Zeta Team to form a sort of barricade between the known ingress points and the rest of the space, trapping Abers' security forces in the lab. And in the same sense, Abers' line of defense kept the Special Forces from gaining further ground.

As the large number of weapons continued to fire, smoke from their heated muzzles rose to the ceiling far above. The incendiaries had added their blue-black smoke to the mixture, turning the air to the color of an indigo midnight.

Zeta had lost two men and Epsilon one, but Abers' men were dropping fast. With several weapons out, Martha advanced into the darkened lab taking cover behind the steel and granite workstations.

It was hard not to strike one of the security persons due to the sheer number of them present. It was a bit like shooting fish in a barrel and was sad in a way. Many of Abers' men were but boys with no tactical experience. Fear was starting to win out over their sense of duty...to Abers?...to the job? and causing them to panic fire their weapons and to second-guess the battle engagement unfolding before them. If their ammo clips ran empty or their guns jammed, they simply dove for cover. These boys were the ones most likely to survive their current predicament.

Abers, in stark contrast to his personnel, had seemed to come alive during the battle. He had armed himself with two semi-automatic M16s that were slung bandolier-style across his back and was wielding two self-loading machine pistols that he fired with a fair amount of accuracy. His aim was concentrated on the Zeta members who were successfully shielding many fighters with their bucklers. He thought to take down their main protection thereby exposing them to his wrath and to the ensuing attack of his brave troops. Abers was clearly a man obsessed.

Martha had made her way slowly and deliberately to Pete's side behind a workstation that was just yards into the lab.

Glancing to her right, she noticed several cryogenic units, one of which had been damaged by wild weapons fire and was billowing a ghostly steam as liquid nitrogen issued out through several holes. The cloud settled close to the floor and was spreading rapidly. Off to her left was Epsilon who were gaining ground, albeit gradually and at the expense of one more man. Touching Pete's arm and motioning that he should follow her, Martha moved into the frozen steam, across a small clear area, emerging close to another workstation. Cautiously, so as not to draw attention, Martha found a view of the battle line, noting that two of Abers' men were laying prostrate, bleeding from severe wounds but still firing on the advancing line. Just behind them, Abers had abandoned his pistols and was firing one of his M16s. Abers had no real advantage since the weapon had to bolt a round in serial fashion and he had to stand up to take aim. As Martha found a view of this scene from between bits of debris littering the tabletop, she discovered that she would have a clean line of fire that could very well take Abers out. Leveling her Mac-10 and honing in on her target, sniper style, Martha took in a breath and held it as she fired her weapon. At the exact moment she squeezed the trigger, a loud pop rang in her right ear. Pete, seeing his advantage, had unholstered his PA-48, set it to cluster and took aim, loosing a round of multiples straight at Abers. Instantly, Abers was jolted by the hits and tumbled down, to his right, falling with the impact of the five rounds that had struck him along his left side. Three of the cadets that were grouped around Abers lost their nerve at seeing their hero fall and almost immediately dropped their weapons and tried to lay down among the debris. Martha thought she heard Abers' voice bellowing out from his place of bloody repose, shouting orders and swearing, but could have been mistaken, what with the ongoing chaos.

The way was now clear for Zeta and Epsilon to move up a few more yards, and they did this with ease. The weapons fire was starting to slow as more cadets surrendered, or were wounded or killed. The losses to Zeta and Epsilon stood at four, but the losses to Abers' personnel were significant and continued to mount. As Zeta and Epsilon advanced through the space, the wounded and those who had yielded were disarmed and securely bound to ensure their immobility.

Martha and Pete made their way to where Abers had fallen and found him bleeding from several punctures as well as from a deep gash over his left eye. He was bloodied, sweaty, and weakened by his wounds and his fall, but he was still conscious and spewing orders and venom. As Pete came closer and was just about standing over him, awareness came into Abers' eyes. Then in a flash, recognition. With his eyes screwed into glaring slits and spittle foaming at the corners of his mouth, Abers spat, "I know you! You're the big security expert who fucked with my systems!"

Pete nodded and smiled and said, "Save it." then slapped a gag over Abers mouth. A Zeta technician stepped up and zip-stripped Abers wrists to his ankles and relieved him of his jammed M16.

As the battle came to an end, Martha looked at her timepiece. It had only been eighteen minutes but it seemed longer. Martha felt like it had been over an hour. Clicking her comm, she asked for status from the team leads. Epsilon answered first. "Prisoners all secure. Epsilon down three with four wounded but mobile." A specialist for Zeta answered next, "Sixteen prisoners secured. Three down. Two severely wounded. Four wounded but mobile." Martha clicked twice to confirm and then looked around.

"Smoke-eaters" had been set to work and several floodlights had been set up and were starting to illuminate the area. A Zeta specialist was attending to the cryogenic unit and seemed to be containing the leaking nitrogen. Other specialists were paying attention to the little pools of smoldering goo that had been created all over the floor area. Some of the puddles were neutralized and others were left to fester until their own demise. As the smoke and pollution cleared, Zeta and Epsilon got their first good look at Lab Three.

The space was huge. It must have been at least one hundred feet wide by three hundred-feet deep. Half of the lab was now covered with broken glass, up-ended machinery and chairs, and littered with more than three dozen captured security personnel and their numerous fallen comrades. There were bullet holes everywhere and in everything.

The point where the fighting had stopped was located at the labs halfway mark and, as the lights were restored and the smoke cleared, Martha and Pete stood facing what remained. Farther into the lab were two long, curved control consoles of sorts. Each console was the mirror image of the other and both appeared to flank what looked to be an eight-foot wide by ten-foot deep glass enclosed area. Radiating out from this glass room were thick glass walls that ran ceiling to floor and away to the lab walls on either side. Each console had several computer stations that were active and displaying various graphs and metered lines across their respective screens. Pete looked at Martha and Martha looked at Pete.

Then Pete said, "We're going to have a bit of fun with all of this, aren't we?"

THE INNOCENCE OF POWER

15
Smoldering Embers

After several team members had swept the area for anyone who may have been hiding under or in back of the larger pieces of furniture, Martha Gainsbrook stepped up to the long, curved console on the right. She noted that two of the computer screens were active and that each seemed to be displaying the vital statistics of a living being. The heart rate displayed on one screen was weak but occurring at regular intervals while the other was strong but irregular. It didn't make too much sense.

She took a seat, laid her Mac-10 across her knees and started to read the labels that were printed in a neat hand and taped next to several of the buttons, equalizer slides and dials. The setup closely resembled that of an intensive care unit found in any well-equipped hospital. As Martha's eyes scanned the control board, she became aware that some of the display graphics were tracking minute chemical processes, possibly those on a cellular level. Not routine for an IC unit.

Standing up and steadying her Mac-10, Martha leaned forward, up onto her tiptoes, to get a better look at the rear of the console and found that all of the wires and cords were gathered into one group and fed through the thick glass wall located about one yard beyond.

The area on the other side of the thick glass wall was darkened, and Martha, peering through the glass, could barely make out a couple of blinking lights and the soft blue glow of a glass-fronted refrigeration unit.

Meanwhile, Pete had stepped up to the glass-walled room in

the center of the thick glass wall, and was starting to understand what it was he was looking at.

Martha spoke, "It's a decontamination room, of sorts."

The room was accessed by a sliding door on the console side and a sliding door on the darkened room side. Each corner of the small room had a showerhead-like apparatus above and a gridded steel panel in the floor directly below it. There were four small nozzles positioned two on either side. Gazing into the chamber, Martha said, "It's my guess that those nozzles were designed to release some sort of mist or liquid into the closed chamber, either with persons in there or not."

The glass box was lighted but the space beyond was not and Martha couldn't see through the darkness. This left her uneasy and almost subconsciously, she reached for her Mac-10 and checked its readiness.

◆ ◆ ◆

Martha clicked her comm and requested that several Zeta members join her. Within seconds, five agents had assembled at the console area, three were checking their weapons but all were alert and ready.

"We've got something here that I'm not quite sure of. It appears to be a quarantine area but there's no indication as to what might be isolated in there. Our bio-suits are effective against smaller pathogens for up to five hours, this should be a sufficient amount of time for us to do at least a basic reconnaissance of the area directly behind this glass wall."

The agents scanned the glass for any signs of damage and could see small nicks here and there where stray bullets had grazed its surface, but most were satisfied that the wall had no cracks or openings that would allow the escape of...what?

Martha had returned to the console and was leaning over fussing with the keyboard and dials on the front panel. Standing up straight, she said, "We'll need to access this lighted glass chamber to find an effective means of ingress, but I would like to be a bit more sure of it before we enter."

One of the Zeta technicians stepped over to the console and sat down. After tapping a key or two and touching the screen, she spoke to Martha, "I can activate the overhead monitor and from there mine down through the screen levels. Should only take a minute."

The tech brought up the overhead monitors and was mining down through the screen levels when she hit upon a schematic for the decontamination chamber and spoke up, "The chamber looks to be made for light use. It will screen and eliminate up to eighty percent of airborne particles and up to fifty percent of general bacteria levels normally found in our environment. It was not designed for the total eradication of bacteria or specific diseases. It's a cautionary measure, not a defense."

Martha thought for a moment then spoke, "Okay. We shouldn't compromise whatever is in there because it could be valuable evidence against Hartfield, but more importantly, we will need specifics as to the nature of 'it' so we can make clear choices and decisions concerning 'its' future." Turning her head slightly to gaze through the glass into the murky depths, Martha said, "Weapons check. Bio-suit and mask check."

Amid sounds of weapon chambers being opened and closed and fresh clips being seated into their places, one agent had started to walk the length of the wall, taking a closer look at it and through it. Two Zeta team agents were assessing the lighted decontamination room with apt curiosity, and the tech at the console was busy flipping screens and searching key words for information on how the chamber operated. Finding enough information to go on, the tech spoke, "Martha, I think this is what we need." Pressing a key or two, the contents of a file was displayed on the overhead monitor. It read...

The Huntley DK5000 is fully automatic.

Entering the three-key code will signal the process to start.

The door closest to the activated keypad will slide open.

Step through and assume position on one of the four grates located in the chamber's corners.

The door will slide closed without assistance.

Stand with feet slightly apart and with arms held out two inches from sides.

Hold this position while the decontamination process is active.

Expect a ten second light misting of a harmless surface agent and fan-like breezes and vacuums. When the process is complete, a soft chime will sound and the opposite door will slide open allowing exit.

At any time, pressing the red override button located next to the

originally activated door may halt
the process.

When Martha finished reading the short missive she turned to face the others.

Pete broke the silence, "The three-key code has been posted on the control pad. It's five-six-four."

Martha nodded. "I don't think we should all go together in case there's booby-traps or other unseen dangers in the darkness. Pete and I and one other, Ames, how about it?" And getting a return thumbs-up, she continued, "We'll go through first, be in constant contact and secure the way for you four to join us. Facemasks secure, standard ops at the start. Is everyone ready? Okay. Stay alert. Whoever's in there probably knows we're coming." And with that, she stepped toward the entrance to the lighted glass chamber, and joined Pete, who had entered the control pad code and was watching the glass door slide open.

◆　　◆　　◆

As they emerged from the chamber doorway into the dim interior of the room beyond, the three agents assumed protective positions and hesitated for a brief moment to let their vision adjust to the low light levels. Agent Ames and Martha cautiously stepped off to the right to clear the doorway for the other agents to follow. Pete had moved two steps to his left and as his eyes began to focus, saw that there was a wall and double doors just a dozen or so steps beyond his position. Holding fast, he kept alert for any movement of the doors and for any sounds coming from the other side.

When the remaining four agents had joined the trio and when everyone's vision was sharp, they positioned themselves into

233

defensive postures, nodded agreement to each other and moved carefully and silently out into the darkness.

♦   ♦   ♦

The work accomplished here would someday be recognized as the most groundbreaking scientific breakthrough of all time. These were the words that occurred to Azekiel Hartfield every time he thought of Lab Three's Isolation & Surgical Ward. Everything else would pale in comparison to his discoveries. His work would herald in a new age of genetic possibilities. At a time when the scientific community had only begun to scratch the surface of DNA-templated chemistry...had barely even begun to understand it...he was shepherding his researchers to possibilities and conclusions. The visions of world acclamation wove their way in and out of Azekiel's thoughts almost daily.

The Isolation & Surgical area housed a delicate eco-system and was dedicated to the monitoring and administration and maintenance of up to five human subjects. Each of the subject areas had been equipped with state of the art monitoring systems, specialized and customized machinery and separate infusion pump systems and pre-programmable medical monitors.

The surgical unit had been furnished with medical imaging, ultra-sound, lasers and infusion pumps, as well as basic life support equipment and standard monitoring systems.

One of the PhDs working in Lab Three had been inspired to build a small greenhouse featuring hydroponics and a photosynthesis spectrum lighting design. Research had been inspired by the theory that some DNA-sourced molecules were compatible with certain plant-based chemicals. Those chemicals were now being synthetically produced and initial findings had led researchers to a new theory involving the digestive enzymes of two very specific carnivorous plant species. What if a plant-based chemical compound could be developed to replace the costly chemicals now used? Wouldn't it save initial costs, provide a more natural method of infusion and be almost undetectable once absorbed? With this goal in mind, the unique and truly beautiful state of the art but also quite basic Greenhouse One was built. It housed two delicate species of plant life: Sarracenia purpurea and Genlisea.

Almost as a hobby, but certainly with a love and respect for the carnivorous nature of the Sarracenia purpurea, several pots of the species had been set among rows of ferns and other forest dwelling plants in an attempt to recreate a more natural habitat for the purple pitcher plant. In contrast to its distant temperate climate cousin, the Genlisea preferred a more aquatic habitat. It had been placed amid shallow rock pools that mimicked its natural preference for rich moist soils where it could sink its white fleshy subterranean leafy tendrils down deep.

All Lab Three areas as well as human subjects had always been closely monitored by two biomedical equipment technicians and, of course, by the PhDs and physicians conducting the ongoing studies. Data acquired through any of the various means was routinely transmitted to the main operations consoles outside of Isolation where it was databased, sorted and displayed on large overhead monitors located throughout the lab.

However, in preparation for a pending relocation to a new and much larger facility, work had been significantly scaled down and only a bare-bones staff had been required for ongoing observation and monitoring of Lab Three's Isolation Ward and greenhouse functions. All other studies and experiments had been postponed until after the move that was expected to take place that weekend.

By this time next week, Lab Three would be up and operational in its new location up state. More space, total secrecy...and off the grid.

◆　◆　◆

Moving slowly into the darkness, some with their night vision visors activated, Zeta team stepped stealthily forward. Pete Malloy, accompanied by Agent Ames, moved to the double doors on the left. Stopping to listen, both men were alert and slightly anxious about what lay beyond. With his PA-48 up and ready, Pete reached out and gave the door in front of him a slight nudge. It easily and noiselessly started to slide open under his touch. Agent Ames copied the move and the door in front of him also slid open a crack. Both men stopped, looked at one another in agreement and listened intently for any sound that might be coming from within. As both doors opened wider and wider, Pete could only hear the steady beat of his heart and his rhythmic breathing. As soon as the opening was wide enough, both men slipped through and silently guided the doors closed again. Hesitating for only a second, Pete reached for his halogen pin-light and quickly scanned the area.

It was apparent that they had entered a surgical room. In the center was an operating table surrounded by various pieces of equipment. Along the walls were long tables with specialized tools neatly displayed under protective plastic wrapping. Just off to his left, Pete spotlit a cryogenic device that was humming and showed the steady red light of its "in use" mode. Switching the pin-light off to thwart the possibility of being tracked by a hidden sniper and moving his position slightly, Pete motioned to Ames to move off in the other direction. From this position, Pete activated the pin-light again and swept it along the wall. They saw additional pieces of equipment and a small table with a console and display screen, presumably, where overviews or techniques could be reviewed in real-time. Sweeping the light across the floor back to the operating table revealed nothing. Pin-light off, Pete and Ames moved forward. Switching the pin-light back on, Pete focused it along the back of the room highlighting more equipment, surgical lighting, overhead monitors, and what appeared to be a video library housed in a glass-fronted case.

Pete moved the small spot slowly along the back wall, taking note of the items highlighted momentarily in the beam. As the light crept into the back corner, Pete was startled when Agent Ames snapped his tactical machine pistol up and aimed it at the place the light was now touching. Pete raised his PA-48 and quickly adjusted the pin-light beam to illuminate what it was that brought Agent Ames to full alert.

For a second, neither man believed what he saw. Spot-lit in the narrow beam of the pin-light was a man. He was sitting cross-legged in a chair with his hands folded neatly on top of what appeared to be a thick, leather-bound book balanced on his lap. He was squinting through the bright light of the beam but otherwise was trying not to move or do anything that could be mistaken for a hostile act.

"Good evening. I'm Doctor Benjamin Hera."

◆　◆　◆

Martha, with her four Zeta agents, headed stealthily away from the glass chamber into the darkened interior. They stayed as silent as they could to not give their position away and alert so they could hear the slightest of sounds before them.

Immediately adjacent to the glass chamber, against the opposite wall stood a huge walk-in refrigerator. One agent crossed the floor and stood at the alert, listening for sounds before stepping into the dull glow of blue light emanating through the frosted doors on the front of the cooler. Inside could be seen several shelves, most of which were filled with specimen beakers, culture tubes, bottles of various colored liquids and Petri dishes that seemed to be teeming with fungi and bacteria, some of which looked to be escaping their outer limits. Labels identified the contents as "Subject One: Peptites Infusion" and "Subject Five: Enzyme Infusion Retrial" and on and on, row after row throughout the shelves. Satisfied that no one was hiding in the walk-in, the agent stepped backwards out of the splash of hazy blue light and back into the darkness to follow the others.

With every step the group took, faint beeps and background noises became more evident. They made their way past tables topped with thermal glassware poised over Teclu burners, scales, autoclaves and burettes suspended above beakers. They moved past a small workstation with its unused power cords and data cables strewn across the desktop.

Several steps further, Martha held up her hand to signal the team to halt. From there, she listened to each of the myriad of sounds that seemed to emanate from everywhere at once. Straining, she made out the whirling sounds and soft beeps of monitoring equipment and the low steady hum of the electricity that powered them.

There. There it was again. Soft. Translucent against the steady beat of the beeps and whirrs. Martha turned her head slightly in the direction of the sound to better hear it. Yes, it was unmistakable now. It was the low murmur of someone in pain. It was almost imperceptible but she was sure. Off to the left, in the darkness, someone was in pain.

Signaling her forward agent to cast a pin-sized light beam in the direction she had indicated, Martha then signaled everyone to stay low and find cover. The small sharp line of light shot out and danced about for a second or two before going out. Then again, the beam came up and scanned another area before going out a second time. The third time it came up, it found what Martha knew was there: a man laying in a hospital bed hooked up to monitoring equipment in what appeared to be an uneasy sleep. His head was rolling back and forth and he was emitting short low puffs of air from the back of his throat that, on first notice, resembled the murmurs of discomfort. On closer inspection, it was obvious that this man was unconscious but possibly only medicated into his stupor of bad dreams.

One of the agents carefully restrained the man's wrists to either side of the bed and slowly moved the monitoring equipment away from his possible reach, in the event that he woke up before their evaluation of the area was complete.

It was determined that the air quality was acceptable and this allowed the team to remove their masks and as their eyes became accustomed to the dimly lit room, those who had donned their night vision visors, removed them too. Stepping through the darkness, listening to and identifying the various sounds coming to them, the team discovered three more beds, all empty with no evidence that they had been recently occupied.

Straight ahead, at what appeared to be the end of the room, small amber lights twinkled from behind the semi-frosted glass walls of an enclosure that, as Martha peered through the darkness, saw to be full of plants. Her thoughts pressed forward. *A greenhouse? What sort of nonsense was going on here?* She tapped her shoulder twice and pointed and two of her men silently moved forward. They were about fifteen feet ahead of the others when Martha saw them stop, stand still and motion for her to join them. As she closed the distance, she picked up on another set of sounds coming from the direction her men were looking. Faintly at first but getting clearer, the sounds of monitoring equipment became distinct but what was that additional sound?

Martha brought out her pin-light and aimed it at the point where the sounds had originated. Another thin beam was added to it and together they encompassed a fifth hospital bed, but this one had a resident. This person, a young woman, was in a deep coma and hooked up to an artificial breathing unit. Martha and the others stood in silence as the machine wound up, and watched as the woman's chest rose, and as the machine released its pressure, her chest would fall. The rhythm was mesmerizing but didn't hold the team's attention for long. Someone stepped forward and secured her wrists to the bed. Turning to the team, all he could do was to shrug his shoulders and jab his jaw in the direction of the greenhouse.

The two forward agents covered the distance to the greenhouse entry, held still for a second or two then slipped silently through the door.

In a short moment, a brief scuffle could be heard coming from inside the greenhouse, and then all went quiet. The agents had come across a young man crouching among the plant benches and had easily wrestled him to the ground, relieved him of his planting spade "weapon" and bound him, wrists to ankles, after gagging him for silence. One of the two agents reemerged from the greenhouse and signaled to Martha that the area was secure. Martha, in turn, clicked her comm unit twice rapidly and twice slowly sending her wordless communiqué to the entire team. At that moment the overhead lights snapped on startling everyone into a defensive stance. They had instinctually lifted their weapons to the ready and were stepping out of direct fire in an attempt to blend into the shadows, each agent looking around for anyone who wasn't them.

A shuffling, clicking noise coming up the passageway made everyone turn in that direction and take aim. Momentarily, three figures could be made out, all together, walking in a cautious, non-threatening manner. Rather deliberate. As the threesome came closer, there was recognition: it was Agent Ames and Pete Malloy with another man between them. Pete had his PA-48 trained on the man and was using it more or less to guide the man forward to join the other Zeta members.

Martha relaxed her grip on her Mac-10 and touched the safety with her index finger, securing it with an audible click. Straightening herself to her full height, said, "Stand down gentlemen, they belong to us."

The trio had closed the distance between the groups to less than ten feet. "Everything back that way," said Pete, indicating behind him with a terse movement of his head, "is secure." Smiling at Martha, as she stepped out in front, Pete introduced his prisoner, "This is Doctor Hera. Lab Three is his baby." Lowering and holstering his PA-48, Pete said, "Doctor, I'd like you to meet Agent Gainsbrook, your new boss."

Doctor Hera nodded his greeting to Martha, who invited him to have a seat in the chair just brought forward by Agent Ames. As he sat down, Martha turned to Pete and said, "Well, it seems that we've seen the entire lab. It ends at the far wall inside the greenhouse. What did you find through the double doors...besides our new friend, the good doctor?"

Pete said, "A very well-equipped operating theater, but not for standard procedures. It looks very experimental and very expensive."

Just then, the greenhouse door swung open. One of the Zeta's was manhandling the tethered young man through the doorway to join the small group gathered there. When the young man saw Doctor Hera, sitting relaxed and unharmed, he started excitedly trying to talk through his gag. However, all he managed to do was to emit a bunch of annoying and garbled gagging sounds that he kept up until his captor looked him in the eyes and shushed him with a finger to his lips. At which, the young man winced, fell silent and tried to shrink smaller.

Doctor Hera spoke up, "That's Henderson. He's our technical expert. He takes care of the medical monitoring equipment in this part of the lab. He does not have access to records nor is he privy to any information pertaining to the work that is being accomplished here." As Doctor Hera spoke, all the stress drained out of Henderson and he visibly relaxed into his restraints.

◆　◆　◆

Two of the agency's best medical professionals and three bio-medical technicians were reassigned to Martha Gainsbrook's team immediately upon her request. They would arrive at the Hartfield and would be escorted through the chaos to Lab Three within one hour of receiving the call from headquarters.

Martha had a table and several chairs brought into the area located directly in front of the greenhouse, adjacent to the bed where the young woman was being kept on life support and who still remained in her deep coma. Two agents, Martha, Pete and Doctor Hera were seated around the table and were waiting for the agency's physicians and diagnosticians to arrive. Agent Ames was standing by watching the proceedings. The conversation at the table started as a sort of get-to-know-you talk with all of the questions being directed toward Doctor Hera.

With the two agents recording the Q and A session, Pete and Martha asked the doctor increasingly difficult questions and as time went on, received increasingly more fantastic answers.

Martha sat across from Doctor Hera calmly observing his face for a brief moment, then spoke, "Tell me Doctor, how long have you been in medical research?"

"I've worked in the field of DNA chemistry and nanoball technology for well over ten years," commented Doctor Hera, "after being in the bio-medical field for fifteen years prior. Bio-medical research was only a passive interest of mine, but when the first in-depth studies on DNA-sequencing and mapping were released, you may remember the excitement this caused among the scientific community, my interest quickly became a passion. It was an old study that had become new again."

Shifting in his chair to stretch out one leg, Doctor Hera asked, "May I have a glass of water?"

Agent Ames, standing close by, nodded to Martha and walked out of the area, back toward the glass decon-chamber. He returned within a minute with a glass beaker and a six-pack of unopened water bottles and set one down in front of the doctor.

"Thank you." The doctor took a moment to open the bottle, pour a small amount into the beaker, re-cap the bottle and slowly sip at the water.

Martha gave him this moment then nudged him, "Please continue. You became involved with DNA research."

Gently setting the beaker down, Doctor Hera picked up the thread, "After ramping up on everything DNA, you see, I was in the fires of passion and could not get enough, I found myself among some of the most brilliant minds of the European scientific society and, subsequently began working in two of the most prestigious research institutions of the time. One was in Belgium and the other France." Doctor Hera was absentmindedly turning the beaker in small circles as he spoke.

Doctor Hera continued, "It wasn't long before I became frustrated with the constant oversight of their governments. Their petty demands for accounting and their unrealistic deadlines for delivery. Delivery! As if my work were nothing more that a commodity to be traded in public auction...a widget of no real value being pushed down an assembly line." Doctor Hera fell silent as his face started to curl up in a scowl of contempt.

Martha looked from Agent Ames to Pete. Silently and with subtle facial movements, they communicated that they understood that Doctor Hera had a deep distain for authority and that they should keep a vigilant eye on him throughout the proceedings. Breaking the momentary lapse in conversation, Martha asked, "So, what did you do then, Doctor?"

Doctor Hera cleared his throat and composed his face and after smoothing down the front of his suit, continued, "So I left. I returned to the states and within a week of my return, Azekiel Hartfield contacted me. That was three years ago."

Watching Doctor Hera closely, Pete asked, "What did Hartfield offer that made you choose to work here? What did he want you to do for him that you couldn't accomplish at a reputable research facility anywhere else in the United States?"

Martha watched as Doctor Hera looked at Pete. From Pete's almost imperceptible reaction to Doctor Hera's intense stare, Martha had the distinct feeling that the good doctor had just analyzed him. And maybe not in a good way.

The doctor continued, "Azekiel Hartfield offered me freedom. Freedom to pursue my research to its natural conclusions.

244

Freedom from government interference. And that, my dear Mr. Malloy, is what sealed the deal for me."

Doctor Hera shifted in his seat and gathered his thoughts. "As to what did Mr. Hartfield want? Well, he did not have specific things in mind, or, I should say, he never stated anything specific directly to me. He seemed to be energized by simply being here, in the lab, inquiring as to what project was being worked on and what it was we hoped to accomplish by it. He didn't hand us goals but he did have one real requirement and that was, any breakthrough experienced in any of the projects was to be communicated to him immediately. And only to him. Lab Three's ongoing work was not to be discussed outside the lab and not with anyone other than Mr. Hartfield. And this included Mr. Sturgess. We were not to discuss findings or matters with him at all."

Doctor Hera sipped the last drop of water from the beaker and poured another small amount of liquid for himself. Martha had been listening patiently to the doctor's résumé but thought it was time for him to overview Lab Three's projects. Martha asked a leading question, "Doctor Hera, what can you tell me about the two persons we've found confined to beds here?"

Doctor Hera continued speaking as if he had not heard Martha's question, "I arranged the lab to better suit my research needs and worked on my DNA-templated fusion trials for six months or more. After that time I found the limitations of experimenting on small animals rather frustrating so began clinical testing on human subjects. That was two years ago, and I've been pretty satisfied with some of my results. Still, other results are not as conclusive as I would like, so further study is required."

The small group fell silent for a minute with everyone looking at the doctor. He, in turn, was gazing at the water in his beaker with a thoughtful expression on his face. He lifted the beaker to his lips and drained it. Setting it back down with an audible clink and placing his hands, palms down, on the table in front of him, he took a deep breath and continued. "I do not know any information of a personal nature about any of my subjects. For instance, she's," wagging his index finger in the direction of the young woman, "Full Subject Three, and the gentleman down the way is Temp Subject Fifteen. I do not track Temp Subjects other than through my notes. You see, Temp means 'Temporary', they are here then they are gone. It all happens rather quickly. On the inverse, Full Subjects can be here for quite long periods of time. Long enough for a trial to begin and be observed for variances and then concluded. Then they become useful again, either unto themselves or as conduits for the next level of research." Doctor Hera finished speaking and withdrew his hands from the tabletop and simply folded them in his lap.

The large, leather-bound book had been placed on the table close to where Doctor Hera was seated. During his conversation, he made no reference to it nor did he even look at it. Its presence now seemed to prick at Pete's curiosity so he asked, "May I look at your book, Doctor?"

To which the doctor said, "Certainly," and slid the book across the tabletop to Pete, "although I doubt you will understand much of what is written there."

Pete handled the book with respect. The pages were gold gilded on their edges and bound using the cotton thread and organic paste method used by bookbinders of two centuries ago. The leather was exquisite with embossed gold lettering and elaborate decoration along the spine. The title on the front cover was simply "Doctor Benjamin D. Hera" but done in a beautiful script. There were at least six hundred pages, but maybe as many as seven hundred and fifty pages of delicate handmade paper between the covers, and as Pete opened the front cover, the binding and leather creaked with authenticity.

♦　♦　♦

The leather-bound book was a journal. The pages were filled with complex mathematical equations, most just outside of Pete's understanding of his fourth year college trigonometry and calculus. The pages were adorned with small drawings and explanatory notes. The first entry was dated some ten years ago and the last entry was made just a few days prior to their meeting. Page after page contained drawings, notes, equations…a collection of relative points drawn from a period of one man's life of learning, theorizing and passion. Scattered among the pages was a word that was repeated again and again. This word was "Innocence". It appeared next to complex drawings of supercharged strands of a DNA double helix with an arrow pointing to a dot between two adenine cells. It appeared on drawings of spinal DNA coiling to the left as well as drawings of recombinant brain DNA coiling to the right. "Innocence." It was peppered throughout the text and had always been written in a careful hand. It appeared that Doctor Hera had stopped writing, picked up a special ink pen and with obvious reverence, wrote the word "Innocence" before retrieving the original writing implement and completing his thoughts and note entries.

♦　♦　♦

The agency's medical scientists and technicians had arrived at the estimated time. Leaving Doctor Hera sitting quietly and Pete engrossed in the journal, Martha met the medics at the main console outside of Isolation and introduced them to their work. "I think things will move faster if everyone has access to their own terminal port and knows approximately what they will be looking for. This is a cursory look at the lab's functions to give us a preview of what may come. I'll ask the technicians to activate each terminal, evaluate for uniqueness of purpose and to carefully preserve the information found there. Use redundancies, please." With a sweep of her arm, Martha indicated the terminals along both consoles and two of the techs sat down in front of the terminal nearest to them and started to work. She touched the third tech's arm, indicating that he should hold back a moment and addressed the two medics.

"Doctors. There are two people in Isolation that will need your immediate attention. They are both abed and are both in what appears to be artificial comas. One is on life support. Neither of their conditions is understood. I'll take you through to them." Turning to the technician, Martha added, "We'll need both bed side monitoring systems checked out, made stable and copied to backup before any dials are adjusted or buttons pressed. Please assist the doctors when that is finished."

As the technicians were activating the screens and more overhead monitors were coming alive, Martha led the doctors and the technician through the decontamination process and down to the place where the two unidentified subjects were confined in Hartfield's Lab Three Isolation Ward.

◆　◆　◆

The post-assault cleanup and evaluation was progressing as expected. The air in Lab Three had been triple filtered and the debris that covered every inch of the floor had been carefully screened for usable evidence and followed by a good sweeping to move it out of the pathways between workstations and ancillary equipment. A dozen additional personnel were on site and busy preserving and cataloging the contents of the lab. The dead had been taken by the agency's medical examiner's staff and the prisoners were being photographed, printed and led, one-by-one, out of Lab Three and up into armored transport vans waiting outside amid the emergency vehicles and tactical vans that clogged the streets surrounding The Hartfield.

After showing the agency doctors to their new patients, Martha rejoined Pete and the doctor at their ad hoc meeting table with full intention of continuing the interview with Doctor Hera. But at the moment, all questions seemed to elude her. Doctor Hera's admissions, so far, implied a much larger body of work, and while Martha was curious, she thought that "slow and easy" might be the best approach to use with the doctor, as it seemed that his mental state was borderline. She felt that he would break if handled roughly. Without a word, Martha took her seat and simply looked from one face to another then turned her attention to the book in front of Pete.

◆　◆　◆

Zeta and Epsilon team members were working among the group, opening cabinets and drawers, assessing damage, carefully looking at everything they had come across. Agent Ames and a second Zeta were evaluating the surgical room and came upon a box of notebooks that had been stuffed under a small side table and hurriedly covered with surgical gowns in what appeared to be a half-hearted attempt to disguise it and hide it. Thumbing through a notebook taken from the top of the box, Agent Ames read a passage on this page, flipped a few pages, read another passage, and flipped more pages. What he got from his brief introduction to the notebook's contents was this: surgeries were all experimental in nature and there were at least five people...subjects...mentioned in this book alone. His curiosity slowly turned to disbelief as he began to realize the nature of the surgery unit and what this meant as part of the bigger picture of Lab Three.

Gathering up the box, Agent Ames spoke to his companion, "These books appear to have been hidden here, possibly in the hopes of escaping destruction and/or our attention. They simply don't belong here and I think they're too valuable to place into immediate evidence where it may take weeks or months to process them. I'm going to walk them up to Agent Gainsbrook to see what she thinks of them. I'll be right back."

♦ ♦ ♦

Martha had decided to keep the box of notebooks and Doctor Hera's leather-bound journal in her safekeeping and to read and analyze them later at her agency office. It would be less chaotic there and would afford her enough time to focus on each one of them uninterrupted.

Enough clock time had passed and Martha felt that the interview of Doctor Hera should continue. "Doctor. We would like to hear more about your work here. What have you accomplished since starting work at The Hartfield and where are your studies leading you?"

A Zeta agent approached the table carrying a tray holding various lab glassware and a hot plate burner which he proceeded to plug into the nearest outlet and set a two quart beaker of clear water on to boil. "Martha, I thought everyone might like a cup of tea right about now. I'm brewing lemon grass and rose hips, my own blend. I'll have it ready in three minutes."

Doctor Hera smiled, "Gentility even among the ruins."

When the tea had steeped, the agent placed it in front of Martha and she portioned it out among the beakers provided and loosely distributed them around the table.

After a sip or two, Doctor Hera continued his tale, "The findings, that resulted from testing my theory on small animals, while frustratingly limited, did prove to me that I was on the right path. Combining my newly discovered neurotransmitter with a specifically coded DNA double helix could work. However, small animals proved inadequate, as they couldn't withstand the monitoring and re-testing processes necessary for each trial. They simply expired before a trial was completed."

A sip of tea, "This is very good," and then, "I do not know how the subjects came to be here. I requested them and they were provided. It was not my concern and I did not worry myself about those details. I had my own concerns, my own work to think about, to concentrate on."

Martha felt disconcerted by Doctor Hera's apparent disassociation with his "subjects". Her conclusions about his mental state were starting to solidify: a closet sociopath with a sharp focus on only what is important to him.

Sitting with both hands wrapped about his beaker of tea, Doctor Hera continued, "Full Subject Three has been here for fourteen months. She is very special." Doctor Hera glanced in the direction of the young woman on life support and his face relaxed for the briefest of moments, into a soft smile. Then catching himself and straightening up, he continued, "She has provided the most important piece to my puzzle. A most valuable piece. You see, with Full Subject Three, my neurotransmitter, alphadroxy

251

thyrolozide X-8, fused successfully with the subject's DNA base pairs to replicate and transmit the resulting output to all cells within the subjects' body. I've coined a term for this, for my alphadroxy thyrolozide X-8. I call it 'Innocence'".

Doctor Hera became very animated when he spoke of Full Subject Three. His face seemed to smooth out as it filled with affection. Then he continued, "I've not been able to freely duplicate this process in other subjects. There's a special quality in Full Subject Three's genetic makeup that compliments and facilitates my work. Much more study is needed though, before my desired results are fully reached."

With that, Doctor Hera fell silent with the expression on his face returning to that of concentration. As he stared at his half-full beaker of tea, his mind was on his work, he seemed to be solving a problem, lost somewhere in his thoughts…very far away.

◆　◆　◆

"Ms. Gainsbrook, may I speak with you for a minute?"

"Yes. Do you have something for me?"

"I think I do."

One of the agency doctors had approached Martha's meeting and was standing about ten feet away. He had waited for an appropriate moment to interrupt and beckoned Martha to join him. As she approached the doctor, he motioned for her to come with him to the bedside of the unconscious man.

As they walked, he gave her a brief update, "The technician successfully restored all monitoring functions and brought up an e-tablet for my use. We ran our John Doe's thumbprint through the agency's database and received an interesting response."

"So tell me, doctor, who's our mystery man?" asked Martha.

"He's none other than Senator Frank Torres." The doctor waited for Martha to work that bit of information and he could see her expression change to that of deep concern.

Martha said, "This is extraordinary. What would Frank Torres be doing in Lab Three Isolation?"

They arrived at the bedside and amid the soft sounds of the equipment that had been mapping Frank Torres' vital signs, the doctor answered, "The monitors are tracking his body's levels of peptites, which are abnormally low. Peptites allow the creation of antibodies, the body's main defense against foreign bodies. His condition is getting more serious as time passes and right now he's running a low-grade fever of 100.4 degrees Fahrenheit. There is little I can do for him until I understand exactly what is causing his current state. Any hasty action on my part may worsen his condition."

Martha stood for a minute at the bedside looking down at Senator Torres. His face was white and drawn into a grimace of pain. Every few seconds a low, guttural sound emerged from his throat. Then she spoke, "Be sure the tech is recording everything properly. I'm sure you will do what you think is right. And thank you Doctor, please keep me informed."

Martha headed back toward the greenhouse area but decided that she should check with the agency doctor who was looking after the young woman in bed number five, so headed there instead.

As she approached, Martha noticed that the doctor had pulled a chair up to the side of the bed. He was studying the screens and streaming outputs of the equipment monitors, which were busy displaying the woman's vital signs and were beeping and clicking as she lay immobile. The only sounds Martha heard were those of the steady and automated rhythm of Full Subject Three's mechanical breathing. The doctor had an e-tablet and was searching a source of text and the overhead monitor was displaying several active windows at once. Occasionally, he would look up at it, then return to his text search.

He was so intent on his studies that Martha purposefully tapped a cart as she passed it so as not to startle the doctor with her quiet and sudden approach. At the noise, he turned to look in her direction and nodded his recognition of Martha and said, "Hello."

"Thought I would see if you needed anything and to ask you about your progress", said Martha.

"I could use a bottle of water if it wouldn't be too inconvenient for you, otherwise, I'm okay. I can't say the same for our young Miss here." Martha clicked her comm and spoke softly, all the while paying attention to the doctor. He took a moment to look at the young woman and to organize his thoughts before speaking, "I had the tech run her thumbprint through the agency but there wasn't an immediate response so they're doing a more in-depth search and expect to have her identified shortly.

"Her condition is serious, as you can see. She's being held in a medical coma on purpose and I haven't determined exactly why this was done in the first place. She doesn't appear to have an obvious condition such as a disease, or to have had some sort of neurological disorder such as a stroke. All of her vitals are normal but I note that there has been a measure of muscle atrophy that would indicate she's been here for a while. I'm unable to determine the exact amount of time because her bed-stay appears to have been well managed."

Martha supplied the doctor with a basic overview of the information she had obtained from Doctor Hera, "The resident doctor indicated that she has been here for just over a year. He refers to her as Full Subject Three. She is part of a long-term DNA study and has been treated more or less like a lab animal."

"Well, that explains quite a lot." The doctor stepped toward the monitor and pointed to a section of the display showing rates of increase in enzymes, amino acids and glutamate rates. "These are unusual areas of interest for monitoring purposes, they display activity on a cellular level and are being fed by this tube, here." Touching a tube and tracing it back to the young woman, the doctor continued, "It's attached to her here, by way of this shunt. I can only guess from its position, here at the base of the neck, that it's in the proximity of the medulla oblongata where it might detect minute changes in glandular output. To what purpose? I don't know yet."

Returning to the monitor, he pointed to a second display section and said, "This is mapping the activity levels of her peptites as they engage receptors in her central nervous system and," following the corresponding tube, "it's connected to this shunt, here," pointing, "between vertebrae C2 and C3."

"Do these things give you any indication of the exact nature of the test or experiment she's being used for?" asked Martha.

"Not entirely. However, I've found some Isolation Unit notes and am reviewing them. It helps to know she's been labeled Full Subject Three. I may be able to search for her more directly, now. Also, I've asked the technician to notify the agency that a specialized medical team will be needed to affect transport and to be available for continued care. They have been placed on stand-by and will wait for your signal to enter the area."

The doctor and Martha had been standing by the monitors, next to the bed where Full Subject Three was laying motionless. She looked serene and except for the mechanical breathing, Full Subject Three resembled a porcelain doll that had been carefully put to bed for a night's rest.

Martha broke their silent vigil, "Thank you, Doctor. Your water will be here in a minute and I'll check back with you in a short while."

The doctor smiled a pale smile and said, "Thank you, Agent Gainsbrook. I'll have more for you at that time."

♦　♦　♦

Doctor Hera had been very busy scribbling notes. The blank pages of loose-leafed paper that were in front of him were filling up with findings and suggestions to himself as to where he would take his test results next. He was a man thoroughly obsessed with his work and he considered everything that had happened at The Hartfield that night...the SWAT Team invasion, the horrendous shootout with Abers' forces, the coup of the lab by Martha's teams and his detention...a small and temporary interruption to his preoccupation with DNA. And the longer his pen flew across the paper, the more he became a man lost to his own thoughts, barely aware of what was going on around him.

The two agents assigned to make note of everything Doctor Hera said or did, sat idle. With their pens and e-tablets at the ready, they observed the situation and periodically reviewed what they had written making sure that what they had captured for the record, was as complete and correct as it could be.

Pete was also lost in thought. He had been intently reading entries and gazing at the drawings in Doctor Hera's journal but looked up at Martha's approach and acknowledged her silent greeting with a nod of his head. Gathering up the book, he stepped around the table and said, "Let's take a walk," and moved in the direction of the entrance to the head of Isolation Ward with Martha setting her pace to match his slow amble.

"Doctor Hera started getting agitated and asked for paper and pen. I didn't see any harm and it seemed to quiet his nerves."

Martha nodded and Pete continued his informal talk. "Doctor Hera's journal is fascinating. It contains ten years worth of notes pertaining to his continuing study and work in the field of DNA. I've read a couple of dozen of his entries that span the ten year period and I'm impressed with two things in particular: the scope of his work and how it has progressed during this time, and the sheer brilliance of this man's mind."

Having reached a part of Isolation where no one was working and where he and Martha might have a quiet conversation, Pete said, "Let's sit here for a few minutes and I'll tell you what I have so far." He pulled a chair up to a small workbench that was up against the outer wall and motioned for Martha to sit.

Pete then pulled a stool out from under the bench and perched himself on it, placing the book on his knees and began, "Some months ago, Doctor Hera successfully developed a matched pair of modified nucleotides that mimicked typical DNA structure and could be inserted into a living DNA helical strand where it would replicate itself. Replicated DNA containing Doctor Hera's experimental pairs...something he has termed 'Innocence'...was to demonstrate a condition where the subject's tendency toward aggression was overridden."

Martha asked, "Aggression as in making war? Or street fighting?"

Pete answered, "No. Not that extreme. Doctor Hera defined aggression as anger, facial expression, raising of the voice and even the desire to act out or strike out, nothing more exaggerated."

Martha's interest started to grow. "That's quite some goal. How would Doctor Hera know he had succeeded?"

Pete patted the book cover and answered, "A positive change

in the subject's glutamate level was proof that the goal had been accomplished on a physical level. Glutamate levels have an effect on the synapse activities in the part of the brain that controls learning and long-term memory. Doctor Hera's early trials indicated that 'Innocence' would change a subject's glutamate levels only temporarily, giving the desired results, but would eventually break down and return the subject to their original state."

Martha said, "Let me get this straight...Doctor Hera somehow pairs his research DNA with a subject's DNA to affect a change but, so far, the change isn't permanent. Is that right?"

"Precisely." Pete, perched on the stool, had dropped one foot to the floor and repositioned the leather book on his knee to keep it from falling. He added, "The problem had became one of longevity. How could Doctor Hera's modified nucleotides be made to bond with the donor's DNA in such a way as to facilitate a permanent replication process? The answer comes in the form of neurotransmitters and enzymes. Doctor Hera found a rare enzyme that seemed to work but shortly discovered that it was more rare than he first believed. Apparently, only one in five thousand persons produce this strain of enzyme chemical. This naturally led the doctor to conclude that if the perfect enzyme were not present, all he would need to do would be to provide it. This was the point where his problem solving ideas begin to also create further problems."

Martha added, "Especially for the young woman in the iron lung, Full Subject Three."

Turning to Martha, Pete said, "Would you like a water? I see that Zeta has put an ice-cooler by the decon-chamber for us." Martha accepted the journal as Pete handed it to her.

"I think that would be good, thank you." Martha opened the

journal and let the pages fall open where they might. As it happened, it opened to the entries dated three months prior and as she let her eyes roll over the ink, the certain truths of it became apparent.

Pete returned with two cold bottles of Pellegrino and cracked their seals. "There's one other detail I've gleaned from the notes. Full Subject Three has the rare enzyme that the doctor had been looking for since he started developing his theory of 'Innocence'. When her enzymes are bonded with a donor's modified DNA strands, it produces the desired results. In lab conditions, the modified DNA does not break down. However, complications arise when this concoction is introduced back into the donor, it seems that the body goes into a type of shock and rejection process. And this is the current state of Doctor Hera's work for The Hartfield Connection."

Both Martha and Pete glanced back toward the meeting table where Doctor Hera was seated and still lost in his thoughts with his hands grasping a pen as a drowning man may grasp for a life preserver. Then Pete said, "I don't doubt that the good doctor is working on that little problem right now."

Martha spoke, "Did you hear that the man in bed number one is Frank Torres? He may be the 'donor' you just spoke of. He's in a medicated coma and appears to be going through a sort of fevered state, indicating that his body is trying to fight something off...foreign enzymes, perhaps?"

Pete said, "If I've got this right, his DNA may have been modified with enzymes from Full Subject Three, put back into him and now his body is trying to reject it."

Pete and Martha fell silent. Both turned to look at Doctor Hera who was still sitting at the table with his head down and his hand flying along the page as he furiously wrote notes and drew diagrams, lost even further to his private thoughts.

Pete then faced Martha and said, "I'm not sure Doctor Hera would be able to answer too many more questions today. We should take the time to review his journal before continuing."

16
All Ye, All Ye 'Outs In Free

As directed, all the team leaders had gathered back at the loft office for the initial debriefing session following the night's extraordinary activities. All were exhausted and dirty from the battle and one or two had medical patches or gauze wraps, but none the worse than that. And no one was more pleased than Martha with how the situation had played out so far. With the exception of the few team members who had fallen in battle, and this truly hurt Martha's heart, her whole team was virtually intact and her spirit was lifted just a bit more as each one entered the office space.

Her e-device had chimed almost non-stop since she had left Lab Three and the Hartfield building over an hour ago. Martha had provided updates to her patrons and had received almost simultaneous inputs from several sources, including team leads that were still in route to the loft office.

Most of the agents returning to the office went to their workstations and brought up their electronics. Three persons started organizing the proposed meeting site in Martha's workspace while two others assembled trays of fruit and powerbars and readied hot tea and cold waters.

When the majority of the leads and members had returned, the gathering in Martha's area started to assemble. Martha was sitting and talking quietly with Pete when her e-device chimed. She glanced at the caller identification and flipped the device to "message". Moments later as she stood in position in front of the group, Martha started the meeting.

"First of all, I want to thank everyone who has worked on this project. You have all done a fabulous and skillful job. Thank you! As of three hours ago, this mission and its ongoing investigations have been reclassified as priority Code Blue Secret Clearance Special Access. You are not to discuss the mission with anyone who does not have that level of access." Martha shifted her weight from one leg to the other and continued, "The Hartfield Connection came under our control." And to that, murmured cheers of consensus rippled through the group. "The upper floors were secured very quickly with no loss of agency or support personnel. Persons still in the building at the time were, for the most part, cooperative and offered little resistance. There was the occasional runner but they didn't get too far and for all their efforts, are now being treated as persons of more interest. The agency has started interviewing all those being held and will be very busy with that process for the next seventy-two hours."

Martha had been standing in front of her desk when suddenly she became aware that her legs were very tired. She leaned back against the cool oak surface and looked at the faces about her. "The securing of the below ground levels had a higher price, but in the end was successful. Per agency standard practice, there will be a routine internal investigation focusing on tonight's activities. Please cooperate fully with this and be sure to submit your reports within the next two weeks.

"What I hope to get from our mission debrief are any suggestions on how we might be able to tighten up our operations...although, from what I witnessed tonight, they'd be hard pressed to find anything to comment on."

Alan raised his hand to indicate that he would like to say something. Martha smiled and said, "Yes, Alan?"

Speaking softly, Alan said, "I'm sorry for our loss of men. I would have liked to have been there to help." Alan sat forward in his chair and clasped his hands together in front of him, then continued, "There's been so much speculation about what Lab Three does. Would you brief us about that at this time?"

Martha pulled out her desk chair and sat down. She was aware that all eyes were on her and as she looked around at the team leads, she was reminded again of all that had transpired that evening and what these people had accomplished in such a short amount of time. She gave a slight smile and said, "After the smoke cleared, we discovered, way in the back of the space, a part of Lab Three that appears to be geared toward a most specialized and as yet, not fully determined, end goal. The agency has placed Lab Three under Special Operations with an accompanying level of clearance. At this time, I'm not able to brief you as to what is going on there. However, I can tell you this much: we found a girl there who had been reported as missing over a year ago—she's under agency medical care and should be okay now; and we found Senator Frank Torres, who appeared to be receiving some sort of medical procedure and who is now also under agency care."

Standing up and stretching her back, Martha added, "Oh, I've heard from our two teams tracking Anne Whitman...she's safe, the teams report no one lost and that everyone is on their way back. They did mention that I wasn't going to like seeing the damage to one of the vehicles because they thought that it would take most of my yearly budget to make it right!

"And one more thing. Everyone. Thank you, job well done. The move back to the agency officially starts first thing in the morning, however, I'd like everyone to go home, get some sleep and come back, day after tomorrow refreshed and ready."

◆   ◆   ◆

As the loft office slowly emptied out, Martha found herself at her desk, sitting quietly, sipping on a fresh cup of hot Earl Gray tea and scanning the first few pages of a composition notebook taken from the box discovered in Lab Three's Surgery Unit. Although her body was exhausted, her mind was fully awake.

The overhead monitors had been shutdown and the ceiling lights extinguished. All that remained were the soft green dots of lights here and there, indicating that some electronics were still powered up, just sleeping. Scattered among the lights of sleeping computers, here and there, a desk lamp was still lit, and the sconces along the walls were on but had been dimmed.

A soft footstep made Martha look up. It was Pete, striding toward her after having just come from the men's room. He had taken a few minutes to splash water on his face, to rinse away some of the sweat and grime of the night's turmoil. Feeling somewhat refreshed, he thought to sit and chat with Martha for a few minutes before leaving for home.

"Doing a bit of light reading, I see," said Pete, as he got closer to Martha's desk.

"Yes. I've managed to put these notebooks into a loose chronological order and picked one from the middle. I guess I don't need the setup, just the basic plotline." Setting the notebook down, Martha got up and said, "Have a comfy seat here on the couch, I'll get you a tea."

Pete sat down, and almost at once, he realized how bone-tired his body was and smiled to himself as he thought of the gymnastics he had been through earlier that evening. Martha returned with a cup of tea and placed a small plate holding a slice of lemon and a few crackers down on the table in front of him, and after handing the cup to him, she took the two steps to her desk, retrieved the notebook and her cup and came back to sit with him on the couch.

They sat together quietly for a few moments before Pete spoke, "Tonight reminded me of a cross-training assignment I once did in cartography. Going in, I had no idea that the terrain we were going to map was in the middle of a civil war, of sorts. Bullets flying, lots of smoke and chaos and there we were, three others and myself, recording geographical data into a specialized geospatial information system. My only hope was that our small hand-held data transmitters didn't fail us."

Martha had been watching Pete's face while he spoke and noticed that the serious lines around his eyes had smoothed out. He wore the look of a man just telling a story. She said, "Did everything work out as planned?"

"Thank our luck, it did." Pete sipped at his tea and held the cup for a brief moment before setting it down on the table. He took in a small breath and said, "My mind is still racing. I keep going over tonight's events as they unfolded against the clock. I'm clear on just about every step I made but almost can't grasp the magnitude of the intentions or the enormity of the implications of what Azekiel Hartfield has been getting into. And to think, this all started for me when I was contacted by the Whitman's about their missing daughter, Anne." Pete relaxed his back and stretched out his legs to full length and turned his head to look at Martha.

Martha had been holding her tea up to her lips, without taking a sip, letting the hot steam waft up to her nose. She was just starting to feel her taut muscles unwind and her mind start to slowly and systematically review the last few hours of activity.

Looking back at Pete, Martha said, "I knew more than that at the start, but neither of us, and none of my patrons, had any idea of the true scope of the thing at the time. I'm betting that it gets a lot bigger as time goes on." Martha took a sip of tea and helped herself to a cracker. Momentarily, she continued, "I've kept a hold of Doctor Hera's personal journal for the time being. The agency has designated it as high security, but I've spoken to them about you and they've granted you a temporary Special Ops clearance for this project only. I know you're very interested in that journal. Would you be interested in a little post-op evaluation?"

Pete raised his eyebrows, tilted his head, and said, "Yes...I...would."

"I thought you would be. I'm thinking that together we can read and evaluate Doctor Hera's journal and this box of notebooks. I'm confident that we have the level of knowledge necessary to put together a thorough cover report before kicking it upstairs. But," turning her face slightly toward Pete and giving a slightly devilish smile, "it does mean that you would have to work with me. Does that sound like something you would be okay with?"

Martha was still smiling when Pete replied, "Yes, and looking forward to it on several levels."

For many minutes, they sat together reading Lab Three journals and quietly sipping their tea, only becoming aware of the late hour when Martha's e-tablet softly chimed an incoming message. She glanced at the tablet's screen, decided that the message could wait for her reply until morning, and pressed the tablet's sleep button, blackening the screen.

"I think I'm exhausted and running on overload," said Pete.

Looking up, Martha said, "I can barely keep my eyes open. I think I'll call it a night. How 'bout we meet back here around noon tomorrow...I mean...this morning? We'll have an early lunch."

Pete reached out his hand to touch Martha's shoulder and said, "Noon. Have a good sleep." And got up from his place and moved to the door to leave.

Martha watched as he strode through the loft office and quietly

266

let himself out the heavy, frosted glass door and into the night.

THE INNOCENCE OF POWER

17
The Fire's Out But The Heat Still Burns

Weeks had passed and the media frenzy that always accompanied these kinds of events had died down. Anything connected with the startling news of the activities of The Hartfield Connection had moved off the front page and into the blogs. A typical sampling taken from the BoldAndBad blogsite reported this:

'There were many arrests following the stunning seizure of The Hartfield Connection building but it seemed that the one man the authorities were most interested in had escaped. Azekiel Hartfield had apparently left the building just moments before the raid, orchestrated and carried out by a top government covert agency, and is reported to have left the country. Although his whereabouts are currently unknown, the government is carrying out inquires and are in position to move if any solid information comes to light. It's been hinted at that Azekiel Hartfield is now one of the government's most wanted, so interest in his whereabouts has been very keen.'

Shortly after the initial news broke, national interest waned, although the town locals still stopped at the cordoned off space around the heavily damaged Hartfield building to watch as authorities came and went.

Mark Sturgess saw the inside of a holding cell for all of an hour before his small team of attorneys posted his $1.2 million dollar bail. As he was leaving the State Department building, he faced media cameras and questions with a confident smile, explaining carefully that he had no idea what Azekiel Hartfield had been up to. He answered all the questions thrown at him by directing them to one of the four attorneys standing with him, who answered with, "No comment," or, "The courts will decide." The most used video from that interview had been the one showing Mark Sturgess climbing into his sleek, superb Mercedes SLR Stirling Moss, flashing a sly but knowing smile and driving away.

Among the more noteworthy persons to be nabbed, was Travis Stratton. After being questioned at length about his association with Hartfield, and apparently, after he talked for almost two hours straight, the authorities let him go. He was supposed to be called before a Grand Jury, but after he conducted several well-publicized media interviews, the Grand Jury decided that he didn't have enough insider information to make it worth their time and had asked for a signed statement instead.

On the other hand, another high-profile Hartfield client was taken into custody and deemed a flight risk, so had been denied bail. Because of her political connections and her foreign associations, Elizabeth Preston quickly became a person of extreme interest. She was quietly transferred to a political facility, abroad, and it's fully expected that she would sing like a caged songbird...after she negotiates the particulars of her near future.

The rescue of Anne Whitman, the reuniting with her parents and her testimony before the Grand Jury sure struck a chord with the country. Here was a beautiful young woman, who in fear of a giant corporation, and in dreadful fear for her very life, had fled the country in a desperate attempt to escape Hartfield's evil and long reaching clutches. The media was all over it. The story had it all: a pretty young heroine, a flight across borders, shoot outs, tearful reunions and damning evidence against a world-class bad guy. There wasn't anything about that story that didn't appeal to the public. After Ms. Whitman had sufficiently recovered from her ordeal, she made the rounds of many of the bigger talk shows and at a press conference, staged by the Douglas Publishing House, and with her parents standing by her side, announced a multi-million dollar book deal. Quite the change going from a girl fearing death in the Canadian back-woods to a newly published writer.

But what was kept from public consumption, the thing that Ms. Whitman was compelled, by the ultimate power of the U.S. government to keep a secret, to never, under any circumstance, ever to talk about was the existence of the original sidecar or any of the information it contained. In fact, she had been placed on permanent censorship with regards to anything that had to do with The Hartfield Connection's other businesses. She faced stiff fines and prison if she violated these instructions but was more than happy to agree. It meant her freedom and with that came a fat publishing deal. The sun was now shining on Anne Whitman.

◆　◆　◆

The story of The Hartfield Connection quickly turned from the idyllic standard of capitalism, a company founded by a hopeful young man that grew into a marvelous example of ingenuity, into an almost unbelievable account of a descent into moral depravity, aided by ego, self-delusion and visions of grandeur.

There was no denying that Azekiel Hartfield had built a success story. His public relations work was quite advanced and showed skill and an intellect that was unmatched in his business circles. Hence his great fortune and the vast rewards that are acquired by a tremendous fortune.

Azekiel's decent into the darker side of business started slowly, almost beyond perception. Someone had told him, "No", and he didn't like it. But instead of getting angry, instead of fretting with right or wrong, Azekiel simply engineered a way around. He got what he wanted and that was all he really wanted in the first place. The lesson was learned and there was no unlearning it.

It wasn't long before the federal government had said, "No". A few years prior to Hartfield's deep involvement with government issues, there was a grassroots effort among the small towns and college kids to put a halt to big government corruption. Laws were enacted that limited the powers of special interest lobbies and controlled campaign spending and as the playing field became more even and mud slinging became unpopular, further inequities came to light. Among the many inequities, one of the worst to be spotlit was the level of deceit with which many politicians were conducting the people's business. Personal gains, job perks, inflated salaries...all came under question and under scrutiny. All fell short of the precepts set forth in the country's sense of fairness for all under the law. It was so obvious that the rich were running the people's business strictly for their own gain. A time of change had come.

After a short amount of time, a committee of psychologists, legal consultants and physicians were formed whose only directive was to create a means of filtering out those who didn't measure up. They became known as The Ethics Committee and after media picked up the story, headlines all over the U.S. proclaimed "People in David and Goliath Battle with Feds" and "Out with the Bad, In With the Good" and "Corruption Flushed Out of Washington". When the hoopla died and the dust settled, what the Justice

Department's Ethics Committee produced had been brilliant. It was a simple two-part test.

One part was comprised of a battery of psychological tests and puzzles combined with reviewer observations and conversations with the applicant that spanned a number of subjects. The test was randomized and the subjects were varied so that no two tests were alike. All tests were devised to provide the exact set of output data so that all applicants were evaluated by the same criteria. The observations and conversations were designed to detect small variations or inconsistencies and would signal deceptions...right down to little white lies.

The second part of the test, was simply a physical examination, not unlike a yearly routine exam done as part of ones own preventative care program. However, there was a minor difference in the exams given by the government and one given by a family physician. The government was interested in the levels of various minute hormones and chemicals that were present in the blood stream, whose levels could be used as data for a behavioral science study and report.

Combined, these two exams and evaluations were unbeatable. They proved the perfect filtering system and, for a time, eliminated the glad-handed corruption from the House, the Senate and the White House. And based on the test's ironclad results, The American Fairness in Government Law was created and enacted. All worked well until corrupt politicians became angry at being denied what they perceived as their rightful due and sought a way back in.

Enter The Hartfield Connection, LLC.

◆   ◆   ◆

Azekiel Hartfield was handling the public relations of several top members of the House and Senate, as well as various staff members and one or two lobbyists. As the political scene in Washington changed, so did the sense and sensibilities of those who sought the services of his company. But Azekiel was smart enough to know that he would never be able to help those applicants that did not display a certain...something...during his interview process. While this represented only a small and somewhat insignificant percentage of his political roster...a percentage he could easily do without...it did bring to his attention another area to exploit. A problem to solve. A game to play.

The situation was perceived purely as the government telling Azekiel, "No", and that clearly wasn't the answer he had in mind. He contemplated the new law and listened to the political complaints and knew there was only one direction to go: deeper and better. And so Lab Three was born with all its gleaming, cold surfaces.

◆　◆　◆

For Martha Gainsbrook and Pete Malloy, the story ran so much deeper than what was allowed into the press. Days ran into weeks and still there was more to discover...deep in various journals, among the numerous encoded files on various computers and e-devices, the now famous Whitman sidecar and any number of personal devices recovered from the Hartfield and its employees. And of course, there were the myriad of data recovered from the three labs that was tantamount to the philosophies of Werner Karl Heisenberg. In addition to the agency activities and reviews, several formal requests had been made to diverse foreign dignitaries for any information they might be able to contribute.

But so far, the requests had yielded very little usable...or credible...information.

The agency's patrons were so pleased with Martha's results that they granted an agency request to deploy three covert teams to several European countries to track and locate Azekiel Hartfield. The patrons also were able to root out several compromised House and Senate members and to expel them for life, going so far as to turn them into political pariahs and hound them into obscurity.

On this day, Martha and Pete were together in her agency office, having closed the loft office several weeks earlier, after the Hartfield operation had been completed. This was a nice office. It was on the fifth floor of the agency's building in the downtown, just a ten-minute walk from Pete's private office. Martha's office occupied a large, northwest corner of the building and had a view of the town's central park with its large trees and wide promenade. Today, the sun came and went as fluffy white clouds passed in front of it signaling the end of spring and the promise of a fine, warm summer.

The office was comfortable, with overstuffed chairs and a leather couch. An armoire had been converted into a credenza and housed a small refrigerator, glassware and a bar-sized sink on the top, with filing and storage on the bottom. Her desk was a large, heavy oak affair done in the craftsman style. And about the office were lush green plants and a modest display of Martha's numerous awards for valor with, notably, a medal of honor among them.

Martha had been curled up in one of her overstuffed chairs, with a Lab Three journal propped up on a pillow in her lap. "I can almost see where Doctor Hera's work would be a valuable tool in the pursuit of cures for various diseases. Although, I would like to know much more before I made up my mind one way or the other." She was watching Pete as he was reading a passage in

Doctor Hera's journal and studying a hand-drawn example of a modified DNA strand as it changed appearance through the four panels that had been drawn at the bottom of the page.

He looked up and said, "This is pretty heady stuff. The potential for 'great' is equal to its potential for 'destruction'. How is something as complex as DNA restructuring to be monitored so as to ensure that it will only be used for benefit? We've been introduced to this path of science through its use for subversion and falsehood, and I don't think that path was the one of least resistance. On the contrary, it was very complex and painstaking, yet it was the path chosen. This is a very serious subject with many, many entanglements that have to be considered. And who's to know which way is true? Or even where to start?"

Nodding in agreement Martha added, "Fortunately, we won't necessarily have to be the ones to answer those questions, although I'm hoping that when our discovery phase is over, we'll be ready to present a couple of brilliant conclusions." Smiling, she waited for Pete to respond.

Pete, almost absentmindedly, turned his gaze toward the windows. After a few moments of looking out the windows at nothing in particular and pondering the enormity of the subject, his attention was momentarily interrupted by the direction that the winds were moving the clouds across the sky. Pete then turned his gaze to Martha and said, with a smile, "I just love science fiction, don't you?"

THE INNOCENCE OF POWER

THE INNOCENCE OF POWER

AFTERWORD

If you liked this account of corporate abuse and government intervention, then you may also enjoy N. K. Hart's soon-to-be-released book, published by Tangible Press, of short stories tentatively titled Women in My Family.

ABOUT THE AUTHOR

N. K. Hart has been in love with stories and storytelling since early childhood. Forays into fiction have included *Guess Who I Am*, *Perspectives* and *One Lonely Day*. A collection of short stories is in the works and quickly to follow, a three-part science-fiction series not to be missed.

N. K. Hart lives in Morgan Hill California with a very nice cat named Awesome.